HOLD YOUR BREATH

B P Walter was born and raised in Essex. After spending his childhood and teenage years reading compulsively, he worked in bookshops then went to the University of Southampton to study Film and English followed by an MA in Film & Cultural Management. He is an alumnus of the Faber Academy and currently works in social media coordination at Waterstones in London.

You can follow B P Walter on Twitter @BarnabyWalter

Also by B P Walter:

A Version of the Truth

HOLD YOUR BREATH

B P WALTER

Published by AVON
A division of HarperCollins*Publishers* Ltd
1 London Bridge Street
London SE1 9GF

www.harpercollins.co.uk

A Paperback Original 2020

1

Copyright © B P Walter 2020

B P Walter asserts the moral right to be identified as the author of this work.

A catalogue copy of this book is available from the British Library.

ISBN: 978-0-00-830964-0
ISBN: 978-0-00-833624-0 (TPB)

This novel is entirely a work of fiction. The names, characters and incidents portrayed in it are the work of the author's imagination. Any resemblance to actual persons, living or dead, events or localities is entirely coincidental.

Typeset in Bembo by Palimpsest Book Production Limited,
Falkirk, Stirlingshire

Printed and bound in UK by CPI Group (UK) Ltd, Croydon CR0 4YY

For my sisters, Molly and Amy

Prologue

January 2020

London passes me in a grey blur. I keep thinking it's going to snow. Part of me would like that – to be stranded here on a train in a snow drift, unable to move forward or backward. Trapped in a vague sort of limbo; a physical manifestation of the state I've been in for most of my adult life. But I've shifted into an unsettling, uncharted realm since I got the phone call yesterday morning.

The voice of the woman at the other end of the line had cut through the dullness of my sleep-muffled brain. Part of me had been waiting for her call, and another part was sure that it would never come; that this sort of thing happened to other people, not me. How stupid that sounds, thinking about it now.

'Am I speaking to Katherine Marchland?' she'd asked in her businesslike tone. 'Formerly known as Katherine Carlson?' I'd told her she was, and she had continued as I'd sunk down onto my bed, clutching at the duvet, hoping it would protect me. 'Ms Marchland, my name is Detective Inspector Cousins of Northumbria Police. I need to ask you to present yourself at Wickton Close Police Station, Newcastle tomorrow afternoon at 3 p.m. to be interviewed under police caution. You are not under arrest at this time, but I have to inform you that you may be liable to arrest if you fail to turn up at the appointed time. You are of course free to bring legal representation with you, or you can access free legal advice through a duty solicitor if you request one to be appointed for you. Please can you confirm you have understood this information?'

By some miracle, I'd managed to say, faintly, 'Yes. I do.' She'd ended the call after that.

Now that I'm on the train, hurtling north at an alarming speed, I'm filled with doubts about the choice I've made. I could have just not gone. Failed to turn up. Left my flat and gone into hiding. Left the country. I imagine myself in a court dock, and then being sentenced to spend time in prison. Being taken down those steps you see in TV dramas, police officers escorting me to a van to drive me to my place of incarceration. Everyone knowing what I did, and why I need to be punished for it.

I can't help it. I begin to cry. The tears start light and slow, trickling gently down my cheeks, then grow louder and louder into constant sobs. Some of my fellow passengers begin to look around. Others try to ignore me, pulling their phone screens closer, surreptitiously edging their headphones into their ears so they can tell themselves that they can't hear me; that I'm not their problem.

I don't care. I don't stop. The panic has settled in now, strong and thick and all-encompassing, the sobs developing into tight, fast breaths. The irregular oxygen supply causes my face to tingle, then to blaze. I'm not sure how many minutes pass before I stagger to the tiny bathroom cubicle and lock myself in, or how long I'm in there for before a kind woman's voice speaks through the door: 'Hello, are you OK in there? Is everything all right?'

I can barely get my answer out, but when it comes, between the quick breaths and the sobs, it's stark and emphatic: 'No.'

'Do you want me to call for help? I can ring the passenger alarm?'

This elicits an angry response from some of the other passengers, clearly enraged by the prospect of major delays to their journey due to the mad woman in the toilets. Let her pass out. Let her hyperventilate. Let her die. I can't really blame them.

'Hello? Are you OK?' The woman's voice continues, sounding even more worried. 'Is there anything I can do to help?'

I've started to focus on the sink in front of me now. The slow-dripping tap. The rock and tilt of the train causes the water to fall in a different direction with each drip.

I feel the panic starting to lessen a little; enough for me to answer this Good Samaritan on the other side of the cubicle door: 'No. There's nothing anyone can do to help me. Not after what I've done.'

Chapter 1

To: KatherineMarchland@gmail.com
From: Susan.Douglas@DouglasEvansPR.co.uk
Date: 2 September 2018
Subject: The Cottage in the Forest Manuscript

Hi Katherine,

I hope you're well.

Goodness. I'm not sure where to start. First, I'm sure you know, but I'm not really working in the book world any more. I've gone into more generalised PR (for my sins), but as I said before, I'm very happy to read anything you write. That aside, this manuscript is, to be frank, rather astonishing.

I'm sure everyone's got something curious in their past, but your story has got me seriously hooked. I'm also so sorry to hear you had to deal with your mother's breakdown so young (btw, I wasn't sure how old you actually are in the book? Ten? Eleven?), and that your father's solution was to take you all to live in the woods. The details you go into – being left to wander the forest alone; the two visitors who are clearly doing something very strange with your mum – is all of this true? Of course, I'm not doubting your word (as you mentioned), and I'm sorry to ask; it's all just so shocking. Have you been burying all these experiences over the years without telling a soul? Are the names all real? And lastly, can I ask: was there ever a police investigation?

The ending truly shocked me – especially if what happened was covered up somehow. Try as I might, I can't get some of the images you paint in those last few chapters out of my head. They're going to haunt me for a long time, I think.

Thank you again for sending this. Let's have a meetup sometime soon. I can advise you on your next steps and recommend some contacts you can approach.

Best,

Susan

Susan Douglas
Douglas & Evans PR
@SusanDouglasPR | 23 Howell Park Gardens,
Hackney, London.

To: Susan.Douglas@DouglasEvansPR.co.uk
From: KatherineMarchland@gmail.com
Date: 3 September 2018
Subject: RE: The Cottage in the Forest
Manuscript

Hi Susan,

Thanks so much for reading. I know life must be hectic at the moment, so I really am hugely grateful for this! And yes, it's all true. Mostly. It all happened when I was ten, when my dad took me and my mother to Northumbria for a couple of weeks in the October half term (when the trip started to run into school time, I believe my father told the school I had flu). The names haven't been changed, at least. I did think about altering them, but something always stopped me. Perhaps because it feels like I'd be doing it to protect the guilty – something I'd rather not do.

Even so, I've decided to present the book as a novel. I just couldn't cope with the attention a memoir might bring, and at least as a novel it gives me a bit of room to string it together into a coherent story. I just wish it was only fiction. I'd be really keen to meet up some time soon and discuss it in more detail if you have the time. Would love to hear any other tips or suggestions you have before I begin submitting it to agents.

Thanks so much, once again,

Yours,

Katherine.

Chapter 2

1987

We're leaving. Go and pack your things.

That's what my father said to me, his suit crinkling as he knelt down onto the patio. I was in the middle of sorting out my ladybird colony and was rather cross about being interrupted. One of the dead members – Tiffany, who had been crushed earlier when I was building them a hut out of rocks – seemed not to be quite so dead after all, and I was enjoying watching her come back to life. Dad was interrupting.

'Kitty, we need to go,' he said, trying to get my attention. I kept looking at the ladybirds. 'Leave that, please. We're packing up the house. You need to come and help.'

'Help?'

I said it as a question, but I didn't really want to hear an answer. I said it like that to make it clear that the very idea was stupid. I wasn't going to help us leave. My garden was my kingdom, even if it was a boring, straight, nearly-perfect square at the back of our house in Grays, Essex. Tidy, Dad called it. I measured it one Christmas, enjoying the crunch of my boots as the metre wheel I'd borrowed from our neighbour Mr Jeffers sliced through the snow drifts. Eight metres, then seven and a half, then eight, then the house taking up nine. So not quite a perfect square, but close.

'Your help is required,' he said, bluntly, before walking away. His blunt days used to be rare and not last long. But recently, he'd become like this more and more, telling me to do things more like a teacher at school. The rest of that afternoon and evening was spent packing up our things. One side of the lounge was for boxes of 'rubbish', the other for 'keep'. Then we stopped for tea. Dad told Mum to order a pizza but she was crying too much to use the phone – her hand kept shaking and her tears went everywhere. He phoned them in the end. Three large pepperoni pizzas with extra cheese. We won't eat it all, he explained. Just so we have some extra for the morning. For the journey.

I think he expected me to ask where we were going. Why we were going. What we were going to do when we got there. But I sometimes enjoyed doing the unexpected: it usually caused more interesting things to happen. Dad dropped a few hints: 'You'll need your wellington boots' and 'Bring your cassette tapes and your Walkman.

9

It will be a long drive.' I responded to all these instructions with my best blank face until he wandered away shaking his head.

The pizzas made us sleepy, but we hadn't quite finished packing and Mum kept having her 'moments'. The biggest came when Dad found her using a permanent marker to scribble over the faces of laughing women on the cover of a magazine. He was holding some wine glasses when he chose to confront her. 'Put down the pen, Marjory,' he said gently. Her reaction wasn't gentle.

Once Dad had bandaged his hand and cleared up the blood, Mum had calmed enough to be settled down onto her bed. Sleep now, she was told, and she did, as if her off switch had been flipped. It wasn't always that easy.

Once Mum had fallen asleep, Dad and I carried on packing in silence. I did it without making a fuss as I didn't want to go to bed; he didn't seem in any hurry to send me there. I think it was about one o'clock in the morning when he finally said we should stop. 'We'll be leaving at 5.30. Get some sleep.'

'Why do we have to pack up and tidy the place? Are we never coming back?'

I didn't think Dad was going to answer at first; he was staring at the floor, kicking the vacuum cleaner cord out of his way. 'We will be, don't worry. We're just letting some people stay in our house for a bit.'

'Who are these people?' I asked.

'People who will pay us money to stay here while we're . . . away.'

I was about to tell him I didn't understand, but he

10

spoke again before I could: 'Go to bed, now. We'll load the car in the morning.'

I left him in the lounge. He was still wearing the suit he wore when he was at work selling his insurance stuff.

It would be the last time I saw him wearing it for quite a long time. But I didn't know that then.

Chapter 3

'Come near me and I'll kill you.'

That's what my mum said when I tried to wake her.
Then she cried when she realised it was me and said she
was sorry. 'It wasn't me who said that,' she said. 'It was
him. It was *him*.' She tapped her neck as she spoke and
shook her head violently. I used to be scared. I still was,
a little. But it was amazing what I managed to get used
to.

Dad was sitting on the sofa in just his pants and a white
t-shirt. He and Mum hadn't slept in the same bed for a
while. Not since she'd started to get more and more upset.
I think Dad had tried, hoping it would make her calmer,
having someone next to her during the dark hours of the

night, but then I would hear shuffling around and then Dad going downstairs before the clock had even reached twelve.

'Mum's crying,' I said to him. For a moment, I thought he was going to cry too, but then he just sat up. 'It's good you're awake. You can start loading the car. The smaller bags and boxes. Not the big ones. I'll do those once I've sorted out your mum.' He wandered away, the light from the window turning him yellow-gold. I sat on the sofa for a bit, then did as I was told. Some of the bits we'd packed that night had been put in supermarket bags when we'd run out of the boxes Dad had brought home with him. I picked some of these up and went out to the car, which was already unlocked, and threw them in, not caring if anything broke. The day had only been new for a matter of minutes, and I was already starting to feel cross. It didn't look like I'd be going to play in the garden, or to the library to get some more books. Nothing seemed certain any more.

The street was completely empty. The sun was still low, the ground untouched by its warming light. Although the summer weather had lasted into September, you could tell autumn wanted to break in and ruin the fun. Before Mum had become like she was now, early last year or the year before, she used to paint the autumn leaves on the trees. Browns and reds and golds. She'd sit outside and paint the trees in the neighbours' garden. I used to sit with her sometimes, making little finger paintings of different plants or animals, often insects and squirrels. Then Mum would beam at me and tell me I'd created another masterpiece and how she'd phone up the Tate at once. Then we'd laugh, and she'd show me what she had created. Her pictures didn't really look like the trees in the way I would sometimes paint them – she used to zoom in on a particular branch and just paint the leaves on that one. Then one day she painted this big, amazing tree – an oak tree, she said – one she remembered from when she was younger. Then, over the top of it, she painted flames. Big flames licking at its trunk, snaking up towards the leaves, and all of them were burning, smoke covering the sky. That was when things started to get bad.

Mum tried to help with the packing of the car but eventually Dad just told her to sit in the front passenger seat and we'd finish the job. She sat there working her way through a pack of garibaldi biscuits while we heaved and stuffed and pushed everything that would fit into the car. We weren't taking *that* much – not as much as when my friend Melanie moved house back when we were both in playgroup and a huge lorry turned up to take all their things – but even so, by the time we were finished packing the car, there was just a small hole in the side for me to sit, all our stuff almost covering the seat. I liked being in there. It felt like I was a dormouse, settling in for hibernation.

'Why are we going away?' I asked. I had been thinking about asking the question since I'd woken up, but sometimes asking my dad questions sent him into a 'flaming rage'. That's what our old neighbour Mrs Slater used to call it. He used to have a go at her about her 'bloody cat' when it left us dead mice on the doorstep. 'You in one of your flamin' rages?' she used to say when he'd try to hand her the corpse of a rodent as she left for the Quicksave to do her shopping. She would never take it from him. She'd wander off, leaving him holding it. Dad used to say 'that woman is a bitch' to himself whenever they had one of their disagreements. I didn't think she was a bitch. She sometimes gave me books from the charity shop. Most of them were about posh girls at boarding schools – the type where they have stables and games they play with sticks – but sometimes a really naughty one would slip in. My favourite of the naughty ones had been a book called *The Count Comes for What He's Owed*. It was about a count in a castle somewhere foreign and he'd been promised a young woman's hand in marriage by her father. I tried to write a sequel myself, in an old notebook I found under the stairs, about when the count started forcing her to have so many babies her body starts to break in half, until she dies giving birth to their twelfth child. I submitted it at school as a part of my writing homework. Mrs Bolton just wrote on it 'See me' in red biro. When I did, she wasn't very pleased. I had to sit outside while Mum had a whispered conversation with her about me. Mrs Bolton had used the words 'unhinged' and 'depraved'. My mother just cried and advised her I was probably going to hell anyway and a 'horrid little story about the sins of the flesh' was the least of her worries at that moment in time. Even so, my paperback of *The Count Comes for What He's Owed* was thrown onto the fire. Mrs Slater was forbidden to give me any more books after that.

'You haven't answered my question,' I said, louder than

necessary, as Dad packed stuff around me and I nestled up against one of my pillows.

'Quiet,' he said. 'I really, really just need you to do as you're told and not ask questions. I will explain when we get there.' I saw, through the gaps in the boxes loaded around me, that he turned to look at Mum, as if he was scared she'd flip. She didn't flip. She was staring into space and humming 'The Lord is My Shepherd' to herself.

'Does Mum know where we're going?' I asked, ignoring his previous plea.

Dad glared at me. 'She knows we're going away for a peaceful break,' he half-whispered to me, 'and while she seems content with that, I ask you not to say anything that may make her upset again.'

After a tense pause, I nodded, and he moved away to get another bag.

I don't know what time it was by the time we were packed – the boxes hid my view of the clock in the front of the car – but it was starting to get warmer. I think it was probably 8.30 or 9. 'Will we be stopping for food on the way?' I asked, ignoring Dad's instruction again. I just got a short 'Yes' from him as a reply.

We set off eventually, driving away from the streets I'd always known and out into the big wide world. I'd only really been out of our town twice – once on a trip to London when I was really young, and another time to France to a place called Lourdes. The London trip was a disaster. A bomb went off somewhere near some soldiers' barracks and everyone started screaming and crying. We didn't see the bomb, but we heard it and saw the smoke.

We were standing outside Buckingham Palace when it happened. I was on my dad's shoulders, back before he was blunt and liable to 'flamin' rages'. Back when he'd pick me up and spin me around and tell me I was special and bright and clever. He'd been especially happy during our trip to London – he'd got some qualifications at his work that meant he could earn a bit more money, and he'd let me sit on his shoulders for ages, not once telling me to walk for a bit because his back was aching. When we'd reached the gates of the palace, I'd been trying to see in through the queen's bedroom window – my friend Gwendolyn had told me she only ever wore knickers made of gold and I was desperate to have a look. Then there was a loud bang and everyone started running and Dad lifted me off his shoulders and shouted at Mum, 'Christ, it's the IRA. It's the fucking IRA.'

The visit to France, a few years later, went a lot smoother. No bombs. No fucking IRA. Although by that time, Mum had started to change. She'd drifted around the place, touching things and crying silently, while Dad shook his head and moaned about the lack of food choices. 'I can't stand hunger,' he had said. 'I wish they had a cure for that, here.'

The food choices on the way to wherever we were going weren't that amazing either. We'd eaten the last pieces of cold pizza early on during the drive, so ended up stopping at a café called Susan's Sausages. Upon sitting down, we were told they'd run out of sausages. When I said to the woman taking our order (she wasn't Susan; her badge said Janice) that they should change their name if there weren't any sausages and it wasn't even Susan talking to their customers, she glared at me and then said to Dad, 'She fuckin' retarded or something?' Dad slammed his fist down on the table and said, 'Just get the food,' and she went off and started crashing things around in the kitchen while a little boy played with chewed Lego bricks on the filthy floor. We managed to get through most of our three portions of ham, egg and chips before Mum started to suspect the chips had been poisoned. 'Marjory, please, just eat the damn chips,' Dad hissed. 'You'll be starving.' She hissed something back about preferring to starve than eat what he fed her.

'Are we going to a hospital?' I thought hazarding a guess might make Dad want to share some more details on where we were actually going.

'Why would you ask that, Kitty?' He was sprinkling a lot of salt onto his food – something I'd learned at school wasn't a healthy thing to do.

'Because that's what Miss Reid said about Mum, after that time she came running into the playground to take me home before the devil could take me. She said "Christ, she needs to be in hospital." So I thought that might be where—'

Dad, whose eyes had flared at the word 'devil', cut me off with another slam of his fist on the table. 'We're not going to a hospital. Nobody is going to any place like that.' He glanced at Mum, who had flinched at the fist-slam, but she carried on moving her food around her plate nonetheless.

'Why not? Miss Reid is a very sensible teacher, you

know. If she said it would be a good idea, I think it probably would be.'

'I won't tell you again, Kitty,' Dad said back, still hissing in a whispery voice. 'People don't come back from places like that. Unless you want your mum to end up like your grandmother—'

He stopped himself mid-sentence, as if he'd realised what he was about to say, then changed his mind. 'Anyway,' he said in a calmer voice, 'hospitals like *that* won't be around much longer. I heard them say so on the radio.'

Dad mentioning Granny had made me confused, since he couldn't have been talking about Mum's mum, since she had died in a car accident when I was younger. I could only really remember her a tiny bit. He must have been talking about his mother, my other Granny who I never met and neither him nor Mum spoke about much. I thought about asking more about her, but decided this might make his mood worse.

After the food, I asked to use the toilet. The moody Janice woman pointed to the back of the café without saying anything, so I found them by myself and peed in peace and quiet, until a little boy who looked around five wandered through the door.

'Hello,' I said. 'Could you go away and close the door?' Then Janice burst in and shouted, 'Tyler, you nasty little pervert, get out,' and he scurried away, giggling. 'Sorry, it's his dad's fault,' she said. 'He lets him get away with murder.' She said all this to me without looking at me. She was tired – I could tell from the dark rings around her eyes. And there was a purple bruise on her cheek that she'd tried and failed to cover with make-up. 'How did you do that?' I asked, pointing at her face. She looked at me as if I was something vile. 'Piss off,' she said, then slammed the toilet door.

I got myself together and washed my hands, then went out to find my parents. Dad was trying to stop Mum from making a scene. She'd become quite an expert at 'scenes' in the past few months. When she'd first started to get bad, a couple of years ago, she used to do it quietly, finding a corner to cry in or waiting until she got home. Then she stopped seeming to care where she was or who was around to see it. She had caused quite a few major scenes in Debenhams, at the swimming pool, in the park, at the newsagents run by the little man with no teeth, and at the theatre when Dad took us as a treat to see *Grease on Ice*. In each of these situations, Dad had shoved us all into the car and said, 'I'm flaming mortified.' He hadn't said it yet, but we hadn't made it to the car either, so there was time for it to come.

'She fucking mental or something?' Janice with the bruised face was saying to my dad.

'No, she's not fucking mental,' he snapped at her, starting to sound stressed. 'Can you just give us a minute?'

Mum was standing on her chair, staring at the floor and jabbing her finger at random areas of the stained tiles: 'There! There! There!' Shouts. Tears. Shrieking.

It was in moments like these I used to try to think of my perfect happy place. A nice little desk with lots of sheets of paper; colouring pens all in a rainbow line, which I could use to draw creatures; a tidy bedroom filled with lots of clean, folded things that would be slightly warm to the touch if you were to rest your cheek on them. I think I must have lived in a place like that once, when I was very small. Before Mum became . . . Mum.

'There's nothing there,' my dad said. He sounded tired.

'I swear it. I swear it upon . . . upon my sweet baby daughter's life.'

It was as if I wasn't there. She didn't look at me. Just kept on with her pointing.

'She thinks she's seen a spider,' my dad said.

I wasn't properly listening. 'A what?'

'A spider!' he snapped.

'Where? Have you seen it?' My mum shrieked.

'There's no bloody spider,' he shouted at her.

'They are the devil's spies.'

'They are harmless insects that are more afraid of you than you are of them!'

'I'm not sure they are insects,' I chipped in, but my dad sent me one of his looks and I sat back down at the table.

'They listen and watch and tell their masters all our secrets.' With this, she clasped her hands together, like she was praying, and began muttering something under her breath. 'He's coming. I can hear it. He's rising. He's rising. He's rising.'

'If she don't come down from that chair and stop with this shouting,' Janice with the bruised face said, 'I'm calling the fucking police.'

'Don't call the police,' he said. 'We're leaving. Marjory, come down, please. I promise you, you'll be fine.'

My mother stared at him like he'd suddenly told her

21

it was her birthday. 'Nathan? Have you come to rescue me?'

'Yes,' he said, instantly. 'Here we go, rescue in progress.' Before she had time to argue, he'd taken her arm and helped her step down off the chair.

'I was tested, just then, Nathan. And I resisted. He didn't rise.'

'I'm glad,' he said, then turned to Janice. 'Show's over. How much do we owe you?'

She murmured something about how she should bloody charge extra for the stress, then totted up the bill and my dad gave her a banknote.

We didn't talk as we left the restaurant, nor when we started driving. Only after we'd been travelling for half an hour did I ask again. 'Dad. Where are we going?'

Chapter 4

Dad ignored me seven times. When he drew in a long, deep breath I thought I'd finally worn him down, but he didn't say anything.

After a while, I said: 'If it's somewhere horrible – like Epping – I won't be happy.' We went on a camping trip to Epping Forest once. It rained. We were forced to either stay in our tent or go to a café near the service station filled with big bald men who drove lorries. I wasn't able to go searching for little creatures once during the whole weekend.

'It isn't Epping,' he said, shortly.

I was encouraged that he at least reacted to my statement, but then he went back to saying nothing again.

'The Shepherd will soon be tempted to leave his flock and give in to his darkest temptations.' My mother said this whilst staring out of the window, pressing her forehead to the glass.

'That's the spirit,' Dad muttered. 'We'll be there soon, now.'

Dad didn't seem to quite understand the meaning of the word 'soon'. It took hours more, through the afternoon and into the night. We passed woodland, towns, and big signs saying 'The North' and 'Newcastle' and 'Northumbria'. We stopped for tea at an old pub with growling dogs. Instead of making a scene at this one, Mum managed to go to the car to have her 'moment'. After a while, though, she started to use the horn to attract our attention and Dad went out to calm her down. I stayed in my seat, picking at the chicken in a basket he'd bought me, but eventually I got unnerved by all the old men at the bar pointing to me, a child on her own in a pub, so I went out to the car too.

'I need to tell you, Kitty,' my dad said when we went back in to the pub to finish our food. 'This holiday may not be like other holidays.'

I stared back at him, unsure of what he meant. 'But we don't really go on holidays. Not any more.' I was tempted to add that even when we did go away, we didn't usually take so much stuff or let people stay in our house, but I decided too many words might annoy him.

He nodded, thinking about what I'd said. 'That's true. But if we did, this wouldn't be like them.'

I dipped one of my chips into the little pot of mayonnaise the waiter had brought. 'Why is that?' I asked.

He didn't answer, just got up to go and pay at the bar. I looked out of the window and watched Mum talking to the steering wheel.

We travelled for an hour more. I know this because I watched the clock on the dashboard of the car turn from 20.00 to 21.00, which means nine o'clock, apparently. We journeyed deep into the thick countryside, through dark trees. They bent and twisted around us, as if they were inviting us into their strange world – though once we were admitted, I did wonder if we'd ever be let out. Mum seemed to have the same idea, because she kept up a steady wailing sound, like a radio signal going in and out, and murmured things like, 'Oh no . . . not into the darkness . . . oh no . . . please.' But she didn't fully 'kick off', so things couldn't have been that bad. I tried to ignore her and nestled my head on the pillow I was clutching. I'd been stealing them from other parts of the car along the journey and now I had a little nest of comfort in the back. It had almost caused a bit of an avalanche earlier, with some of the books Dad had allowed us to bring slipping from their bag, but he didn't notice. He was too busy trying to navigate, glancing at a map in the gloom whilst driving with the other hand.

Finally, a little bit after nine, Dad announced, 'We've arrived.' He looked over at Mum. 'Marjory. We've arrived. Remember. Our little holiday?'

She just nodded and looked at her hands. He sighed and got out of the car. I was sleepy – I'd been dozing on and off since the pub. 'How far have we travelled?' I asked.

'Far,' Dad said. He sounded tired and annoyed. The

window to my left was completely dark. I tried to look past all the stuff into the front of the car, but I couldn't see anything out there either.

'We've fallen. And I don't think we'll be able to climb back out again.' I heard Mum speaking in a flat voice, then saw the shape of my father move to the right and open the car door.

'I'll come round and get you out, Kitty,' he said before he closed the door.

He did as he promised, half lifting me out of my little nest in the back, more gently than I expected. 'I realise this might all be a bit strange. And it might get stranger. But it's all for the best.' He nodded as he spoke and didn't look me right in the eyes. Just off over my shoulder, into the darkness.

'Where are we?' I said. I looked around, making out the outlines of trees. They surrounded us. I gasped. I couldn't help it. We were in the woods. In the middle of the woods. I didn't know what woods, or forest, it was, but we'd been driving for a whole day and a bit, so we could be anywhere. Then I looked directly ahead and saw a building type of thing. A house type of thing. It was like a cottage, only a little bit larger. You could tell it had an upstairs because of the windows.

'Come on,' Dad said. 'Let's go and wake the place up.'

'Waking the place up' wasn't as nice as it sounded. The house, which had strange-looking plants crawling up its walls outside, and strange-looking wallpaper crawling up its walls inside, was like something in the old picture books I used to get out of the library. Ones that involved little children getting lost in woods. At least I had my dad with me. And my mum. Although, with each day that passed, she was becoming more of a child than I was.

'There are spiders,' I said as I looked eagerly around the living room.

'The devil's creatures!' my mother shrieked.

Dad sent me one of his sharp looks and put his arm around Mum. 'Don't worry. We'll get rid of them. Won't we, Kitty?'

I frowned at him. 'So long as I can keep them and make a spider colony.'

He huffed and puffed a bit and settled my mum on the sofa while he and I began to bring some of the boxes and bedding in from the car.

'Prioritise the stuff we'll need for tonight and the morning,' he said. 'Then we'll bring the rest in tomorrow.'

I thought about telling him that it was hard to 'prioritise' stuff like that when we couldn't really see what was in the bags unless we unpacked them, but I decided not to. He'd given me too many sharp looks already today. One more could be the final straw for the both of us. I did as I was told, even though I didn't want to, and tried my best to bring in just the things I needed. Sometimes I got it wrong ('Kitty, why the hell would we need our wellington boots for either bed or breakfast?') but it all had to come in eventually, I said, so I didn't know why he bothered complaining. While I did this, he took the majority of the bedding upstairs. I heard him rifling around up there, then a loud creaking noise. He must be moving the furniture, I thought. In the end, bored with bringing things in, I went up to have a look. The stairway groaned as I trod on it and I imagined how many wonderful animals must be living underneath it. Rats and mice with razor-sharp teeth and spiders the size of dogs.

There were three rooms upstairs. A big one, which Dad was in now, a smaller one and a bathroom. I thought about Ebenezer Scrooge, going about his house after seeing the face of Jacob Marley in his door knocker, and wondered if I too would see any apparitions. Part of me hoped I would. It was one of those things that seemed to only happen to people who wouldn't enjoy it. They just screamed and spent the rest of their lives boring everyone with how they ran away instantly and would never go back in the room or house or hotel or museum or wherever they'd been ever again. I would try to talk to a ghost. I think I'd have a lot to say. Like whether all this was worth it, just to reach the other side, and if they had food in the afterlife. Mum and I played ghosts once on Halloween. My classmates at school were having a party, but I'd had flu that week and was still feeling tired and worn out by little things. So Mum made our own party: we had sheets with holes in and watched *Casper* cartoons on the TV. Later on in the evening, I said something that spoilt things a little. I said to Mum I'd like to have a little ghost as a pet, like Casper. He'd float around when I'd want him to, then when I didn't he would be invisible and sit on my shoulder, so nobody else would know I had a little friend, but I could still talk to him and he could speak to me, like a voice inside my head. She'd gone quiet when I said this. Then she took off her ghost sheet and said she needed to have a lie down.

The sound of her crying lasted for most of the next three cartoons. After that, I started to understand Mum probably did have a little ghost on her shoulder, or inside her head. But it didn't say nice things.

'Kitty, come in here and take the other end of this sheet.'

I went into the room Dad was in and watched as he struggled with a large bed sheet, trying to wrap it over an ancient-looking mattress, only to have the ends ping off each time he tried to secure them. I held it still for him and he finally got it all secured. 'There, that's done.' Without speaking, he picked up all the pillows and duvets from the floor and tried to make them look tidy on the bed. 'Right, now for your bed, Kitty.'

We went back downstairs to get the remaining bedding stuff, but Dad froze statue-still as soon as we got to the lounge. 'Where's your mother?' he said, loudly and angrily.

'I don't know,' I said. I tried to sound defiant and not worried, but I was scared. It wasn't too much of a worry when she went off wandering when we were at home. This was a rather recent thing, and I got the feeling Dad wasn't quite sure how to deal with it. I don't think he wanted to lock her up or force her to stay in the house all day while he was at work, and mostly she just kept to the lounge or the kitchen. But sometimes she wandered, usually to the local shops, just to try on some clothes. She never bought anything, but the staff now knew her by name and were very nice to her. They would allow her to sit down in one of the changing room cubicles for a bit if she got upset, then telephone for my dad to walk down the street to get her and help her home. But we weren't at home now. And Mum couldn't have gone to Debenhams. We were alone, in the middle of the woods in a fairy tale house, and it was dark and strange. And worst of all, I think it was me who had left the front door wide open.

Chapter 5

'Holy fucking Christ,' my father said. He turned to me.
'Was she down here just now, before you came upstairs?'

I nodded.

'Stay here,' he said. 'She can't have gone far.'

I sat on the sofa Mum had recently left. There was still
an indentation in the middle from where she had been
sitting. I stared around at the odd place in front of me.
There was a television, smaller than ours at home and
with a thick layer of dust on top of it. There was also a
fireplace, with a rusty metal thing around it. I looked
forward to watching logs burning on it.

I was about to go and put some wood in it from the
little pile by its side, hoping Dad would see it and be

inspired to build a fire, but then I heard noises from outside: Dad shouting my mum's name, then another shout from her, then her voice, loud and clear. It sounded like she was walking around the side of the house. 'I need to check to see if they're listening,' she said to my dad, speaking as if she thought he was stupid, while at the same time annoyed he was bothering her.

'There isn't anybody out there to listen to anything. Even if there was anything they'd want to listen to! Marjory, please, come back inside.'

'He has *thousands* of spies, Nathan. *Thousands*. Do you want to know how many I see every night in my dreams?' She shouted these words, coming closer still. I twisted round on the sofa and leaned over the back so I could see out of the dirty, green-tinged window. I could just about make them out. She was standing out there, clutching something – I thought it was a stick. And Dad had his hands out, trying to take it from her. 'I see their eyes. Their EYES. You know what that means, don't you? You know what they tell me to do.' Then she burst into tears. Loud tears with serious sobs and lots of words I couldn't properly hear.

Dad walked over to her. For a second, I thought she was going to run him through with the stick, but he just put his hands round it and took it from her. She let him. She was too busy crying.

At first, when I started to see Mum cry more and more, I wanted to cry too. I didn't really know what was happening, or why she got so upset, but I used to think there must be something really serious to worry about if a grown-up was crying. Because crying was something children did. Adults only cried when something was really bad, I thought. But when I started to see my mum cry about four times a week, I stopped finding it as upsetting as I once did.

'It's OK, Marjory. Why don't we just go back inside? We need to make this place a home.' Dad was doing his best to be kind, now. And, finally, she let him, and wrapped her arms around his shoulders, her sobs turned into silent crying. I turned around and sat back on the sofa properly to watch them as they came in.

'Hello Kitty Cat,' she said. 'I'm sorry about my little moment.' She sniffed and dabbed at her eyes with the back of her hands, as if she was trying not to disturb the make-up she wasn't wearing. 'I just got so upset at the thought of someone listening.' She sat down and Dad murmured something about a glass of water as he left the room. 'Do you know what I mean by listening?' she said. Her eyes were going wide again. I thought about calling Dad, but before I could he was back and giving her a drink.

'Have some of this,' he said, and Mum did as he said and took a sip of the water.

'Better?' he said.

'It's not from the stream is it?' she whispered, urgently. Dad looked confused. 'No, it's from the tap.'

'Are you really, really sure?' She gripped his hand, stopping him moving away, staring at him as if desperate for him to reassure her.

'Yes, I'm very sure. I haven't seen a stream.'

'We passed one on the way,' she said, sipping at the water and flicking little looks at me that I found more disturbing than the crying.

'No we didn't,' Dad said with a sigh. 'And it was dark. Even if we did I don't think you'd have seen it.'

Mum muttered about 'all-seeing eyes' and then went quiet, concentrating on her drinking.

'Why don't you go up to bed, Kitty?' my dad suggested. 'We'll carry on with the unpacking in the morning.'

I nodded and got up. 'Goodnight Mum,' I said. I went to give her a kiss, but she didn't look up. She was staring into the water in the glass as if it were the most interesting thing in the world. 'Night, Dad,' I said, walking past him. I didn't offer him a kiss, as he'd made me cross too many times today.

'Goodnight,' he said.

I went up the creaking stairs and made sure I pressed hard on the loosest ones, hoping some dust or wood flakes would snow down on any creatures inside. Perhaps they'd come out and play during the night.

My duvet and things were all on my bed. I didn't know where my toothbrush was – probably in one of the hundreds of bags and boxes either downstairs or in the car – so I just used the stiff tap in the bathroom to wash my mouth out (five spits, one gargle) and then went back to get into bed. On the landing I could hear my dad saying something to my mum about sleeping downstairs if she 'promises not to go walkabout'. She replied straight away, 'Oh dearest, why on earth would I want to go walking about in the woods at night? Anything could be out there.'

Once in my room, I spent a good few minutes trying to put the bed sheets on myself. I eventually succeeded, feeling a little proud at how good I was starting to get at doing things like this without help. I then got under the covers and tried to sleep straight away, but it didn't work, so I just started counting the drips of water I could hear falling outside the window. Then the drips became rain and the rain became a downpour. I burrowed into my bedding and pretended I was a little mouse, caught in the fields in a storm, in need of a large leaf or a den to shelter under and stay dry and warm. I need to stay safe and sheltered, I thought to myself as I finally drifted off to sleep. After all, Mum was probably right. Anything could be out there.

Chapter 6

January 2020

The police station is a drab, seventies build – the sort of thing that might have looked edgy and modern once, but now looks depressing in a harsh, Brutalist way. Part of me had expected a row of uniformed officers holding sub-machine guns to be waiting for me at the doors, the type you see patrolling London underground stations or key tourist attractions. But of course, they don't bother with the likes of me. I'm not an immediate threat. It's the past that matters now. Not the present, or the future.

The woman on the desk looks at me with all the emotion of a robot. I explain who I am and who I've been asked to see. She glances at a screen that's turned away from me, then at a tablet device on the desk in front of her, then tells me to take a seat. I do as I'm told, sitting next to a young man who cracks the knuckles on each hand, as if to warn me not to even think about messing with him. One of his hands, I notice, is badly bruised and cut, like he's punched a wall. Or a face.

'What you fuckin' looking at?' he asks me in a thick Newcastle accent, then, without waiting for an answer, he asks, 'Want a smoke?' and brings out a packet of cigarettes. I look down at them, noticing the box is stained with something dark and sticky-looking, perhaps spilt beer, then jump when a voice above me says, 'No smoking in here. It's illegal.' A short, burly police officer rounds on us both, as if we're two naughty school kids. I object to being grouped in with the unsavoury-looking man next to me and start stammering about how I hadn't intended to take one, but another voice cuts me off.

'Katherine Marchland?'

Another figure has appeared to the left of the short man. This one's also male, but younger – he only looks about twenty-six or -seven – and much taller. 'I'm Detective Constable Malik. Please come this way.'

He doesn't smile exactly, but his mouth thins into a shape that I think is meant to be comforting. His movements are gentle and courteous as he holds the door open for me, leading us deeper into the building. The light quality is poor – the corridor is windowless and lit by dim white strips, with some of the bulbs blinking as if they might give up the ghost at any moment.

'Just in here,' he says, and opens the door to a small room, also windowless. I recognise it instantly as a police interview room from any number of television dramas. It even has one of those dark-glass sections in the wall, presumably for people to watch behind it unseen. The only thing different is that I can't see one of those big old cassette recorder decks on the desk, although I can see something long and thin hanging from the ceiling, so I presume it must be a microphone hooked up to a recording device somewhere out of sight.

'Do take a seat,' he says, motioning to the one he clearly wishes me to sit in, then asks, 'Would you like some water?'

I nod, grateful for the offer. 'Yes please. Thank you.' Maybe things aren't quite as bad as I'd thought. This man seems kind.

He opens the door, presumably to go out and get the water, but a woman walks straight through it before he can exit. 'Ms Marchland? My name's Detective Inspector Tamara Cousins. I'll be leading this interview with DC Malik.' She's short, and quite a bit older – maybe early forties. Whereas the younger officer is clearly a local, with a pleasantly soft Northumbrian note to his voice, her accent is a surprise – rather posh and tight.

At this, DC Malik leaves the room and returns seconds later with a plastic cup filled with water. 'Are we all set up?' DI Cousins asks her colleague.

He nods. 'Fine to go ahead.'

'OK, for the recording, present in this interview we have currently speaking Detective Inspector Tamara Cousins and Detective Constable Leon Malik.' She then looks at me: 'Please confirm your name and date of birth.'

'Katherine Marchland,' I say, a little shakily. 'I was born on the 4th September 1977.'

'I gather you were formerly known as Katherine Carlson – although I understand Marchland is a name you have created rather than one you acquired through marriage – and you live at Number 2, Station View Walk in the London Borough of Barking and Dagenham?'

I nod.

'Could you answer "yes" or "no" please for the recording?'

'Yes.'

'Good. Ms Marchland, you do not have to say anything but it may harm your defence if you do not mention when questioned something which you later rely on in court. Anything you do say may be given in evidence.' She's looking right at me, watching for a reaction. I don't give one, just stare back, trying to ignore the rush of panic sweeping through me. 'As I explained on the phone, you're not under arrest at present, and I'd also like to make it clear you're free to leave at any time. Do you understand everything I've just said to you?'

I nod. 'Yes.'

'Splendid. I've got here that you are currently employed as a staff writer on a newspaper. *The Dagenham and Rainham Advertiser.* Is that right?'

'Sort of. I do bits and bobs. Sell some advertising space, write some copy.'

She nods, looking at the papers in front of her. 'The purpose of this interview is to help us understand your perspective on certain incidents which have come to our attention.' Her eyes flick back up to my face and stare directly into mine. 'In other words, Katherine, we've seen the video.'

She holds my gaze for a couple of seconds, then presses on. 'What you say in this interview will be recorded. We will take into account what you tell us today when we decide whether to pursue formal arrest and any potential criminal charges. You have not brought any legal representation with you, and I believe you declined the offer of a solicitor to be appointed for you?'

I nod again. 'Yes.'

She produces a folder from her bag under the desk. 'I trust you have an idea as to why you're here?' It's said like a question, and she raises her eyebrows at me.

'I do. I'm here because . . .' I take a deep breath, trying to stop my speech becoming shaky, 'because of what happened in the woods. All those years ago.'

Chapter 7

1987

I woke up to blood. Tiny, tiny drops of it on my pillow. I examined them through my sleep-blurred eyes. Then I felt the sting of a cut in my finger. It was small, like the droplets of blood, but it was there. It took me a few minutes to discover what it was – a discovery that rather pleased me. There was a large stag beetle, the size of a small mouse, climbing up my wall near my bed. I knew they would come. Animals usually sought me out. I think it was because they knew I wasn't a threat. I was curious rather than predatory.

'Hello,' I said to it. 'What shall we do with you, then?' I scooped him up in my hands, feeling his pincers trying to cut me again. I let him cut me. I didn't mind. After all, he was here first. I was the one trespassing on his territory.

I walked down the stairs, giving them some celebratory creaks (maybe more creatures will come, I thought). Dad was in the kitchen, a small, cold place, colder than the rest of the house, which was odd as I'd always thought of the kitchen as being the warmest, filled with stoves and ovens. In spite of the cold, Dad was just in his pants, brandishing a screwdriver over the old toaster from home as he leaned over the rough, stained kitchen table.

'Dad?' I said, watching him from the doorway.

'Morning, Kitty,' he said, not looking up.

'How old are you?' I asked.

He looked up then, clearly surprised by my question. 'I'm thirty.'

'How old were you when you stopped crying when you hurt your hand or got a cut or fell over?'

He looked a little irritated now, and turned back to the toaster. 'Er . . . I don't know. Probably your age.'

'I've been bitten by a beetle more than once this morning and I haven't cried once. I haven't really felt the need to.'

He gave me one of his confused looks. He often looked confused when I told him things I found interesting.

'Mum cries all the time though,' I said, a little quietly.

'Well, Mum's different,' he said. He seemed to be finished with the plug part of the toaster now and went to plug it into the wall. 'The bread's stale,' he nodded towards the loaf. 'We should have got some on the way last night but I didn't really think about it. So we'll toast it. Then it will taste fine.'

'Will it?' I asked, rather surprised by this new information.

'It will. Come and sit down.'

I looked around the kitchen and found what I was looking for. I dragged a small but deepish bowl from the countertop and dropped the beetle into it. 'What the hell is that?' he said, looking at the bowl in disgust.

'The beetle. The one I just told you about.'

'We don't want it in here. Throw it out in the garden. You can't carry on with this weird animal adoption thing, Kitty. You're getting too old for it now. It may have been, I don't know, cute or eccentric when you were young. You're ten years old now . . . it's just not normal.'

He stopped, then turned away as if he'd changed his mind.

'Why?' I said, folding my arms. He was starting to upset me, but I tried not to show it.

'It's just not . . . something you should be doing.'

I kept my arms folded. 'Mum used to say my creature curiosity was the sign of a mind that one day would do great things – because I'm *interested* in things. In animals, in wildlife, in—'

'OK, OK,' he said, holding up his hands. 'I'm sure that's all very true. But your mum doesn't like little creatures any more, does she? You've seen how she can react to them. Just . . . just chuck the beetle out, all right?'

'After the toast,' I said, sitting down. I could see him deciding whether to argue further or not. He chose not to. It was for the better, I thought.

He left me to my breakfast, muttering about unpacking

some clothes and going for a pee. He was right about the toast. It didn't taste stale, although I had to cut off a little green bit on the side. I accidentally ate some of it before the amputation and it tasted like plants. Strong ones, with a bitter, furry taste. The rest of the two slices was fine, though.

Dad came back quicker than I expected, dressed in a t-shirt and one of his older pairs of jeans with a few holes in them. 'Where's Mum?' I asked immediately.

He let out one of his I-would-prefer-not-to-talk-about-it sighs. 'She's still asleep.'

'Do you need me to wake her?' I went to stand up.

'No.' His hand shot out to stop me. He gripped me – not too hard, but firm. 'Please, Kitty. Just let her sleep. It's still very early. It'll be the only peace and quiet I'll get all day.' He looked sad when he said this, and the lines on his face seemed more *there* than usual. Jemimah Prince at school once described my dad to her mother as 'a young popstar dad' compared to her 'crumbly old git of a dad'. Jemimah's mum didn't seem too impressed with this description and told her daughter to keep such rude evaluations about her father to herself. She said her comments about my dad were 'inappropriate' and then frowned at me, as if I'd said them. I didn't really know what to think. I didn't think my dad looked like a popstar. I suppose his tallish thinness and dark-brown hair made him more noticeable than the chubbier, slightly grey-haired dads I sometimes saw at school plays or Christmas fetes, but to me he was just my dad. Nothing more remarkable than that. But now, I wondered if Jemimah were sitting at this table at this moment and saw those lines on my dad's face, with his tired, dark eyes and sad expression, whether she'd still describe him in the same way. I thought it unlikely.

'Let's go and take your beetle outside,' he said, sounding kinder now. 'We'll say goodbye to him together. OK?'

I nodded and counted the burn marks on the kitchen table while he went to find a jumper from the car. I had already got dressed, but Dad had something draped over his arm and seemed keen for me to take it. 'You'll be a bit cold,' he said. 'Put your mum's coat round you.'

I'd worn Mum's coat before and I had always liked how much it smelled of home – when home was a happy place, a place I liked to remember. A little while ago, probably just over a year back, Mum and I would spend most Saturday mornings going to the shops to buy ingredients for a pie, then spend the afternoon making it. Rolling the pastry together, filling the insides with apple in sugary syrup from a tin, her telling me what a clever girl I was when I made a pattern on the outside that went all the way round the rim. Thinking about this made me a little sad, so I wrapped the coat around me, bunching it up so that it didn't trail along the ground, and tried to press the thoughts out of my mind. I followed Dad as he carried the bowl with the beetle in and walked away from the house through the trees. Their branches went high – higher than most trees I've seen – and although it was autumn, most of them still had their leaves, dark green and spiky, sticking to their branches. 'Here we go,' Dad said, kneeling down by one. 'This is far enough away from the house. Let's let him out here.' He handed me the bowl.

I didn't say anything as I let the beetle go. I would have been sad if I was at home. Friends like a large stag beetle were hard to come by, though perhaps not quite so hard as human friends. One of the nicer teachers at school, Mrs Clifton – she taught another class but helped out at break times – once took me aside at the end of lunchtime play and asked if I'd like it if she helped me make some friends and how she was worried she always saw me on my own. I said I was fine as I was, watching the butterflies on the bushes and the birds nesting in the trees. She went away eventually, but part of me wondered how things would have been if I'd said yes, I would like some human friends. But I missed my chance, and she didn't ask again.

'No! No! No!' I heard the shrieks and dropped the bowl.

Dad jerked around quickly, then immediately started walking towards the little house. 'Come in, Kitty,' he said sharply.

'I will not do it!' My mother's shouts echoed around me and I watched my dad go inside the house. Heard him trying to calm her.

I turned back to the beetle. He wasn't moving. Just standing on the trunk of the tree. Poised. Unsure. Sensing danger.

I know how you feel, I thought. Then I put my cut fingers into my mouth and sucked them gently as I went back inside.

Chapter 8

We spent that first day getting unpacked. Mum even started to feel better enough to help at one point, although she kept getting distracted. Most of the boxes she opened led to her sitting cross-legged on the floor examining her own collection of mugs or balls of Dad's socks, as if they were really interesting things from another planet that had just been discovered.

We had lunch later – about 2.30, according to the old metal clock above the fireplace that was already there when we arrived. Lunch consisted of toasted stale bread again, with Marmite this time, and Dad said he'd drive to the nearest shops later and get us some supplies. I think he was getting tired of checking each slice for mould before he bit into it.

'Can I come with you?' I asked. I was keen to see the world outside the woods. Just to make sure it was still there.

'No,' he said, gruffly.

'You want me to stay here alone?' I was annoyed with him, mainly because he was doing this stupid thing where he didn't look at me properly. He did it when he was going against what he knew I wanted.

'You won't be on your own,' he replied, quietly. 'You'll be with Mum.'

I looked over at Mum, who, having cut off all her crusts, was now eating them one by one, leaving the main (and best) part of the slice of toast on the plate.

'She could come too.' It seemed like a reasonable suggestion to me.

'Just stay with her. We'll see if we can get that old TV working.'

I didn't jump for joy at this. He knew I didn't really care about TV. 'I think I'd still rather come,' I said, simply.

'And I'm the adult so what I say bloody goes,' he said, angrily. He was looking at me now, his eyes sharp and filled with warnings. I often ignored signs like these and he would get into a rage where he'd go white and then red and then white again and have to go and lie down.

'I wish Mum was the one who was still normal,' I said.

I heard him drop his knife with a clatter. I didn't look up. I was staring at my plate. Trying not to move.

'Are you trying to upset me, Kitty? Is that what you want? I'm doing my fucking best, you understand! I'm—' He stopped. Got up. Then walked out of the room.

I heard him putting his coat on in the little hallway cloakroom thing. He took a long time doing it. Mum was already crying, but not making as much of a fuss about it as normal, just wiping her tears on the plastic bag the bread was in. 'I'll be back in about an hour, hopefully.' Dad didn't come back to say this. Just called it from the doorway. 'Do not let your mum go outside. Keep the door shut. Keep talking to her. OK?'

I let a few seconds pass before I finally called out 'OK' in response. I heard the latch and the door slammed. And then he was gone.

And I was left at the kitchen table, watching the 'o' of the word 'Hovis' go all blurry from my mother's tears.

Eventually, I finished the unpacking. I thought I might as well do it on my own, even if I couldn't quite reach the high things and the chairs didn't look too safe to stand on. I got the things all packed away – saucepans in the cupboard, clothes in the rough, scratchy old wardrobes and drawers. Mum even helped me fold my cardigans neatly, humming the theme tune to *Coronation Street* as she did it. With the clean, though slightly tatty, carpets and light green curtains now feeling a little more familiar, the place had started to feel more like a home. Just not our home.

I didn't hear the door go. I was sitting on the stairs, so wasn't far from it, but I was concentrating on encouraging out a large spider I'd seen crawl into a hole at the bottom. I thought it would make a nice replacement for the beetle I'd been forced to cast out earlier, so I spent a good few minutes trying to coax it into a bowl, though without success. I'd just given up and had gone to put the bowl back in the kitchen when I saw that Mum had disappeared from the lounge. I went through, into the hallway. The front door was open, swinging in the breeze. It was starting to get dark. Darker than I had expected. How long had passed since Dad left? It must have been more than an hour. More than two, if it had got dark already?

I ran and put on my wellington boots and a coat, then went outside into the twilight. Although not as new-cold-crisp as it had been this morning, the wind was blustery and I hugged my coat close to me as I walked around the outside walls of the house. 'Mum!' I shouted, peering around the corners, hoping to see her crouched on the ground, playing with some leaves or something. Right around by the back wall, I did find something. But it wasn't Mum. It was on the wall. A word in big, black letters, scrawled in what looked like paint.

LEAVE.

I knew I probably shouldn't have, that I should have gone back inside immediately, but the glinting of the letters made me do it: I reached out and touched the bottom half of the 'L'. My fingers came away wet. It smelled like paint. And if the paint hadn't dried in the blustery wind, that meant it hadn't been done very long ago. My mind started racing. I remembered a creak I'd heard just before I found the spider – a sound I'd dismissed as a tree moving in the wind. Could someone have sneaked up on us in the dark without me knowing? Was someone watching me as I stood there, at the back of the house, just a tiny insignificant figure amidst the enormous woodland?

'Mum!' I shouted again. I heard a noise to my right. A strange scratching noise, as if someone was scraping something against the side of the house. Someone I couldn't see. I looked all around me, but I couldn't focus on anything. It was like the forest was closing in, the light getting dimmer by the second. A flurry of birds suddenly erupted from a nearby tree, screeching and squawking, and I felt my pulse increase, my temperature drop and goosebumps break out across my skin. I tried to call for Mum, or Dad, or anyone, but my throat was tight and croaky. In the end, I just ran.

I ran as far away from the house as I could in my wellington boots. When I was completely out of breath, I crouched down behind a big thick tree trunk and peered around it. The house was a small speck of light through the trees. I watched and waited for a little while, listening hard to the rush of the leaves and the wind. Then I saw something move, up near the house. Did they go inside? Or had they gone round the other side again?

My heart was pumping, my thoughts racing, wondering if it was one of the murderers I'd seen pictures of on TV and in the newspapers Dad read. Or if it was someone else. Some*thing* else. It was the worst 'or' in the whole horrible world. Because it would mean something really, really bad. It would mean Mum was right. They were listening. The trees were listening. The animals were listening. And they didn't want us here. They were not going to let us live.

I ran again, blindly through the woods until suddenly the trees vanished and I was standing on a road. A long, winding road, with trees either side. It was completely empty – no cars, driving or parked. No signs. No glimmer of light to suggest the house in the distance or the direction I'd come from. Nothing. I'm lost, I thought to myself with a flash of fresh new panic, wondering how long it would be before the wolves or cannibals would arrive to eat me. I walked along the edge of the road – away from the house, I thought, but I wasn't completely sure. Then, out of the corner of my eye, I saw a light. A glinting light. It was a car.

I once saw someone in a film waving down a car. They had put their hand out and the person driving stopped and the other person got in. I thought that was maybe what I should do, but before I'd decided I saw the car slowing anyway, so I just stood there, at the edge, watching it crawl to a stop. There were two people in the front seat and the driver wound down their window. It was a woman. She looked like she was about to speak, but before she could, the passenger-side door burst open and a man jumped out. A man I knew. I'd been crying already without realising, but at the sight of him I immediately burst into full, gasping tears.

'Dad?' I sobbed.

'Kitty! What the hell are you doing out here? What's happened to you?'

He was staring at me as if I looked a fright – and when I looked down I saw that I did. There were mud marks on my coat, one side of it was scratched so much the material had almost ripped, and my hands were cut and bleeding.

He saw that I was crying, trying to speak, and he came round to me and clasped my hurt hands. 'Kitty, darling, tell me. Where's Mum?'

I shook my head, and the tears rolled down my face.

I saw the worry growing in his tired eyes. Then he looked back at the woman, now standing by the door of the car, looking at me with big, curious eyes. She was rather beautiful, and slightly older than Dad. Her hair was short and modern-looking and she was wearing a brown leather jacket. 'We need to find her,' Dad continued. 'Let's get back to the house.' The woman didn't say anything, just nodded and got back behind the wheel. Dad led me by the hand to the car and helped me into the passenger seat.

'Drive,' he said, and she zoomed off. The trees blurred past the window. I was pulled away from them by Dad, who was trying to ask me questions. 'Kitty, when did you last see Mum? Where was she when you last saw her?'

I tried to think about it, about how much time had passed, but I couldn't get my thoughts in order. He got impatient. 'Kitty! Please, answer me.'

'I . . . I think she was in the lounge. I left her painting her nails with her favourite violent colour.'

'Violet,' he corrected automatically. 'And how long ago was this?'

I shook my head again. 'A little while. I forgot what the time was. You were gone so long. Why were you gone so long?'

He looked at me and I thought he was about to say something, then he turned back to face the way the car was going and carried on looking ahead.

It didn't take us long to get back to the house. The car wound into the thicker parts of the trees and up towards the front door – still open, as I had left it.

'There's something else,' I said, but he didn't wait to listen.

'Marjory!' he shouted at the top of his voice and ran into the house.

'Don't worry,' the woman said, turning round to face me. If she had been a new class teacher, or one of the team of women who gave me milkshakes at the café in the high street, I probably would have liked her. But right at that moment, I just wanted to get back in the house with Mum and Dad and close the door. 'I'm sure your dad will find your mother soon.'

'How do you know?' I asked.

She didn't seem to know what to say to this straight away. She paused for a moment, then said, 'Whatever will happen, will happen.'

A noise to my left distracted me, and I turned to see Dad running out of the house. He still looked frantic. 'No sign of her in there,' he said.

'I'll get Kitty inside,' said the woman in a businesslike way. 'I'll come and help you look for her in a sec.'

He shook his head. 'No, both of you stay—'

A scream stopped him mid-sentence. Then another. Then a cry. It sounded just a short distance away.

'Marjory!' my dad shouted.

Another scream answered in return.

Then he set off running and I followed, even though the woman was shouting at me to wait. We kept running and I realised we were going down a slope. At the bottom of it was a river, the water glinting and flickering, a big shimmering line through the woods. And in the stream was Mum. She was floating on her back, her arms slowly caressing the water, the movements making her look like an angel.

Except that angels didn't scream.

'Fuck!' Dad shouted and looked around him. I'm not sure what he was hoping to find – maybe a boat which he could use to sail out to get her. 'Stay on the bank, Kitty.'

'But—'

'It's deep around here. Do as I say.'

He threw down his coat, pulled off his shoes, socks, and jeans, and started wading in.

'Christ!' he said. The water must have been cold. He should have kept his trousers on, I thought to myself. Then I remembered that there are few things in the world worse than wet jeans. Mum always used to say so when I was younger if we were caught in a rain storm in the park. Back when she did trips to the park.

Mum's screams got worse as Dad grew nearer to her. He took her hand and pulled her back to the edge of the water. She was shivering, and so was he, although Mum didn't let it interrupt her wailing. 'I need you to walk, Marjory,' Dad snapped at her. I was alarmed to see something dark on her arms, dripping down into her clothes, but as they came closer I realised it wasn't red like blood, but rather deep, dark black.

It was paint.

'What the hell is this?' he shouted when he saw it.

'At the back of the house . . .' I said, struggling to get my words out, 'I think she's painted on the wall. It said LEAVE.'

He glanced over at me, his face filled with worry. 'Kitty, go back into the house,' he said, but I didn't move. I was watching Mum walking slowly, leaning on his side, crying as she did so. As her breathing got slower, I managed to work out what she was screaming. 'Poison. Poison. Poison. It burns him. It burns him. It *burns* him.'

Chapter 9

'I told you to watch her, Kitty,' Dad said as he helped Mum up the stairs to the bedroom and began towelling her down.

'You didn't actually,' I murmured. I watched him as he helped Mum out of her wet clothes, looking at her nakedness; her pale, white skin, slightly shrivelled from the water, now clean after Dad had washed the paint off. Once she was dry, he helped her into her night clothes and then got her into the double bed.

'Let's let her sleep,' he said. 'Come on. I need to introduce you properly to Amanda.'

I followed him downstairs. The spider I had been trying to befriend earlier had come out to see what was going on, peering down from the side of the banisters, his legs wrapped around the flaked white-painted wood. I stopped to look at him, stretching out my hand to see if he'd crawl onto it, but Dad snapped at me. 'Kitty, I told you to come.'

I left the spider for another time and followed him through into the lounge. The woman – Amanda, apparently – was sitting on the sofa, looking comfortable and relaxed, as if she'd always lived here with us and we were all one big happy family.

'Hello Katherine!' She smiled a wide smile, her hoopy earrings swaying as she turned her head to look at me.

'It's Kitty,' I said, staring back at her. I didn't smile.

'How lovely. It's such a pleasure to meet you in person. I've heard so much about you from your father.'

I looked over at Dad, who had sat down in the armchair near the fireplace. 'Amanda was kind enough to give me a lift back. My car broke down when I went to the shops earlier. We'll need to go and get it in the morning.'

I nodded, but remained silent. If all she did was give Dad a lift from the shops, why was she still here sitting on our sofa?

'Are you two friends?' I asked, looking from one to the other. There was something odd about all of this and I didn't like not being told things.

'We're . . . yes, we're friends,' Amanda said, nodding. 'Your father actually helped me a lot with an insurance issue I had with my flat down in Thurrock, near where you both live. That's how we first met. I mentioned I was originally from up here and he should say hello if he

58

should ever visit. And lo and behold, there he was, on the side of the road, with a broken-down car.'

I frowned at her. I wasn't quite sure which bit of her explanation to argue with, but something about it sounded false.

'It's quite an interesting place you guys have moved into,' she carried on, looking around her. 'You'll need to stand on a chair or two to reach those cobwebs up there. But I'm sure you'll help your father get it all spick and span.' She gave me her smile again. I didn't return it.

Dad glared at me from his seat, as if he thought I was showing him up or something. I didn't care. He'd left me all alone and he must have known that what had happened was a possibility. It wasn't my fault Mum escaped. He never said to lock her up or anything. It wasn't like she was our prisoner, after all. Not like one of those Colditz people Mr Gregory showed us at school on a video he brought in.

After a minute or two of sitting there in silence, Amanda eventually got up. 'Well, then. I better get going. Lots to do. Got three dogs at home. Yappy little things. They're not even mine – my sister's. Just one night left before she gets back from her holiday and I can return them. They're one big nightmare as a pack, I can tell you. Rather terrify me. They've probably ripped up the house in protest by now.'

I turned my gaze on her. 'I'm never terrified by dogs. I like animals.'

She nodded, raising her eyebrows slightly. 'Good. That's good, Kitty. I'm pleased. Well, I might borrow them off my sister one day and bring them round these woods for a walk as a special treat.'

I wasn't sure if she meant it would be a special treat for me or for the dogs, but I didn't ask.

'Right, off I go then,' she said, walking towards the door. Dad jumped up to follow her. 'I hope your mother has a calm night and feels better in the morning.'

Dad said a few things to her at the door that I couldn't properly hear, but I did make out the word 'tomorrow'. The door closed and Dad came back into the lounge.

'Time for bed,' he said, not properly meeting my gaze.

Tomorrow arrived sooner than I expected. It felt like I'd only closed my eyes for a short few minutes before I opened them again, light shining in through the dirty window, some creature tap-tapping outside it. A magpie. It seemed pretty determined to undo the latch on the window and join me in my bed, but I didn't dare let him in. Little animals, like spiders and beetles, rarely caused a fuss. Usually my parents didn't know I had one. But something as big as a bird wouldn't go down well. Plus, there was every chance Dad would still be cross about the previous night.

The memory of last night was liquid. It rippled when I tried to touch it in my mind, just like the folds of water that lapped against the side of the stream down the hill through the woods. I thought about Mum screaming, and Dad and that woman talking in whispers. The water on Mum's body. The damp leaves clinging to her skin like black bruises; the trails left by the paint running down her arms. I felt bad that she escaped, but at the same time there wasn't really much I could have done. And Dad had been gone for hours. Hours and hours. I didn't mention last night how unfair the situation was, because I didn't think I needed to. I made a plan to drop it into conversation if he started complaining about the next little creature I adopted.

Breakfast downstairs didn't go well. Mum started off talking quite normally for once – or normal for her – not mentioning her ordeal in the river. Instead, she lectured me and Dad, in a quiet, matter-of-fact sort of voice, on how bread made by a baker who hadn't washed his hands both 'prior and after' kneading the dough could quite likely pass on 'Satan's stain' to those who later consumed it. She said this was particularly likely if 'the baker had taken part in fornication or similarly wicked deeds' before the bread's flour was sifted. I was a bit confused by this, but it clearly annoyed Dad; he seemed to take it as a dig towards the loaf of bread he had brought back from his hours-long trip yesterday.

'I don't think Hovis let their sodding factory workers do anything wicked before sifting the flour,' he remarked sternly, taking up two thick slices and buttering them generously. Mum poked about at her slice, which had been meticulously toasted to the right shade by Dad, as per her instructions. In the past, it would have been me being fussy over how my bread was toasted, and Mum telling me to 'stop being silly' when I objected to it being undercooked or burnt. She'd always give in though, toasting me a nice slice just the way I liked it, with extra chunks of orange peel she'd scooped out of the marmalade jar, just for me. Now, I felt like we were going in opposite directions, as if someone had reversed her timeline to make her become younger as I started to get older, her slowly becoming the child again. A child who needed an adult to sort out her fussy little problems. And bigger problems, too.

'Please eat,' Dad said, sending one of his cross glances her way.

Mum shook her head and pushed her plate away. 'I think it would be better if I went back to bed,' she said, looking not at Dad but instead over towards the ancient-looking refrigerator in the corner by the wall.

I thought back, then, to one time when Dad had tried to encourage Mum out to eat breakfast in the garden, on a warm sunny day in late spring. She wouldn't go. She'd been terrified someone was outside waiting for her, convinced the unusual invitation for 'al fresco dining', as Dad called it, was a sinister trick. She accused Dad of calling for people to come and take her away to somewhere she could never come back from. 'Promise me,' she'd pleaded, 'you never will. Promise me you'll never call them.' He'd promised her then. Promised her never to send her away. I had a feeling it was a promise he would one day have to break. That he couldn't keep indefinitely. But for now, at least, he seemed to be keeping his word.

With Mum now ignoring his attempts to coax her into eating, Dad got properly cross. He threw down his bread and lined up the different types of spread on the table – raspberry jam, Marmite, blackberry jam, peanut butter, on-the-comb honey – saying each one's name out loud. Mum still refused to properly look his way, and flinched as each jar landed on the wood in front of her.

'Surely there is one of these you could possibly fucking contemplate eating,' he said, starting to shout now. 'One of them must free the bread from Satan's fucking stain or whatever shit you're about to come out with next.'

He didn't normally say words like this to Mum and she seemed upset by it. Tears started to fall down her face and she began muttering something containing the words 'Jesus', 'God' and 'forgiveness'. Dad then got a bit sad too, and started to say he was sorry. He tried to hug Mum, but she screamed and he went back to his seat and ate the rest of his toast in silence. I chewed on the little pile of toast squares on my plate and tried to think nice thoughts.

After breakfast, Dad announced that today would have a 'bit more structure' compared to yesterday. For a second I thought he was about to apologise properly for leaving us alone for hours, but he didn't. 'Today, we're going to have some visitors. Some very nice, very important visitors who are going to want to talk to us.' He turned to me now. 'Or, specifically, Kitty, they're going to be talking to Mum. So there might be some moments where you'll have to go and amuse yourself. I'm sure you'll find things to do up in your room. Or, in fact, it might be better if you went exploring for a bit. Only nearby. Not too far. Our visitors are going to want to have a nice long chat with your mum and me without any disruptions.'

'I don't cause disruptions,' I said. 'I just sit by and watch them happen.'

Dad looked a little confused by this. 'Right,' he said at last. Then he made a big fuss of tidying everything, preparing for the guests, getting everything tidy when it was already quite tidy, while Mum sat there, like a strange statue, not moving a muscle.

Chapter 10

Mum was upstairs asleep when the guests arrived. She'd started muttering again about returning to bed and eventually Dad gave in and went upstairs with her to settle her down. A little while later, I heard him greet people at the front door and I heard a voice I recognised. Amanda had returned. She was, apparently, one of the guests, along with a strange-looking, and very round, old man. 'Hello Katherine,' she said from the doorway to the lounge as Dad brought them in.

I said nothing.

'I hope you're all rested after last night's excitements?'

She said it like a question, but I thought it a foolish one. I just stared at her until she looked away and started to take off her coat. Dad should have asked her for it at the door, but he often forgot these things. It used to annoy Mum. Back before Mum started to annoy Dad. Back before Mum started to make Dad look stressed and pale white all the time.

'Shall we all sit down in the lounge here for a bit of a chat?' Amanda asked, settling herself down on the sofa and patting the seat next to her.

'Do you live here?' I asked. It was something I'd been wondering since we'd arrived; whose cottage this was before we made it our temporary home.

She laughed a little. 'Goodness me, no. But the owners of it are acquaintances of mine. Your father got a very good rate from them.'

I looked over at Dad, who had been talking to the old man, offering him something to drink. 'Tea. Proper tea, milk in first, there's a good chap,' the old man said. His voice sounded a little posh, but old-person posh, not really-rich posh, and he sat down in the armchair by the currently dead fire.

'And you must be Katherine,' he said to me. This made me jump, as he wasn't looking towards me, since the chair was facing the other way. I could only just make out the tip of his white hair, barely covering his bald spot, poking over from the top of the chair's frayed top. I hadn't accepted Amanda's invitation to sit next to her, but I decided to leave my position by the doorframe and walked over to face the old man in the chair.

'My name is Kitty,' I said, sternly. 'I rarely answer to Katherine. Only in emergencies.'

He seemed to find this funny. 'Oh very good, very good,' he said, laughing.

I looked down at his clothes. They were completely black, except for a white bit that could be seen under his collar at the front. I recognised it as a dog collar and pointed.

'You must be a vicar.'

'Well, well, well, you are a clever one,' he said, then laughed again.

I lowered my hand, unsure if he was mocking me. I didn't like to be mocked.

'Well? Are you?' I said in a way Dad would have called rude if he wasn't busy in the kitchen making the tea.

'In a way, in a way,' he said, smiling.

'In what way?' I asked, but that set him off chuckling again.

'Why don't you come and sit down with me,' Amanda said from over on the sofa.

I ignored her. 'Why are you here?' I asked the old man. He didn't stop smiling, but he did narrow his eyes a little.

'I think that subject is best discussed when your father is back in the room,' he said. He nodded a little after saying it, then looked towards Amanda. 'I think my daughter over there offered you a seat. You should probably take it.'

'Your daughter?' I stared between Amanda and the old man. 'But she's old. How can she be your daughter?'

I saw both of them look at each other, then they laughed again. I was starting to get really tired of the laughing.

'Oh, Katherine, how blunt you can be,' Amanda said. 'I'm not that old. I'm only thirty-seven.'

'And I am a good three decades older than that. And a bit more,' the old man said, winking at me. People winking at me made me feel weird, so I walked away from him and took the seat next to Amanda that she'd been patting for a while.

'I see you're all getting on like a house on fire,' Dad said, coming into the room with two mugs on saucers. He set them down on the scruffy coffee table in the middle of the room, and then hovered by the old man's chair. 'So, what are we all talking about?' he said. He was trying to look cheerful, but I could tell he was worried about something. Dad never smiled this much these days. There was something very odd about his face right now.

'Katherine was just suggesting I'm getting on a bit,' Amanda said, then laughed some more. 'Practically called me ancient!'

Dad looked shocked. 'You didn't, did you Kitty? That's very rude.'

I glared back at him, anger rising in me. 'She's lying.'

Amanda, still smiling broadly, waved her hand. 'Oh it's nothing. I dare say to someone of Katherine's age I probably do look quite old.'

'Even if she does insist on wearing that infernal leather jacket of hers', the old man said, shaking his head a bit. 'Trying to be one of the young, hip, trendy ones, I'm sure.'

'I do try,' Amanda said, winking at me. Why were all these people winking, I thought as I looked from her to the old man.

'Well, I don't think you look ancient,' Dad said. He was putting on a nice voice, a bit posher than normal,

68

so he sounded more like these people and less like how we all normally talked. I'd heard him do this before, like when he talked to people at the bank or the doctor's. It seemed strange he'd be doing it now though with this odd pair.

'Well, that is enough merriment for now,' the old man said. 'If we're all settled, let's just give Katherine here a rundown of what to expect over the coming days.'

I looked at him with a strong, fixed gaze. Unlike most people I did this to, he didn't look away. Although I was sure I didn't like this man, I couldn't help but be a little bit impressed.

'Yes, that sounds sensible,' Dad said.

'Right, OK then. Katherine—'

'Kitty,' I cut across him.

'Kitty. Yes. Quite.' He nodded, as if giving me permission to be called what I wanted. 'Well then, Kitty, my daughter Amanda and I are going to be staying here, in your lovely house, for the next week, maybe a little more. The length of time isn't fixed. We'll be coming and going, as there isn't space for us all to sleep here at any one time. Amanda will be more "residential" than me. My bones are old, and I'm not quite as adept at sleeping on a sofa as I once was.' He paused, as if waiting for me to laugh, and when I didn't he smiled and carried on. 'As you may have guessed, this concerns your mother.'

My eyes flicked to the ceiling, where I could hear Mum shuffling around. There was the occasional clunk of something heavy; I suspected she might be rearranging the furniture. She had a bit of a preoccupation with nightstands and bedside tables. She liked them to be as far away from the bed as possible.

'We don't want to upset you, Kitty.' Amanda was talking now, but I carried on looking at the old man in the religious clothes. 'But your mother is exhibiting some behaviour that some may call . . . well . . . disturbing. And my father and I – and indeed your father, too – believe we might know how to sort it out.'

I said nothing.

'The sorting-out part,' the old man now said, 'will be what we'll focus on, at least for the next few days. This might take a bit of trial and error, and I don't imagine we'll achieve success straight away, or even particularly quickly. This is why I said there's no fixed time to us being here. This is very rough work. Interesting, of course. Very interesting, and your mother is a particularly fascinating case. I don't think I've really encountered that many similar, aside from a young woman from Baghdad who—'

Amanda coughed quietly, and the old man very obviously changed what he was about to say.

'So, anyway, will you allow us to take up your lovely home? And you won't mind if we need you to be absent for a little while while we try our best to help your mother?'

I thought for a little, and then looked up at Dad, who was staring into the distance, as if in his own world. 'This isn't my house. I don't think it's lovely. And I don't really have a choice about you being here.'

Silence greeted these words for a bit, then the old man started laughing again, 'Well, I do like a young girl to know her own mind, and it sounds like you certainly do. Thank you, Kitty, for being so honest.'

I nodded once, short and sharp. 'I'm not a liar.'

'Certainly not. I never would have thought it.' He smiled widely at me again. 'So, I think it's time to bring down your mother and let us have a chat with her. I think, so long as your father agrees, it might be useful for you to remain for this introduction. Your presence might help put your mother at ease. But I understand if you wish to leave if she responds badly to us and it starts to become upsetting for you.'

Dad left the room without really reacting to the old man's words. I heard him going up the stairs and then some mumbling from one of the bedrooms.

'Do you get upset, Kitty?' Amanda said, in what she probably thought was a kind, child-friendly voice. 'About your mum? About her . . . moments of distress?'

I considered this for several seconds, then answered her. 'I used to. But not now.'

Amanda nodded and looked as though she was going to say something else, but then the sound of two people on the stairs signalled Dad's return, accompanied by Mum. She wasn't screaming just yet.

'Hello, Marjory,' Amanda said warmly, standing up from the sofa and going over to her. She held out her hand and Mum took it, not looking at her, but peering around the room, as if hunting for something. Amanda clasped Mum's hand between hers and said, 'We've been looking forward to properly meeting you. We didn't get the chance to speak last night.'

At the mention of last night, Mum's gaze snapped to Amanda and she looked worried. 'Have you come to take me away?'

Amanda looked worried too for a moment, then said, 'Oh no. No, no, no. Definitely not. We're here to help you. We have no wish to take you out of this beautiful woodland property you have.'

'It's not beautiful,' I murmured, more to myself than to Amanda, but Dad hissed 'Kitty!' at me. I glared at him, and then looked at the floor.

'I'm Amanda, and this,' Amanda said, gesturing to the old man, who was also rising from his chair, 'is my dad, Father Tobias Kent.'

The effect on Mum was instantaneous. She yelped as if she'd been kicked, then fell to the floor and clasped the man's black clothes, saying, 'Please, *please*, help me.'

He lowered himself slowly to her level, knees clicking, and took hold of her hands. 'That, my dear, is the very reason we're here.'

She was shaking now, and tears started to roll down her face. 'Please. We don't have much time. When . . . when he finds out you're here . . . he'll be so *angry*.'

Father Tobias Kent nodded. 'Then we'd better get started straight away.'

Chapter 11

I was sent out into the woods soon after the introductions had been made. Mum's sobbing became loud and close to hysterical, and Amanda decided it would be better for me to go and play.

'Play with what?' I asked. She laughed as if I'd made a joke, but I didn't really see what was funny.

'Explore! Make a fort from sticks! Just don't get lost. Stay in the nearby vicinity of the house, or your dad will worry.'

She closed the door, leaving me outside in the cold. I wasn't sure my cardigan would be enough to keep me warm. Amanda hadn't said how long I should stay out for.

I began by checking the outer walls of the house for

creatures, and I was pleased to find a patch of snails around the back wall. I removed them from their place on the concrete and lined them up on a large thick log that was resting next to a nearby tree. The log must have been an upright tree itself at some point, I thought to myself. I wondered how it fell. I could fell a tree, I thought, as I watched the snails making their tracks across the damp, rotten bark. That would have made all of them in the house sit up and take notice.

I wandered a bit further into the woods, following the route we took last night when we were looking for Mum. Dad had slipped slightly on the wet ground as it turned into a slope, and there were marks where he must have skidded. I followed them, realising where I was going, but it was still a surprise when I reached the water and had to stop myself walking on. I raised my eyes from my shoes and looked ahead at the river, the water smooth and still, though obviously moving. The trees hung so low and the cloud so thick that there wasn't much difference in light here than there was deep amidst the trunks of the trees.

'Be careful,' said a voice. 'You'll be swept out to the ocean.'

I looked around me and saw a girl over on the other side of the stream. She looked about my age, and was dressed like me too, in a cardigan and boots. But her hair and skin was deep dark brown, rather than light like mine. She was smiling, and seemed to be waiting for me to respond to her warning of peril, so I looked down at the water and asked, 'Does it really lead out to the ocean?'

'I'm sure all rivers do,' she said, knowledgeably. 'And

this one moves quite quickly. Isn't it strange how it runs through the woods so quietly? It's like a secret.'

These words made sense to me instantly. I liked this girl.

'My mum said it is poison.'

The girl laughed. 'She probably just doesn't want you to go into the water. Maybe she's heard about the enchantments.'

'Enchantments?' I looked up at the girl now. She was throwing things – acorns, by the look of them – over the stream towards me so that they landed with a scatter-thud by my feet.

'Yes. Apparently a witch placed an enchantment on the stream. Anyone who disturbs its calm surface will be cursed with terrible, painful skin for the rest of their life. Apparently it will speed up ageing too. In some cases, you die instantly.'

I picked up one of the acorns out of interest. There was a hole in it. A hole possibly made by a creature. 'Who told you these things?' I asked.

She shrugged. 'People talk. I listen.'

I nodded. I knew exactly what she meant.

'Walk down the river with me and you'll come to a bridge. Then you can cross over to my side.'

'OK,' I said, and started to walk in the direction she was, moving along the side of the river bank.

It didn't take that long to get to the bridge; an old wooden thing that creaked as I stepped onto it, but didn't look like it was going to break. At least not just yet. When I reached the other side of the stream, the girl offered her hand, as if we'd only just met. I suppose we had.

'My name is Adah,' she said.

'My name is Kitty,' I said.

We shook hands.

'You look serious,' she said.

'I didn't know there were other young people around here.'

She laughed. 'Well, there aren't many. And I'm only here while my aunt decides what to do with me.'

Adah sat down on the raised end of the bridge and I sat next to her, taking care not to squash a woodlouse that had appeared from the depths of the folds of wood. I let the woodlouse run over my hand and then asked: 'Why does she need to decide what to do with you?'

She let out a sigh, but it didn't really sound like a normal sigh. Not like the ones Dad did when he was stressed. It sounded almost pretend, like she was doing an impression of an adult.

'My aunt has been looking after me since last year when my parents died.'

'Oh dear,' I said, surprised by how calmly she said this.

'Yes. It is a bit of a nuisance.'

I was surprised again. Surely she should be upset? She looked about my age – I didn't think she was more than ten – but the matter-of-fact way she spoke reminded me of an adult more than a child. At any rate, there weren't any tears in sight. Just a calm face.

'Why is it a nuisance?'

Another sigh. 'Because she doesn't care about me. She's awful. She's called Andrea.' When she said this name, she made a twisted shape with her mouth, like she had just tasted something sour. 'She keeps telling me to "fuck off and get lost".'

'Does she hurt you?' I asked, very curious about the answer. I'd never met a child like Adah before.

'No, she doesn't hit me. Just tells me I'm a waste of space. I ran away once to a big city. She didn't come to look for me. I stayed away for a night. I slept in a disabled toilet in a park.'

I frowned. 'Didn't the police send you home?'

She shook her head. 'Nobody saw me. I did wonder if the police would come looking for me, but nobody seemed to care. The next morning I felt too cold, so I went home. My aunt was in the lounge watching TV and just said "Christ, I thought I was fucking shot of you."'

'She sounds horrible.'

'She is.'

'Were your parents nice?'

She shrugged. 'I suppose. Nicer than her.'

'What were their names?'

'My mother was called Nikki and my dad was called Jep. I've got my mum's hair and my dad's eyes. I'm pleased it's that way round. My mum was black, so I've inherited her hair and I can do fun things with it when I'm bored.'

I looked at the beads she had in it now. She was right – it did look fun. 'Was your dad not black?'

She shook her head. 'No. He was white and Jewish.'

I nodded. 'There's a Jewish boy in my class at school.'

'Where do you go to school?'

'A long way away. In Grays.'

'I don't know that place. Is it all grey there?'

I nodded. 'Yes. Very. My parents have always lived there, I think. Even before I was born.' I shuffled a little and reached forward to put the woodlouse on the ground. He had died in my palm. I didn't kill him. It was just his time.

'What are their names?'

'Marjory and Nathan.'

'And what are they like?'

This was a question that could not be answered in my usual short way — not properly — so I opted with: 'Like normal parents who are suddenly not normal any more.'

She chuckled. 'That doesn't sound very normal.'

I nodded. 'I know.'

Adah seemed intrigued. 'Tell me something that they've done that isn't normal.'

Part of me didn't really want to go into details with someone I'd just met, but almost against my will, I could feel examples crowding to the front of my mind, keen to break out. 'OK,' I said, slowly, 'well, there was a time last year, when my dad got me a programme about whales from the video shop in the high street, and it was one of those big video cases with two tapes in. Well, one of the tapes wasn't the right video. It was this film called something I can't remember — something like *The Heretic* but it may have been called something else. Anyway, Mum discovered it just as I was putting it in the machine, and she burned it. Not just the tape, the whole video player. She did it in a bucket in the garden. My dad was furious. It took us months before we got a new player.'

Adah watched intently throughout this story, but once I'd finished she just shrugged. 'It was probably a naughty film.'

I didn't feel Adah quite understood what I was trying to say. How the whole thing had been so frightening: how Mum had ripped out the video machine from its sockets; how she'd filled a bucket with some liquid she'd found in the shed; how she'd made the tape machine, with the cassette inside it, burn so bright and with such black smoke that one of the neighbours had threatened to call the fire brigade. Dad had arrived home amidst the chaos. He said it was just a bonfire gone wrong, but once he and Mum were alone they'd had a shrieking row in the kitchen.

'There have been other things,' I said, feeling a need to impress upon her the sense of spiralling disorientation I'd felt over the past two years. 'One time she wouldn't let me go to school swimming lessons until the local priest came and did something to the swimming pool. I don't know what she wanted him to do, but in the end my dad told her the priest had visited the pool the previous day and done whatever was needed.'

Again, Adah seemed resolutely unmoved. I couldn't quite work out if I was frustrated by her or admired her. 'Well, at least you got to swim,' she said with a little shrug. 'I've never learned. They tried to teach us at school, but on our first time in the water I got in a scrap with a girl who threw my shoes in the water. We both had to sit on the poolside from then on.'

I nodded, trying to look thoughtful, deciding not to continue trying to make Adah understand the strangeness of my home life.

★ ★ ★

We walked about her side of the forest for a while until we got to a winding track that clearly led somewhere proper. 'Where does this go to?' I asked.

'To the street, eventually. Where the houses are. But it's still a long way, even once you've got through the trees. It's where I live. I'm going that way.'

'I don't think I should follow. I think my dad would worry if I was away from the house for too long.' I looked at my little red watch Mum got me for my birthday when I was eight. I wasn't completely sure what the time was when I left, but I could see at least a couple of hours had passed.

'Where is your house?'

I turned back, about to point, but then decided it was pointless, since we'd come quite a way and you couldn't even see the river from here, let alone the house. 'Back there somewhere. It's in the middle of the woods. Perhaps not quite the middle, but it feels like it.'

She nodded. 'The house in the woods. I know it. I didn't think anyone lived there.'

'People do now. Us.'

'I'll have to come and see it soon.'

She looked as if she was about to say goodbye, but she grabbed me and pulled me off the path and behind a tree. 'Shhh!' she said.

'What?' I whispered.

She peered out from behind the tree, looked for what felt like a long time, and then pointed. I followed her hand and could see something; something moving. Up a tree. It was climbing up the branches. I couldn't work out what it was. Was it an animal?

Then it became clear: it was a human. A teenage boy, quite a bit older than me and Adah.

'Who is it?' I asked.

'Levi. He's always climbing trees.'

I stared at the boy, who was dressed in shorts and a t-shirt that looked rather too summery to be worn at this time of year. He had a thin face, with a harsh jaw. I imagined he could be quite cruel or rough if he wanted, although of course I didn't have anything to back up this assumption. 'Does he live in the woods?' I asked. It seemed like a reasonable question to me – after all, I lived in the woods – but Adah laughed and said 'No, he doesn't live in trees. Just climbs them. He lives in one of the houses, not far from me.'

I nodded, even though I still didn't really know where these houses were. In spite of her descriptions, the woods felt like they took up the whole world, and everything else outside them had vanished as soon as Dad had driven us up that winding road towards our weird cottage.

'I should go,' I said.

Adah nodded. 'OK. Just follow the river to the bridge and you'll find your way back. Make sure you don't fall in though. Or touch the water at all.'

I looked at her, confused.

'It's evil,' she explained. 'One touch of it, and bad things will happen.'

I didn't like this. It was too similar to what I'd heard Mum say when she came out of the water. Thinking about it made the back of my neck go prickly, so I changed the subject. 'Is it safe to walk past the Levi boy? Will he throw acorns at me?'

Adah giggled again. 'It's safe. And if he follows you, you can always just scream.'

I looked back over at the tree and could see his eyes, little dark holes watching me as I took a few tentative steps away from Adah.

'All right,' I nodded. 'If he follows, I'll scream.'

I'd never properly screamed before, but as I left Adah and turned to walk back into the depths of the wood, I got the feeling that I might be rather good at it.

Chapter 12

The Levi boy didn't make a sound as I hurried past the tree he was sitting in. Part of me was disappointed. I was even more disappointed to find that nobody was out shouting for me or even looking for me when I got back to the house just after midday. I peered in through the grimy window and saw them all sitting in a circle having cups of tea and passing round a plate of yellow things – scones, I thought. I tapped on the window and waved at Mum who was sitting in the armchair that Father Tobias had been sitting in before. She let out a loud shriek that made both Amanda and Dad spill their tea. I ducked down so they couldn't see my face, but after a few seconds I heard the front door unlatch and

Dad came stomping round and told me I was being disruptive.

'We've only just got her settled!' he shouted at me, then looked sad, as if he was cross with himself that he'd got angry.

'I made a friend,' I said. 'In the woods.'

'Come on Kitty,' he said, taking hold of my cardigan arm and pulling me round towards the front door. 'I haven't got time to hear about whatever bloody beetle or grasshopper you've befriended.'

'Can I have some lunch?' I asked, not bothering to tell him I'd made friends with a real human this time.

'Yes, of course. But in the kitchen. Amanda and Father Tobias haven't finished talking to Mum yet.'

I wasn't a fan of being banished, but I also wasn't much of a fan of eating with other people, so I didn't complain. I was led through the back door, which made it impossible to see what was going on in the lounge properly – or have a chance to have one of the scones – and Dad closed the connecting door as soon as we were inside.

'I'll do you some hooped spaghetti and toast,' he said, opening the cupboard.

'More toast,' I murmured.

'Yes, *more* toast. And you'll eat it and be grateful.'

I filled my cheeks with air and let it out slowly so that it sounded like a very slow sigh. Dad didn't comment. Eventually I asked: 'What are Amanda and Father Tobias talking to Mum about?'

Dad stayed silent for a bit, then, once the toast had popped up, said, 'They're trying to help.'

I frowned. 'I think you've said that before.'

'Then it should be enough!' he snapped.

'Why are you getting cross?' I glared at him to show that I was not impressed.

'I'm not cross, Kitty. I just . . . I just really want this to work.'

'Want what to work?'

He paused for a minute, then said, 'Mum's treatment. She's not very well, and we want her to get better.'

I let my frown deepen. 'I thought *doctors* were the ones who made unwell people better. Doctors in hospitals. Not strange church people who come round to eat scones.'

For a moment, I thought Dad was going to shout at me. He even opened his mouth, his eyes flaring. But then he stopped himself. 'I think we've covered that subject, Kitty. Doctors and hospitals can only do so much. And sometimes not the right things. It's much better if we help Mum to get better here, quietly, ourselves, with the help of our visitors. Just eat your food and then go and play upstairs for a bit.'

'All right,' I said, then asked in a quiet voice, 'So when will we be going home?'

Dad scooped out the spaghetti hoops from their pan on the hob and put the toast next to it on a plate. Now it was in front of me, it did look rather nice. 'You'll be going back as soon as we're done here. Anyway, it's half term at the moment, so I don't know why you're worrying. Most kids want the holidays to carry on for ever.'

'Is this going to carry on for ever?'

He slammed a mug he'd just picked up back down onto the table, and everything on its surface trembled.

85

'Enough questions, Kitty. Please. Just . . . eat your food, then go upstairs, OK?'

I nodded.

'Good girl,' he said, his tone a bit calmer now. He was probably feeling bad about getting cross. 'I'll come and find you when our guests have gone.'

I ate the food so quickly I barely tasted its sugary saltiness until the very last bit of tomato sauce from the hoops had gone. I put my plate and fork in a line by the sink next to the saucepan, to show that I could be helpful sometimes, then went into the cold, dark hallway and climbed the stairs. I didn't bother creaking them on purpose this time.

Upstairs in my room, I took my time taking out some of the plastic animal figurines I had packed to take with us. There wasn't any way I was going to allow them to be thrown onto the rubbish pile when we were sorting all the stuff out. They were precious, even though both Mum and Dad had, in the past, got angry when I'd left them on the stairs and they'd trodden on them in the night. Apparently the antennae of some of the beetles and snails were quite painful.

I put them in rows along the little ledge above the bed by the window and I took some time thinking of new names for them. I did this every now and then, because I forgot what the original names were and it was just easier to have a mass renaming. It meant I could do a series of Christening ceremonies, too, which were always fun – I'd tap the plastic creature on its back (or on its wings, if it had them) and say its name four times. Then I would move it to make its head nod, set the little friend back down, and carry on with the next one.

After the Christenings, I started reading an old paperback book from a box Dad had brought up to the landing yesterday morning. It was a mystery novel by Enid Blyton, part of the Famous Five series, following the group as they go to stay on Finniston Farm. I started to wish we'd gone to stay on a farm. A farm full of animals I could have gone to talk to and make friends with. Horses in barns, barns that were so big you could spend all day exploring them, stroking the creatures and collecting all the spiders and the mice that would be lurking under bags of grain.

I got almost halfway through the book when I realised it had started to get dark outside. The light coming in through my window was already more of a dull grey and I was straining my eyes to see the words on the page.

Instead of turning the light on straight away, I opened my door and went out onto the landing. I expected there to be lights coming up from the hallway, but it was still dark down there and the door to the lounge was shut. I tiptoed down the stairs, stopping halfway down when one creaked loudly. Nobody came bursting out, so I just carried on. The uncarpeted floor of the hallway was cold on my bare feet and I trod carefully and quickly until I was in front of the door to the lounge. There was no light coming from inside. Have they all gone out and left me? I wondered. Then, from underneath the crack of the door, I saw a flicker of light – a small dancing glow. They must have had the fire burning and the main light switched off. But why? Why would they want to sit there in the dark?

Then I smelled it. A strange, sweet smell, not like anything I'd really smelled before. It reminded me of an old antiques shop Dad had taken us to a few times; like old flowers mixed with perfume and something a bit medicinal. I didn't like it. It scared me, and I worried the lounge was burning and that what I could smell was their bodies being turned from skin into ash. I reached out and quietly opened the door.

I couldn't quite work out what I could see at first. They looked like shapes rather than people. Then I realised. Mum was sitting in one of the straight-backed chairs from the kitchen. She was in the middle of the room and the main sofa, armchair and coffee table had been cleared away to the sides to make a space in the centre. Dad and Amanda were standing at different ends of the room, Dad facing Mum's front and Amanda her back. And Father Tobias was with Mum, bent over her, his hands stretched out, offering her something small in his hand.

'Please . . . keep it away . . . he'll be here soon.' Mum was whimpering the words out rather than shouting them. And then she began to shake violently, her arms juddering. She tried to press herself into the back of the chair, holding her hands over her head, as if terrified of what was in Father Tobias's hands. I tried to look closer, to see what Father Tobias was holding, but the door gave a massive creak as it opened further and they all looked around. And then Mum screamed. 'No! No! No!'

Dad ran across the room and pushed me so hard I fell against the hallway wall. He slammed the door behind him, then turned round to help me up.

'You hurt me,' I said, trying not to cry. I really wasn't a fan of crying.

'What's going on?' Amanda said, appearing from behind the door. 'Is Kitty OK? What happened?'

'Get upstairs. Now!' He hissed the words and he looked so angry I ran away from him, back up the stairs.

'Calm down,' Amanda said, but Dad ignored her.

'You can forget about any tea! Go to sleep.'

I flew into my room and slammed my door. I lay on my bed crying for I don't know how long. Now he'd mentioned tea, I felt my hunger rise, and the tears kept coming. I had never been refused food as a punishment. Never. It was the type of thing my parents wouldn't think was right. But there were a lot of things that used to be wrong and were now right, apparently. Like taking me out of school and not telling me when I'd be back home, and making me pack up all my things and expecting me to like living in a cold, dark cottage. I started to think about the lounge downstairs – about Father Tobias, holding something out towards Mum. Her pleading with him to put it away, holding her hands over her head, trying to shield herself. And Amanda and Dad just standing there at the sides of the room. Watching.

I must have fallen asleep at some point – just a little bit. But then I heard voices. Voices in the hallway down the stairs. I wasn't sure how much time had passed. I tried to listen to what the voices were saying, but they were talking deliberately low. I crept out of bed and sat down next to the door, raising my hand and pulling on the handle. It inched open with tiny creaks, and then a loud one, so I stopped. But it was enough for me to be able to see the landing, just a little.

I saw a warm glow of light at first – they must have turned the main light in the lounge on. Then I heard Dad say, 'She'll be all right now she's asleep. Sleep seems to be the only thing she's able to do.' I heard a door close – the one to the lounge? – and then silence for a second. Then:

'Right. Well. I'd better leave you two in peace.'

It was Father Tobias's voice. And then I heard Amanda's.

'We've still got some things to discuss. About the next steps.'

'Right. Of course,' Father Tobias said. 'Well, I'll see you both tomorrow morning.'

The front door closed, a bit quieter than normal. Then there was an odd sound. Like the rustling of clothes. And then a breath.

'No, not here. Not while Marjory's in the house. We're lucky we got her off to sleep so easily.'

It was Dad. He had his kind voice on. Gentle. I could barely hear it. I could hear it enough to tell there was something slightly different about it though. It wasn't a type of gentle I'd heard before.

'OK,' Amanda said, 'I'll get the bed made up in the lounge. And you'll be OK with Marjory upstairs?'

'Like you said, it would be best to have someone with her throughout the night.'

A few moments of silence passed, then Amanda said, 'Well, come and find me if you need to.'

Dad said goodnight quietly, then I heard him start to walk up the stairs and make his way to the main bedroom. I hadn't seen him spend the night in the same bed as Mum for a long time, and it made me wonder what had happened in the lounge earlier to make him think she needed someone to be with her all night long. Perhaps he was worried she would escape again, and that we'd lose her in the forest and never see her again.

Once the house was still, I got back up and got into my bed, pulling the covers up over my head. I tried not to let my thoughts stop me from sleeping. It was difficult at first, but as I tried to focus on nice things, like one day owning my own insect and reptile emporium, I steadily felt myself start to drift.

To my surprise the next morning, I didn't dream about Mum or Amanda or Father Tobias. I dreamt about Adah. Of her wandering through the forest. Climbing trees. Going too close to the river's edge. At one point, I think she vanished, and I found her cardigan swinging from a branch, and that boy Levi was pointing and laughing at me, saying that she vanished sometimes – like a spirit in the night. Eventually, I found her sitting under a tree, playing with a pile of acorns. She shared them out and we played with them for ages. She was smiling and laughing, and I smiled and laughed too. I was happy.

And then everything folded together, as it does in dreams, like a concertina in your mind; and I was left with nothing but darkness.

Chapter 13

January 2020

'Please could you outline for us, Katherine, why your father took you out of school, packed up your things and drove you and your mother to Northumberland, right into the middle of Barret Forest, a place many miles away from your home?'

I nod. This at least isn't too difficult to answer. 'It was because of my mother. He didn't take me out of school, it was mostly in the half-term school holiday. After that, I only missed a week of school, and he just told them I had flu or something. Mum's mental health had started to deteriorate quite rapidly. I'm not too sure when it began, but steadily, throughout my childhood, her reactions to things started to become disturbing. She'd become

92

frightened by seemingly innocuous coincidences; she'd spot patterns in people's behaviour and think they were part of a conspiracy to spy on her, like if the milkman came at a different time two days running. She'd accuse him of being one of the devil's spies.'

DI Cousins nods. She shifts the folder on her desk and I see there are actually two there, bundled together, the one underneath the first looking much older and faded-beige, whereas the one on top looks crisp and new. She opens the newer one and stares down at a page of what looks like bullet points, although it's tilted away from me, obscuring a full view. 'We'll be speaking to your father about this, of course, to get his take on it all, but could you tell us a little about your mother's delusions, paranoia and hallucinations – did they have a religious dimension to them?'

I nod. 'Yes, although I wouldn't say to the point of them making much sense.'

She looks up, lines creasing her forehead. 'How do you mean?'

I shuffle in my chair, changing my position slightly. 'Well, I'm no expert, but I think a lot of people who have, say, religious mania or obsessions at least stick to their own set of rules. My mother, on the other hand . . . she was unpredictable. There was no knowing what would upset her next. She'd always been religious, I think; a lot more so than my dad. My memory doesn't go back too far beyond her illness, but I can remember her praying and going to church before that and seeming perfectly content with it. It was later when it started to get extreme. She went from occasional references to God and Jesus to more frequent comments about the devil and sins. It all seemed to relate to there being something inside of her. A bad force, a demon, one of "Satan's offspring", as she sometimes referred to it. Some other dimension of her psyche, I suppose.'

'That must have been quite scary to witness,' DC Malik says. Part of me is relieved he's spoken. I was finding the penetrating gaze of DI Cousins a bit intimidating, and his words have a soft, sympathetic edge to them.

'Yes, it was,' I say. 'It . . . it was something that affected me very deeply. I think I've only recently come to understand now how much I've been affected by it. And why I wanted to write it all down. I felt I couldn't keep it all buried any longer.'

DI Cousins looks at me for a bit, then continues with a new question. 'Can you tell us who was in the cottage with you?'

I nod. 'Well, there was me and my dad and my mum. But we were joined by two others: Amanda, who, as I'm sure you're now aware, my dad was having an affair with, something I think began when she was living in Essex some months before we went to Northumbria, and an older man – Amanda's father – that I knew by the name of Father Tobias. Although he rarely stayed over. He used to come and go most days. To do . . . what they were doing . . . to Mum. Their sessions.'

I see DC Malik shift in his chair a little, moving his neck as if it were stiff and he was trying to click it. DI Cousins, meanwhile, leans forward and asks, 'And can you tell me, Katherine, what these sessions were?'

Our eyes meet, then I look away. I try to focus on a little flake of something white – maybe the remnants of a tissue – floating across the corner of the desk, propelled by the collective force of our breaths. 'You've read my book, I presume. You know what they were doing.'

Even though I'm not looking at her, I can still feel DI Cousins's eyes on me. 'I'd like to hear it from you, in your own words.'

I pause. Take a deep breath, then answer. 'Exorcisms. They were performing exorcisms.'

Chapter 14

1987

When I first woke up the next morning, I felt like it must have all been a dream. But upon opening my eyes, I could see very clearly it wasn't. I was on the floor. I must have fallen asleep down here, curled up by the door. It wasn't a dream. Or a nightmare. Everything was real.

My cheek was pressed against the rough wood of the floor, and from my position I could see under the bed. It was mostly just a big dark space, with scuff marks across the wood, probably from where the bed had been moved around the room a few times. There was something there though; right at the back, towards the wall.

I got myself into a long, thin position, like a worm, and stretched out, edging my hands forward, trying to reach whatever it was; but it was too far away. So I crawled on my front until I was halfway under the bed. That's when I got a hold of it. And as I touched it, I realised what it was. It was a magazine. Its pages were thin and glossy to touch, the pictures a mass of colour. But it wasn't the kind of magazine I normally liked to get – ones with zoo animals or wildlife that came with free little plastic pots taped to the front to put little creatures in. It was full of naked ladies. Lots of them, on each page. Some of them were holding their very large – too large – breasts and poking their tongues out. I carried on flicking through and at the midway point there was an image so big it took up two pages, like the pull-out photos of pandas I got in my *Wild Forests of the World* magazine I saved up to buy at the newsagents, except that I couldn't imagine ever putting this on the wall. It was of a woman sitting on a black stool. She was wearing nothing but a feather boa and had her legs wide open.

I knew all this had something to do with 'sex'. Some of the boys talked about all that at school and, from remembering parts of their discussions, I realised what I was holding must be what they called a 'dirty mag'. But even so, the whole thing seemed very, very odd, especially since the women were all sitting in very strange ways. It couldn't have been comfortable for them at all. I decided this must be some very unusual kind of dirty mag that only people who liked very special, rare things would get, like the *Creatures of the Deep* magazine that Mum had to place a special order for at the newsagents because it wasn't a title they regularly stocked.

I skipped past the rest to the back pages. These were divided into lots of little boxes, about eight on each page. They all had a different woman in them, all of different ages, some young, some a lot older – like Mum's age – and they all said things like 'CALL FOR A GOOD TIME' or 'PHONE STACEY NOW – SHE'S WAITING FOR YOUR CALL' and then had what looked like a phone number next to them. I decided these were probably not aimed at people like me, so I closed the magazine and put it in one of the little drawers in the old bedside table, next to two of my Famous Five books and a figurine of an antelope.

I went down the stairs boldly and with purpose, trying to show I wasn't afraid of what I might find. The lounge was no longer dark and scary, but lit warmly from the main light and a lamp I hadn't seen before on the window-sill. It was still dark outside and the place had a cosy feel. I noticed that the sofa, chair and coffee table had been moved back to their normal places facing the fire. On the sofa, though, there was a pile of blankets, all neatly folded, at one end. Although it was still quite early, I wasn't the only one awake.

'Hello Katherine,' said a woman's voice from the kitchen. I peered round in its direction and saw Amanda coming through the connecting doorway, smiling widely. 'You're up early for a Saturday.'

I eyed her suspiciously. 'What are you still doing here?' I asked.

She looked taken aback for a second or two, but

recovered, smiling to show she wasn't cross. 'I stayed the night. Slept down here on the sofa.'

She gestured to the blankets. Now I knew she was a liar too.

'And Mum?' I asked, looking her in the eye. She seemed to find this a bit uncomfortable so walked away back into the kitchen as she said, 'She slept upstairs with your dad, of course.'

She busied herself putting breakfast things on the table. Jam, butter, marmalade, knives and plates and, in the centre, stacks of toast. She must have been doing this for some time, I thought, since the toaster takes two slices and wasn't exactly quick.

'Do help yourself. You must be hungry after being sent to bed without any supper.'

We didn't call it supper, we called it tea or dinner, but I didn't bother correcting her. I just sat down, then jumped as I heard a whirring and clunking.

'Looks like your dad's having a shower. That old boiler does make an awful racket doesn't it? Must be ancient, like everything else in this place. Aside from the things you brought with you. They're all right, of course.'

She was still smiling a lot, but I didn't offer a smile back. I just took a bit of toast and started to put more butter onto it than Dad would ever have allowed.

'Where's Father Tobias?' I asked. Amanda had her back to me, washing something up in the sink, so I couldn't properly see what she thought of this question.

'He went home. He was getting tired. It happens, when you're old. I stayed to have a chat with your dad.'

I crunched some toast. The butter was saltier than the one we normally got at home.

'And what did you talk about?' I asked.

'Oh, just stuff. To do with your mum. Things to do with making her better.'

She set a clean but dripping plate down on the sideboard to dry and came over to the table. 'How is your toast?'

'It's fine. So what were you doing with my mum in the lounge? When she was in the middle.'

Her eyes widened slightly as I said this and her smile started to look a bit false. It took her a moment to talk again, but then she gathered up my hand in hers. Her hands were smooth and soft and her fingernails were painted a deep red. I had never painted my nails, but Mum used to do hers if she and Dad were going out somewhere nice, like the local pub for a meal with friends for a birthday or something. I would sometimes look at the bottles of nail polish in her bedroom, wondering if she'd like it if I painted her nails for her. I'd almost tried it out once, when she was sleeping, but I'd worried that if she woke up to find her nails a different colour she might start screaming.

'You want your mum to get better, Kitty.'

The way she said the sentence didn't make it sound like a question, but I decided to treat it as one.

'Yes.'

'So, the best thing you could do for your mum right now – the very *best* thing – would be to let me, your dad and Father Tobias carry on with what we're doing and not make things difficult. You're not a difficult person, are you Kitty?'

I crunched on the crust of toast and watched her for a bit. She waited patiently as I brushed crumbs from my hands and then said, 'I don't think I'm difficult.'

Her smile widened. 'Good. I didn't think you were. The moment I saw you I thought: there's a girl who knows what's *best*.'

She kept on saying 'best' slowly, making sure she was looking into my eyes as she said it. I decided to ask her about this.

'So, how do I know what *best* is if I don't know what you're doing?'

She looked irritated for a second, then picked up a bit of toast from the stack on the table and started buttering it slowly. 'When I was a girl, Kitty, there was a man in our village who didn't quite fit in. Do you know what I mean? He was odd – a loner, and not in a good way. Being alone can be a wonderful thing; managing one's time without the pressure of others can be a joyful way to live, if you do it right. But this man wasn't doing it right. He used to watch people. Watch people in the street. Watch people in the park. Watch people . . . by the children's school . . .' Her eyes flicked up at me as she said this last bit, then returned to her toast. 'Anyway, one day he went a bit too far. He tried to talk to a girl over the playground railings at the school. That in itself may have been harmless. Inadvisable, perhaps, but harmless all the same. But the man wasn't properly dressed. And so it became inappropriate. And the man had to go away somewhere. He no

101

longer watched people around the village. No longer spoke to children over the playground railings.'

I stared at her, puzzled by what she was telling me. 'So, are you saying my mum will be taken away somewhere?'

She put out a hand onto my arm and rubbed it firmly. 'No, no, no, Kitty. Let me finish what I was going to say. What I meant was that it is my belief that that man didn't need to go away somewhere. I think, if he'd had some *support* he wouldn't have needed to be taken away at all – he could have been helped if people had just stepped forward and steered him towards a healthier, easier way of life.'

I stared at the table, trying to work out what she meant. 'So, you're saying you're doing that with my mum?'

Amanda beamed. 'Exactly. We are an *intervention*. Do you know what that means? We're intervening before things get so bad more serious steps have to be taken. OK?'

I paused, thinking. Then nodded.

'Wonderful.' She was about to start eating her thoroughly buttered toast when I asked:

'So, will you make the demons go away?'

Her hand stopped halfway to her mouth, the toast wavering slightly in the air.

'How much has your mum mentioned about the, er, demons?'

I looked at her as if she was silly – because it really was a silly question. 'All the time,' I said. 'And she says "Him" a lot. As if there's one of them. She says "He" won't like it or "He" will hear. Is it a demon she's talking about when she says that?'

Amanda kept her hand in the air for a few seconds more, then set the toast back down on her plate without eating it. 'I suppose you could say that, yes. After a fashion.'

I didn't know what to say to this. So I said nothing.

Amanda and I ate our toast in silence, then a clomping down the stairs told us Dad had finished in the shower and was fast approaching. He arrived looking happier and younger than I had seen him look in weeks, like he'd been traded in for a calm, sprightly dad and the stressed, tired-looking dad had been thrown away.

'Morning, you two,' he said. 'You been having a natter?'

'Yes, we've been having a very nice time.' Amanda beamed at him, ignoring the fact we hadn't been speaking for a good five minutes. And 'very nice' seemed like a strange way to describe the conversation we did have. I didn't mention this. I didn't want to seem difficult.

'Good, good,' he said, sitting down. 'It's so nice not being the first one down and already having the kitchen all warmed up. And look at all this toast!'

He greedily took up two of the chunky slices and reached for the butter. 'You're spoiling us, Amanda.'

'Oh I do try,' she said, and laughed. I didn't laugh, because nothing was funny.

'So, Kitty,' Dad said, 'today it's very important we don't have any interruptions. OK?'

I didn't respond.

'Do you hear me? It's very important, for your mother's sake, that we're allowed to carry on helping her without any disturbances.'

He sounded a bit stern now, and to stop him doing his properly-angry voice, I looked at him and nodded.

'OK, then. Well, maybe you could start the day off with a little walk, like you did yesterday. Did you have a nice time exploring?'

I thought about ignoring this question to punish him for sending me to bed with no tea, but it was easier just to answer. 'No.'

He rolled his eyes and chewed on his toast for a bit. 'Where did you go? Find any nice bugs and insects to befriend?'

'No,' I said again. 'And it's usually them that befriend me.'

Dad said nothing to this, so I continued.

'But I did meet a girl. And I think I befriended her.'

He looked more interested now. 'Oh really? That's interesting.'

'Why is that interesting?'

He shrugged. 'I didn't realise there were other children out here. I thought we were alone.'

I reached for another slice of toast and pulled towards me three of the four different types of jam Amanda had laid out for us. 'You'd prefer it if I was the only child in the woods all alone?' I didn't look up as I said this, but I suspected Dad had rolled his eyes again.

'Christ, Kitty,' he said. 'Do you have to always make out like you're some poor, lost neglected soul? I thought you liked being by yourself. All your teachers say so.'

'The teachers I may never see again,' I mumbled, unscrewing the jam lids.

'You don't need that many jars of jam, Kitty,' Dad said, reaching to take two of the three jars away.

'I was going to create a mixture.'

'I don't think so.'

'Why not?' I set my knife down with a clatter to show I was annoyed. He was doing that thing where he avoided my gaze again.

'Because it's impolite.'

I was about to leave the kitchen in a silent huff, but then something popped into my head. 'Are you just saying that because *she's* here?' I jabbed my finger towards Amanda, who was now sipping from a mug and trying her best to do an impression of a kind, pleasant woman at a tea party.

Dad looked enraged, so I got up from the table and walked out of the room before he could speak. I climbed the stairs, stomping all the way, then went into my room to get my favourite fluffy towel. I was going to run myself a bath, just like Mum used to do for me, and put all kinds of shampoo and soap things into the water. And I didn't care if anyone else needed to use the bathroom.

The hot water only lasted long enough to fill the bath half-way, so it wasn't quite the cosy activity I'd planned, but the warmth and comfort of it still made me happy, if only for a little while. I washed myself, and then my hair, having fun twisting it into different shapes. I was almost about to get out when a knock came on the bathroom door.

'Is that you in there, Kitty?'

I didn't reply.

'Kitty!' Dad shouted through the door so loudly it was as if he was in the room with me.

'What?' I shouted back.

'I was worried,' he said in a quieter voice.

'What, in case I had drowned? Would you care?'

He muttered something which sounded a lot like 'for fuck's sake', then I heard a strange whimpering sound. 'Your mother needs to use the bathroom,' he said.

I splashed about for a bit, considering this request. 'Can't she just wait a second?'

I heard him sigh. He could be very impatient sometimes. 'This is testing my patience, Kitty. I've barely been able to encourage her up the stairs because there's a spider on the landing.'

Although I was well aware how she felt about spiders I was still rather cross he wanted to spoil my nice early-morning bath time.

'Couldn't you just move the spider?' I called back. 'If you do, could you take one of the little plastic pots I put on the shelf in the kitchen, the ones with the coloured lids, and keep it safe for me so—'

'I haven't got time for your fucking pots. Open the bloody door, Kitty.'

I heard Mum let out a little cry and start saying something about Satan's spies.

'Yes, yes, all right,' Dad said to her. 'Kitty, for the last time, open the goddamn door.'

I heard Mum make a whimper at 'goddamn', but I had finished my objections. I got out of the bath and pulled my favourite soft-blue towel over me and opened the door.

'You do bloody rile me sometimes, Kitty,' Dad said as he pushed past me, pulling Mum in by the hand. She sat down on the loo immediately and I heard the tinkle of her weeing. 'Come on, let's give your mum some privacy,' he said, putting his hand on my shoulder.

'Wait,' I said, and moved past him. 'I need to let out my bathwater.'

Mum's reaction happened so fast, it scared me. She lurched forward off the toilet seat and grabbed me, shaking me, her face looking both terrified and sad at the same time. 'You mustn't!' she shrieked, her eyes looking straight into mine. 'You mustn't go near the water. You mustn't touch the surface of the river. He's been punishing me since . . . I tried . . . but I've been punished . . .'

'Kitty, come away,' Dad said, taking my hand, but I was fixed to the spot. 'Kitty, I said come on. Marjory, please, sit back down!' I saw him looking down and I followed his gaze and saw a trickle making its way down Mum's legs from under her dressing gown.

'Terrible things,' Mum sobbed. 'Never touch it. Terrible things. He'll know. He always knows.'

'Who always knows?' I asked Mum, but Dad wasn't going to let me say any more.

'Enough! Kitty, go and get dry and dressed in your room. I'll sort your mum out.'

I padded back to my room and closed the door. I could still hear Mum moaning from the bathroom and Dad trying to calm her down. I got dressed in warm clothes, as I expected I'd probably be sent out again soon. When Dad and Mum finally went downstairs, I followed them.

Mum was settled on the sofa by the time I walked in. She was dressed in one of her big jumpers, fiddling with a stray thread on one of the sleeves. Amanda, meanwhile, was in the armchair, knitting, as if she were in her own sitting room. I watched her hands go in and out, moving the wool and the needles together.

'Father Tobias should be here within the next ten minutes,' she said, without looking up. 'So you may not want to get too comfortable, Kitty.'

'Comfortable?' I said the last word as if I'd never heard it before; it was a very strange word to use. She kept doing this, Amanda. Using bad choices of words to get her meaning across. I wondered if it was a plan to make me feel even more uncomfortable.

'What Amanda means,' said Dad, as he shifted some of the furniture around, making more space in the centre, 'is that it probably isn't worth you getting settled. This will all be boring adult talk from now on.'

'It didn't look boring from what I saw.'

'So,' he continued, ignoring me, 'perhaps you should go out and explore again.'

I thought about what he'd said. 'Perhaps? Do you mean I don't have to?'

He set down the old coffee table with a thud and looked at me like an angry man. 'I've had it up to here with your cheek today, Kitty, and it's not even ten o'clock. I think you should go out and play. Right now.'

I stared at him, then marched over to the windowsill where he'd stacked a mixture of books untidily, grabbed three of them and hurled one at him.

'Right!' he shouted, running towards me, but tripping on the coffee table he had stupidly put in his own way.

I ran, out of the lounge, through the hallway, out the front door, and then collided with something big and solid but also rather squashy.

'Well, well, well, what's all this?'

It was Father Tobias. I took my face out of his clothes and stepped away. He smelled of smoke and spicy things – a surprisingly homely sent, like mince pies at Christmas.

'Kitty, come back here and apologise!' Dad shouted.

'Why?' I turned back to him. 'It's you who I threw the book at.'

'Well then come back and apologise to me!' he screeched.

'You threw a book?' Father Tobias straightened up and looked at me, as if he were appalled. As if he'd never heard of anything so shocking in his life. 'This is a very sad state of affairs, young lady. Very sad indeed.'

I realised now he was carrying a briefcase. He set it down into the leaves and twigs on the damp ground, and lowered himself so we were face to face.

'So then, Katherine. Tell me, which tome caused you such unimaginable distress that you decided to cast it away from you with such violence?'

I frowned at him. 'I didn't see the cover.'

'It was *Watership* fucking *Down* and it bloody hurt,' shouted Dad from the doorway, looking murderous; then he seemed to notice how silly he sounded and changed his voice a bit. 'I'm sorry, er . . . Father Tobias – do come inside into the warm.'

I watched Dad as he tried to tidy his hair with his hand. 'Why do you keep going all posh?' I called over to him.

'Kitty, if I hear one more word from you this side of teatime, I swear—'

Father Tobias held up a hand and Dad stopped talking instantly. 'I think Kitty and I understand each other. She knows, in her heart of hearts, that God doesn't like little girls who use bad words and throw books at their fathers. Especially ones as remarkable and profound as Richard Adams's leporine classic.'

He must have seen me frown at the word 'leporine', as he went on to clarify, 'That means relating to rabbits or hares.'

I ignored this, unwilling to let him think I was impressed or grateful by the explanation. Instead I hissed 'I didn't use a bad word.'

'Ah, but the book throwing is a sin, one that I don't think even you can deny. Come, my child, which other books do you have about your person?' He gestured down at the three remaining paperbacks in my hands. I held them up and he took them in his hands.

'Goodness, this is quite a mixture. *The Pale Horse* by Agatha Christie. Are you familiar with the works of Mrs Christie, Katherine?'

I shook my head. 'Well, her books might be a little grown up for you, but the language is simple and she spins a jolly good yarn. I haven't read this one myself, but it probably features a Belgian detective or an old spinster going to a big manor house to solve a crime.'

I just stared at him. He paused for a moment and I heard a huff from the doorway. Dad was getting impatient. But Father Tobias didn't seem in the mood to rush. He turned over the second book in my pile. '*The Mysteries of Udolpho.* My my, Katherine. This is some heavy reading material. And the last one . . .' He examined the final volume. '*The Scars of Dracula* by Agnes Hall.' His mouth twisted a little. 'Have you read Bram Stoker's original *Dracula*, Katherine?'

I shook my head.

'No. I should think not. You're far too young for things like that. And besides, this one looks to be mass-produced fluff, using Stoker's character just to turn a profit. It wouldn't be of interest to you. I suppose it's one of your father's books?'

'It's not *his*,' I said, glancing at my dad, who was still looking like he'd like to start shouting again. 'It's mine. Someone from where we live gave them to me. Before we came here.'

Father Tobias looked troubled. 'Well, I think your father should perhaps look after these two,' he paired *The Mysteries of Udolpho* and *The Scars of Dracula* together and put them under his arm, 'and you can maybe read them when you're older. The Agatha Christie, meanwhile, I'm sure is harmless enough. Miss Marple never comes across anything too shocking.'

I took the book from him and ran off into the woods.

'Kitty, come back here!' Dad shouted.

'Let her be,' I heard Father Tobias say.

I was soon out of earshot. I only stopped running once

I was safely behind a large tree and I heard the sound of the front door closing.

I got cold quite quickly in the woods. When I'd run off, I was only wearing one of my cardigans. Though it was a rather snuggly, large cardigan, it still wasn't sturdy enough to keep me from shivering. Part of me wished we'd come to the forest in summer, not autumn, although I'd always preferred the colder, darker times of year. I liked the falling leaves and the conkers and walking past the shops with all their lights on as it got dark earlier and earlier.

I stayed out hours – hours longer than I planned – but I blamed my book. Once I'd found a relatively dry spot to sit, under an old oak tree, I settled back to read *The Pale Horse*. I quickly became immersed, although part of me was a little confused. Father Tobias's descriptions of what the book might be about didn't really match its contents. There weren't any old ladies called Miss Marple and as far as I could discover, nobody was Belgian. Instead, it was a strange and slightly frightening story about three women who, one of them claimed, may have the power to kill from afar. These weren't ordinary women. These were witches.

The thought scared me a little, as did other parts of the story, especially the list of names of people who were dead, or destined to die very soon. I got to about halfway in when I realised I could no longer feel my fingers and decided it was time to go and get a proper coat. I walked back to the house. It wasn't far; I'd only run a little way along, stopping before it sloped down towards the stream. The front door was on the latch so I walked into the dark hallway quietly, hoping I wouldn't be heard or discovered. Part of me expected to find something strange, but there was no sign of the weird burning scent that filled the hallway yesterday. The door to the lounge was closed and I could hear voices, but I couldn't quite catch what they were saying. I decided not to linger, and reached for my coat on the peg by the boots, next to an umbrella I hadn't seen before.

That was when I heard it.

'YOU VICIOUS LITTLE CUNT.'

It wasn't a normal voice. It was a roar. A roar of fury, hatred and terrible, terrible things. And it was coming from inside the lounge.

I stayed completely still. I didn't move a single finger. The coat swayed as it hung from my hand, the yellow, waterproof fabric making a slight sweeping sound. Then I heard another voice – Father Tobias's.

'Come back to me, Marjory. Step out of his vile bonds. Step away from his evil stare.'

His voice was commanding and strong, but the other voice was stronger, harsher. And it frightened me like nothing else had in my entire life.

'MARJORY WILL BURN FOR HER SINS. WE WILL TEAR OPEN HER HOLES AND FILL THEM WITH NEEDLES. HER EYES WILL BE GOUGED OUT BY MY FOLLOWERS. THEY WILL FUCK HER BRAINS AND SPILL THEIR SEEDS INTO HER BROKEN SKULL. THE EDGES OF HER SMASHED JAW WILL DRIP WITH THE SEEPING WHITENESS OF THEIR JUICES.'

I felt my hand start to tremble and I slowly lowered the coat and pressed it towards me. I dared not move any more, but I wasn't sure if this was from the fear of being caught, or fear of that voice and the things it was saying.

'I order you to leave this pure, innocent woman,' Father Tobias said, his voice shaking a little.

'SHE IS NOT AN INNOCENT. SHE HAS DONE EVIL THINGS IN HERE. AND SHE HAS ENJOYED THEM. AND SHE WANTS TO DO THEM AGAIN. AND AGAIN. AND AGAIN. UNTIL SHE SPLITS IN TWO.'

I ran. I could not stay. It was impossible. The voice had made me want to scream and cry at the same time. I didn't close the door – I just left it open, swaying in the breeze.

Chapter 15

I ran through the woods, not caring that tree branches were snatching at my clothes, at my skin, ripping and scratching and tearing. It reminded me of the time the other day when Mum went missing. It felt like she was missing all over again. Missing in a different way. Missing when her body was still there. And her voice . . .

I tried not to think about the voice. But I knew, deep down, that it must have come from Mum. That it was like all those things she'd been saying for weeks – months – now, only this time it sounded like a man; deep and rasping, like an old man who had smoked for a very long time.

I stopped running, then dropped to my knees. The ground was even colder than the air around me and the damp leaves chilled me as soon as I fell onto them, the moisture coating my face and hair.

MARJORY WILL BURN FOR HER SINS

The words tumbled into my head and rattled round until I couldn't bear it. I screamed. And screamed and screamed.

HER EYES WILL BE GOUGED

I couldn't stop hearing them. I couldn't get them out of my mind, no matter how hard I cried, no matter how long I screamed.

HER BROKEN SKULL

The words bloomed into pictures – horrible pictures, pictures of the worst possible things. Of Mum's head, broken on the ground. Her eyes hanging out. And then someone striking a match and trying to burn her body, only it wouldn't burn, because it was wet from all the blood—

'Bleeding Christ, will you just shut up!'

The voice made me jump. It was a real voice. Not the terrifying hammering voice shaking around my head. It was a girl's voice. Someone near me, right now, here in real life. I looked up from the ground, trying to brush the leaves away from my face. Some clung to my eyelashes, making it hard for me to blink.

It was Adah.

'You shouldn't say "Bleeding Christ",' I told her, sniffing slightly as I stood up.

She shrugged. 'It's what my aunt says. "Bleeding Christ, shut your fucking mouth".' That's one of her favourites.'

I was shivering. I tried to keep as still as possible so

my teeth didn't chatter. 'I just don't think it's a nice thing to say.'

She tilted her head to one side, as if she was trying to work out a puzzle. I was the puzzle.

'Because it's blasphemous?'

I wasn't too sure about this, so dodged the question. 'There are better things to say when you're surprised. Like "Oh my goodness" or maybe "Oh my gosh" or something like that.'

She laughed. 'That sounds a bit posh. *Oh my gosh!*' She said the last bit with a similar voice to the queen. I didn't find it that funny, but she kept on with her laughing. '*Oh my gosh, one should shut one's fucking mouth!*'

This did make me laugh, just because it sounded so silly, and Adah seemed pleased she'd managed to get some sort of reaction from me other than disapproval.

'I don't think you should be making all this noise in the woods. You never know who may be listening.' She said this in a hushed voice, as if sharing a secret.

'What do you mean?' I said, feeling a prickle of something on my neck. Fear? Or just a flake of bark or leaf?

'I mean,' she said slowly, 'the whole wood is filled with evil spirits.'

I didn't want to hear this, not after what I'd heard in the house, and I felt a rising sense of panic flooding me, filling me up from the inside out, until it reached the surface of my skin and sent a wave of goosebumps down my arms. 'It isn't . . . there's not . . . you're being silly.'

'It is. Filled to the brim. Particularly one. A woman who died. In your house, I think.'

117

The blood was pumping within me so loud, I thought I was going to go deaf from the noise of it. 'In the cottage?'

'I think so. Her name was Jadis. She was a witch. A real one. Lived in that cottage. Used to sell things. Rope, mostly. My aunt said there were some who reckoned it was made from people's hair. Children's hair. But that was never proven.'

I stared at her, transfixed. The wind started to gust around us, blowing more leaves towards me, but I let them snag in my hair. I didn't care. 'What happened to her?'

'She died. One day, she walked into the river, screaming. And apparently all the birds flew out of the trees and started to join in – screeching and screeching, until finally she stopped. And her heart stopped too. And then her body fell beneath the surface of the river and that was the end of her. Or the end of her *body*, I should say.'

'Why just her body?'

Adah smiled; a crueller smile than normal. 'Because her spirit lives on. Around us. Everywhere.' She opened her arms wide and circled on the spot, as if conducting an orchestra or gratefully receiving applause, and the wind gusted again, as if in response to her movement. 'The whole forest is full of her spies still. Even some of the trees are on her side.'

Ever so slightly, I felt a small memory bell start to ring inside my head. Something was stirring in my mind. But it went quiet again, just as quickly.

'Are you trying to scare me? Because it's not very nice if you are.'

Adah stared back at me, deadly serious. Then her face broke out into a smile.

'Oh come on! I'm being silly. That's what my aunt said if I tell her stories like that. I'm being "silly". Well, she's right. Surely being silly is the best thing to be. I'd hate to be dull and serious all the time.'

'What you said sounded serious to me,' I said, trying to keep my voice strong and clear, although I felt like running away and leaving this strange girl to all her strange things. But she ran forward and took my arm.

'Let's go across the stream and into my side of the forest. We can climb a few trees if you've got time.'

Part of me wanted to say no and leave her in the woods and go back to the cottage. Then I thought of what I heard there, in the lounge. And that strange, deep voice.

SHE HAS DONE EVIL THINGS IN HERE. AND SHE HAS ENJOYED THEM. AND SHE WANTS TO DO THEM AGAIN.

I shook my head to get rid of the words. 'OK, I'll come.'

Adah grinned. 'Excellent. Let's go.'

She moved away from me, down towards the slope leading to the stream, in the direction of the little bridge. I waited for a second and glanced back to where the cottage would be, if I followed the trail through the woods. Then I turned my back on it, and walked forward, slowly, following Adah towards the water.

Chapter 16

Adah followed through on her promise. We did climb trees.

She was slightly taller and stronger than I was, so she helped give me a lift up. And then I was in, climbing through the branches, although they started to creak a bit too much the nearer I got to the top. I thought I'd get an amazing view from up there, but no – there were just loads of leaves from all the other trees, all of them tightly packed next to each other. It was as if down on the ground wasn't the real forest, just a dress rehearsal for the main stuff up in the skies.

'What's it like?' Adah shouted up to me.

'A lot of leaves,' I answered. 'Although some of them look as if they're going to fall pretty soon.'

'That's because it's autumn,' she said, as if this was a really interesting piece of news I wouldn't have thought of myself.

She came to join me eventually, and we spent a little while talking about how awful our family members were.

'My aunt can be so mean. Sometimes she throws bottles at my head. Glass ones. They never hit me, of course. She's too drunk to be able to aim properly. But once one smashed just above my head and one of the pieces cut me quite badly. I've still got a mark on my shoulder.' She pulled at her jumper to expose a bit of flesh. Along the top line of her shoulder I could indeed see a thin red mark. 'I sometimes wonder if there's any glass still in it. It itches quite a lot, and sometimes if I press down on it I get this weird tingly sort of pain that doesn't go away for a bit.'

'Couldn't you see a doctor?' I ask.

She looked at me as if I was stupid, but didn't say anything.

We sat for a bit in silence, playing with leaves, picking them off the branches, shredding their dry stems, watching them float down one by one.

A rustling and shaking made us both jump.

'What is that?' I shrieked, and Adah looked scared too for a second, then started to laugh.

'It's only Levi. Look!' She pointed down. I saw him instantly, darting about near the trunk of the tree, running back and then thudding his weight against it, causing the whole thing to shake worryingly.

'Stop it, you degenerate!' Adah shrieked down.

'What did you call him?' I asked, watching the boy stop what he was doing and look up, grinning. He had a strange face – one that might look nice and friendly on someone else, but on him it looked wicked and full of mischief. He had deep, hazel eyes and frighteningly white teeth.

'I called him a DEGENERATE.' She shouted the last word down at him.

'What the fuck you on about?' Levi called up.

'It's what my aunt calls him,' Adah said. 'Which I think is a bit rich, considering she spends most of her time glugging from a vodka bottle.'

Levi was positioning himself on the lower branch, preparing to climb.

'Er, no, I don't think so. We don't want any dodgy teenage boys up here,' Adah said with conviction, although I could tell she wasn't really that annoyed. When he carried on climbing, she even moved further up the branch she was resting on so he had space to haul himself up and sit on. Once he'd settled, he turned his gaze on me.

'So, girlies. What's the game, then?'

Adah tutted. 'There is no *game*,' she said, scornfully. 'We were talking before you rudely interrupted us.'

He looked at her blankly. 'I'm not rude.'

'You *are*. We were having a private conversation and you started sticking your oar in. Or your foot,' she said, giving his dirty trainer a tap, since it was pushing up against her jeans.

'I wonder if you girls are secretly plotting,' he said. 'Plotting to take over the forest. Seize it as your own territory.'

Adah let out another tut and rolled her eyes. 'It's already our territory. Although as I've already explained to Kitty, it actually belongs to Jadis, Queen of the Woods, whose spirit still floats on the wind and whispers on the river.'

He looked disbelieving. 'Surely it would make more sense to float on a river and whisper on a wind, not the other way around?'

Adah turned to me and made a can-you-believe-his-cheek sort of face. 'He thinks he's so clever,' she said. 'Just wait until the Day of Judgement comes. He'll be sorry then.'

'Why will I be sorry?' He gave me a smile then, as if he were letting me in on a game he was playing.

'Because naughty boys like you will get what's coming for them.'

'What have I got coming for me? What have I done wrong?'

Adah made a face as if she was deciding what she wanted to say. Then she started scratching the tree bark with her fingers and, not looking at him, said, 'I've seen what you do in the wood shed.'

'What do I do in the wood shed?' There was something hard and not that nice about his grin; it was almost becoming a smirk.

Adah looked up at him. 'Things. Nasty things. In the wood shed.'

Levi frowned at her, then turned to me.

'So, who the fuck are you then?'

His use of bad words made me worried – I wouldn't normally want to be in a tree with someone who said words like that so easily – but I decided to ignore it for the moment and instead said to him: 'None of your business.'

He laughed. 'It is my business. If you're in my forest.'

'I've told you,' Adah said, sounding impatient. 'It isn't *your* forest. It belongs to—'

'The wicked old witch who died in the cottage, yeah yeah, I know,' he said, batting away Adah's words with a flick of his hand. 'I'm more interested in the right here and the right now. And in the now, this is my forest, and what I say goes. And when there's a stranger – some new blood – wandering in the wild, I want to know about it.'

He said all this while staring at me. I matched his gaze.

'My name is Kitty.'

'Kitty? *Kitty?*' He said it like it was the most ridiculous thing he'd ever heard. 'What type of name is that? Kitty? Surely your parents didn't call you that?'

'Oh clear off, Levi. You've got the weirdest name of anyone I know.'

'At least mine's a real fucking name. Her one's like something you'd name a furry animal. Or an old lady.'

'Old ladies start off as little girls. Or haven't they taught you that at school yet?'

He sniffed loudly and then reached for something in his pocket. I was startled to see him draw out a packet of cigarettes. Dad used to smoke, but he hadn't for years, and even my memories of him smoking had faded into a memory. But the smell of it, as he lit one and breathed out, filling the leafy air with a grey haze, took me back to when I was very young, when I would play on the swings and Dad would smoke on the bench nearby. Mum used to say he'd smoke there to try and 'distance himself from the herd', whatever that meant. I thought it was because most of the other kids were at the playground with their mums, so if Dad took me, I think he felt left out of the all-female parents' gang. They'd all stand around chatting and he would feel awkward on his own. Smoking gave him something to do.

'I can't be dealing with school right now. I got real things to cope with.'

Adah let out a disbelieving splutter. 'Like what? What on earth would *you* have to cope with?'

He let out a stream of smoke quickly, looking cross. 'Don't you carry on with none of your cheek, young missy. I got things, you know. Real things. I'm trying to get some cash quickly so I can leave this place. Fuck off back to Doncaster where I was born.'

Adah was still looking at him with disdain, shaking her head and smirking a similar smirk to his. 'And how are you going to do that? Sprout wings and fly? And what about your foster parents?'

He let out a sharp bark of a laugh. 'If anyone could sprout fucking wings I bet it could be me. But no, I'm going to buy a motor. And anyway, them lot don't care. They're having a baby of their own. Didn't think they could, before, but now they're all obsessed with that shit – buying prams and all. It's like I'm not there. I stay out all night in my cabin and nobody gives a fuck. As soon as I've got my motor, I'm gone.'

It took me a few seconds to realise he meant a car.

'You'll never afford it,' Adah said with confidence. 'Bet you can't. Bet you die before you're able to afford one.'

'Bet I don't.'

'Bet you do. You can't drive at your age. And where you going to get the money from anyway?'

'I have my ways.'

The sentence sat quietly between us for a minute, then Levi turned to me and said, 'Adah's right, though. About your cottage. I don't know about an old woman, but there's something . . . I don't know . . . *weird* about it.'

Adah scoffed, 'Something weird. Don't be ridiculous.'

Levi looked highly displeased. 'It was you who fucking started it with your strange talk. I'm just agreeing. I think there's something fucked about the place. Something not right.'

Adah twisted her mouth a bit, as if she were considering his reasoning. 'Like when you have a rabbit caught in a trap and it's broken its leg and it just won't die,' Adah said, nodding slowly.

'Who said anything about rabbits?' Levi muttered.

'I think I want to go home now,' I said. The image Adah had created of a struggling rabbit, unable to walk from a broken limb, had disturbed me beyond comfort. I didn't want to go back to the house. I didn't want to walk through the woods for the rest of the day. But I knew I couldn't stay in this tree listening to these two freaks bickering on about things that upset me for hours on end.

'Oh no, don't go,' Adah said. 'We're sorry, we didn't

126

mean to make out that your house is bad or anything. Levi was just being silly.' She kicked the boy in the shin and, although he still looked grumpy, he nodded immediately.

'See! Everything's fine. Let's stay and count the leaves.'

I shook my head, my arms reaching out to pull myself from the little area of trunk I'd been sitting on. The bark scratched my ankle as I slid my feet out and tried to stand.

'Careful, you'll knock us both to our deaths!' Adah protested.

'I'd quite like to die,' muttered Levi. 'Sooner rather than later.'

'I just need to get out,' I said. I tried to get myself into a position where I could lower my legs down whilst holding on to a branch with my arms, but immediately I felt my shoes slip and I was clawing at the tree with both hands, trying not to fall.

'Hold on, I got ya,' Levi said. He helped me back up and I sat on the middle bit of the trunk, panting and trying not to cry.

'Right, if we're really getting down, I'll go first and help you two girlies down after.'

Adah tutted. 'Thinks he's a big strong man, doesn't he, Kitty?'

I decided not to point out that he might well have just saved my life, and nodded, meekly.

Levi clambered down effortlessly to the ground and then called up. 'OK, then. Who's first?'

'You go first,' Adah said. 'I'll hold your hand until he's got your other half.'

She did as she promised, and within seconds, I was being helped down from above and below until each foot one by one made it to the damp, leaf-strewn floor of the forest.

Then he went to help Adah down, but came up against her protestations of 'I can bloody well do it myself, little boy!'

'Little boy? I'm like four years older than you! Or more!'

Adah tutted loudly, but accepted Levi's hand. He helped her down the last few unevenly placed branches so that all three of us were finally back on the ground, as nature intended.

'Do you want to go home?' Adah asked gently, looking at me with kind eyes. I had the mild sense that I'd become the child of two parents; Adah and Levi. I wasn't sure I was a fan of this arrangement, so I shook my head. 'I'm fine. I just wanted to be on the ground.'

'Well then,' Adah said, 'I think we should explore young Levi's hideaway.'

'What!' he barked, looking affronted.

'Yes. Let's do it. Let's go to the wood shed.' Adah nodded as she said it, and folded her arms to make clear that, to her, a decision had been made.

I looked at Levi, who was kicking bits of twig and leaf up with the tips of his trainers. 'Will there be spiders?' I asked.

Levi looked up quickly. 'Yes. Yes there will be. Lots.'

Adah laughed. 'I think Lev's trying to put you off, Kitty. He doesn't know that spiders are your friends.'

The boy looked sullen again.

'All right,' I nodded, folding my arms like Adah. 'Let's do it. Let's go to the wood shed.'

Chapter 17

The wood shed was smaller than I had imagined. I had hoped it would be an almost barn-like place, filled with chopped logs and saws and clunking mechanical stuff built to skin tree-bark off like a knife through butter and to create perfect planks, ready for house building. But it wasn't anything like that. It was just a shed. A cabin sort of thing. And there weren't any logs in it.

We trekked for what felt like hours through the woods, although I suspected it only felt so long because I was hungry. When we arrived, I hung back, watching Adah as Levi bounded up to the shed. 'You going to tidy away your filthy mags first?' Adah called out, pausing at the worn-out trail of pathway-like earth before we got to the door.

'Sod off,' Levi said. He opened the door and went in.

'Come on,' Adah said, taking me by the arm. She led me, firmly but not harshly, into the wood shed. Aside from it being smaller than expected, part of me quite liked it inside. Although Levi looked like one of those boys my mum would have called 'rough' back when she was well, he'd made it homelier and cosier than I would have thought likely of him. There were three or four blankets, some of them a bit scraggly, but they looked soft and comfortable enough. There were also cushions. These could have done with replacing as they were partly ripped, but the effort to make the area on the floor nice and comfortable, rather than dirty and wet, lessened the worry I'd been feeling ever since I heard that voice back at the cottage.

'Close the door!'

Levi's shout made me jump, taking me out of my thoughts. I did what he said quickly.

'I'm not used to having girls in here,' he said, shifting the blankets around. It took me a few seconds to realise what he was doing: he was tidying, embarrassed by the place and the mess we'd found it in.

'Is this place all yours?' I asked.

'Yes. Well, no. I don't know whose it is, really. It's been empty for years. But I come here when my foster parents get tired of me and start throwing stuff.'

I felt awkward about this confession, and it seemed Levi did, too, as he kicked his trainers off, settled down on one of the blankets and didn't look at us for a bit. Adah sat down, too, so I joined her. In the quiet, I heard

131

rain begin to patter its way through the trees and onto the roof. Although it wasn't night yet, the single window at the back of the shed was dirty and covered with leaves, so didn't let in much light. Levi lit a heavy jar candle he had in the corner. Its glass was cracked and the label was partly torn off, but I think it said something about Christmas and had holly wreaths on it. Sure enough, in just a few minutes, the smell of Christmas trees filled the cabin. It reminded me of when I was very small, so small I could barely remember, when Mum used to lift me up to put little chocolate Santas on the branches of the tree in the lounge.

'There's something under here,' Adah said, digging about under the blankets and pillows. She pulled out a battered paperback book. It had a deer on the front; Bambi from the Disney film. 'Why've you got this here? It's for kids.'

'We are kids,' he murmured from his nest in the corner.

'*We* are kids,' Adah said, gesturing between herself and me. 'You're a *teenager*.'

She said the word teenager as if it were some sort of disease most would want to avoid catching.

'Give it here. I don't want you messing it up.'

Adah laughed. 'It's already messed up. The cover's all bent and—'

'I said give it here!' Levi leaned forward and snatched it from her.

'All right, all right,' she said, clearly a bit hurt by this. 'I was only looking.'

'It was my mum's. Well, it was mine. But she gave it to me.'

Levi looked sad. Adah nodded. She looked sad too.

'Do you want to read it to us?' Adah asked, quietly.

Levi let out a short, low laugh. 'What is this? Fucking story time at playgroup?'

'You don't have to,' Adah said. 'I just thought it might be nice.'

He looked like he was thinking about this, his eyebrows screwed up a little. Then he pulled out the book from where he'd shoved it behind his back, and opened the first page.

'OK.'

We sat, listening to the story. It must only have lasted five or ten minutes at most – the book wasn't long, and it was filled with pictures from the film – but it was like we were lost in another world for hours and hours, days and days. When Bambi's mother was shot, even though we all knew it was coming, it was as if a jolt ran through us all, like we'd felt the bullet ourselves. Like we'd felt the pain. And I looked over at Adah and I could see that she was crying. Tears running silently down her face. I reached out my hand and she reached out hers and our arms met in the space between us. And we held hands for the rest of the story. This is what it must feel like to have a best friend, I thought to myself as I felt the warmth of her hand in mine. Being able to be close and together without actually needing to speak. And for a few moments, it was as if we'd skipped the time and experience that go into building a strong friendship, and had already arrived at some destination I'd never reached before. Like we'd grown old together, in the space of that afternoon.

Once it was done, I saw Levi's eyes look shiny. But it may have been the candlelight.

'It's a happy ending,' Adah said.

'Yeah, 'tis,' Levi said, nodding, as if trying to convince himself of something.

We sat in silence for a little while longer, then, when the patter of the rain on the roof had got so strong it was like a chorus of applause, Levi said, 'I should be heading back home.' From what he'd said before, I doubted he had any real need to get home, but I got the feeling he wanted us to leave.

Adah nodded and turned to me. 'Will your parents be cross you've been out so long, Kitty?'

I shook my head. 'They wanted me to go out and explore the forest. And I have.'

She yawned a little and straightened up. 'I'm getting hungry. I'm afraid you shouldn't come round mine, really. My aunt wouldn't like it.'

'It's OK,' I said, 'I think I should go home now.'

Adah turned to look at Levi, still sprawled on the floor, his legs half uncrossed.

'Aren't you coming?' she asked, and he shook his head.

'You guys go. I'm going to just stay for a bit and tidy the cabin.'

Adah didn't reply, just turned round to open the door. I followed her through it.

'Bye,' I said. He didn't said goodbye in return. Just gave a vague nod, his eyes not on me.

I expected Adah to start walking away from the cabin, but she raised her finger to her lips, telling me to be quiet. 'This way,' she mouthed, and then started to pick her way through the fallen branches and masses of plants that covered the back of the wood shed. Once we'd reached the other side, she made a gesture, telling me to crouch down and be quiet, then she pressed her eyes to a crack in the wooden wall.

'What are you doing?' I whispered in her ear.

She flinched, as if caught at something, then peered back through the gap. After a moment, she took her eyes away from it and then leaned in close to my ear and whispered, 'I wanted to see if he gets them out.'

I looked at her with a confused face, which was enough for her to come back to my ear and carry on whispering. 'His dirty mags. I wanted to see if he has them hidden in there. I've seen them before when I've spied on him.'

I nodded, as if I understood, but I didn't really. I thought of the dirty magazine I'd found under my bed. Did Levi have one of those?

I felt along the wall of the cabin and found a crack that was big enough for me to see through as well. And sure enough, he proved Adah right. He stuck his hand under the blankets, fished around for a few seconds, and pulled out a magazine. Even from the small crack in the wood, I could tell that the woman on the front wasn't wearing anything and was clutching her chest with her mouth open. I was about to whisper to Adah about the magazine I'd found inside my house, thinking perhaps it would give us some common ground – show that I had

135

at least seen things like this before – but before I could say anything, Levi did something that took my attention back to inside the cabin. He stood up and pulled down his tracksuit bottoms, revealing his underpants. I shot a quick look at Adah, but she was staring intently through the wood. I looked back and saw Levi had dropped his underpants too, and there it was – his bottom. The first boy's bottom I'd seen, apart from my dad's. And Dad was old. He was thirty. Dad's body belonged to an old person. But Levi's didn't. And, as we watched, I thought I vaguely knew what he was doing. I didn't really want to think about it, but we kept watching, Adah silent next to me.

And then something happened. I saw it happen, and at the same time, I didn't see it, because it was as if my brain went black suddenly. All of a sudden, the forest was in my face, trees, branches, like last time when I was running. And now I was running again. As fast as I could.

When I got to the stream, I stopped myself just in time. A few more steps and I would have touched the water. But I didn't, and it was fine, and then Adah was there next to me, panting, out of breath, shaking my shoulders, asking what was wrong. Asking if I could hear her. But I could barely hear her. Instead, my ears were ringing with the words I'd heard earlier when I stepped into the hall. And no matter how hard I tried, I couldn't make them stop.

I'd begun crying without realising and suddenly Adah was hugging me and I was crying into her shoulder. Crying and crying and I could tell she wasn't sure what to do except let me cry.

Minutes later, she led me along the stream to the little bridge, where she'd taken me on our first meeting, and we sat down on the steps. As we did so, the rain stopped and the sun came out. Beams of light fell through the branches, as if a giant was pouring liquid gold onto the trees above, just for us. To make our seat on the bridge that little bit less horrible. That little bit kinder.

'I'm sorry I showed you that. I didn't realise it would upset you,' Adah said, looking seriously at me. I looked at her, trying to take in her deep, dark-brown eyes, but I was holding myself back, trying not to cry, and I found I couldn't look at her for long.

'I've seen him do it before. I used to spy on Levi for ages before he started talking to me.'

I nodded, although I wasn't sure what the nod was supposed to say.

'All boys do that. You must have heard about it at school. It's not as if it's, like, that weird or anything.'

I brushed my tears from my face and nodded again. I didn't want to say anything. If I could just sit here and let her talk, I'd be all right. After a bit, Adah patted my arm.

'Shall we walk back to the cottage? We can walk there together?'

I looked over at the other side of the stream. 'Don't you live that way?' I said, pointing. 'Shouldn't you get home?'

She shook her head, looking a little sad. 'I'm going to go home. But I don't need to. My aunt would prefer it if I didn't ever again, I think.' Before I could respond, she stood up. 'Come on. Let's go.'

My legs were aching from running, but I slowly got up and we walked in the direction of the cottage. I felt the wind start to gather strength again and the coldness of it stung my face, my cheeks still raw from the scratches of the branches and plants I must have knocked out of my way.

'Tomorrow,' said Adah, 'if you come out again, I think you should wear a thicker cardigan under your coat. It's getting colder. Nearly November.'

'Soon be Christmas,' I said under my breath. It's what Mum always used to say at this time of the year. When it was getting cold and people complained about the short days and long nights. *Soon be Christmas*. Not that last Christmas was much fun. I'd hoped it was when she'd start to enjoy things again. Noticing the signs of the season, seeing the snow outside or the smell of roast turkey. But she spent most of it crying in the downstairs bathroom. The colour of the paper Dad's Christmas present had been wrapped in had upset her greatly.

We arrived at the cottage to find Amanda outside, smoking.

'Hello, Kitty,' she said, doing her warm, aren't-I-so-friendly voice. 'And my goodness, look, you've made a new friend.'

'Yes,' I said flatly, with a little sniff.

I saw her eyes flick over me. If she noticed I'd been crying, she didn't say anything. Instead, she turned to Adah and said, 'What's your name, sweet one?'

'Adah,' Adah said brightly, and put her hand out. Amanda shook it, grinning widely. I could smell the smoke as she came close, together with something else. That strange, sweet smell I'd noticed before. Coming from the lounge.

'Well, it's very lovely to meet you, Adah. I trust both of you have had a nice time out playing in the woods?'

Adah grinned. 'Yes we have. Jolly good fun. Endless fun.'

There were times when I thought Adah repeated things she'd heard other people say, rather than coming up with them herself. This was one of those times.

'Great stuff,' Amanda said through a lot of teeth. She'd reapplied some more deep red lipstick since the morning. It made the rest of her face look pale. 'So, Kitty. I think it's time you came in and we all had a bit of a chat. OK?'

I just stared back at her.

'OK?' she said again.

'Where's my dad?' I asked, taking my eyes off her and casting them around. The front door was closed and the curtains were drawn.

'He's inside. We'd like to talk to you. All of us together.'

I thought about this. 'And have some food?' My stomach was now seriously starting to pain me, the hunger arriving like a big, crushing wave, hurling me against sharp rocks, again and again. It's only then I realised how much time had passed.

'Of course! It's a bit late to call it lunch, now it's nearly four, but you can have an early tea.' She smiled even wider, then said to Adah, 'I'm sorry, sweetness, we're going to have to end your day of forest play here for today. Kitty has some things she needs to do.'

Adah smiled back. 'That's OK. I better get back off home now too.'

'Good, good.' Amanda beamed at her. There was so much smiling going on, it was making me feel very uncomfortable. I didn't think anyone should be smiling at this moment.

Amanda opened the door, swinging it wide, then stepped forward and took hold of my shoulder. Before I could properly think about shrugging it off, she'd chucked her cigarette away with her free hand and grabbed hold of my other shoulder to guide me inside. The last thing I saw before the door swung closed was Adah, standing amidst the falling leaves in her turquoise coat. Giving me a little wave.

Chapter 18

January 2020

'I think it's best we talk a little about Adah Okafor and your relationship with her.'

DI Cousins says this sentence in a very businesslike way, apparently oblivious to the effect it has on me. I feel the hairs on my skin prickle and my temperature starts to drop so rapidly I have to draw my thick woollen cardigan round me. I try not to visibly shiver. DC Malik notices. I see his eyes move, but he doesn't say anything.

'Ms Marchland?' DI Cousins prompts, when I don't answer.

'Erm . . . yes . . . I'm sorry.' I pull my sleeves down so they cover my cold hands, trying to stop the wave of ice taking hold across me.

'Are you quite all right?' she asks, sounding more impatient than caring.

'Yes. I'm sorry. It's just . . . the subject of Adah is a very difficult one for me to talk about.'

Both police officers stare at me for a few seconds, then DI Cousins says, 'Well, you've managed to write a whole *book* about your experiences, so it can't be that hard.' She doesn't bother trying to cover her frustration. 'And anyway, you've come all this way to do this interview, so you may as well speak to us openly.'

Her words echo around us for a few beats before she adds, 'It really is for your benefit, Katherine. Help us out now, and we might be able to avoid this becoming very, very serious.'

I look up at this. 'It *is* serious.'

'Serious for you, I mean. And your future. So please, talk to us honestly and answer our questions fully.'

I watch her blank face, the lines starting to crease around her eyes as middle age takes hold.

'I only came,' I say, choosing my words slowly and carefully, 'because you threatened to arrest me if I didn't agree to come in for questioning.'

I see DI Cousins's nostrils flare a little, but it's DC Malik who responds.

'Katherine, we really are just trying to get to the truth in all of this.' His tone is soft and calming, and he places a hand on the desk in front of him, almost as if he were laying a hand on my arm. 'Avoiding our questions now is only going to delay that, and as my colleague says, that might make things difficult for you. Not cooperating might send a negative message when we have our meetings with various other people about whether or not to take this case further. Do you understand what I'm saying?'

His hazel eyes seek out contact with mine, and eventually, grudgingly, I give in and look at him properly. 'Yes,' I say.

He gives me a small smile and nods.

'Thank you,' he says, still speaking in a slower, kinder voice than DI Cousins had been moments before. 'Now, I realise this must be terribly distressing for you, having all these old memories brought up, but one of the most important things for us, as I'm sure you can imagine, is working out where Adah fits into this puzzle.'

As I give him a little nod, to show I understand, a few tears slip from my eyes. I don't brush them away. I just let them fall.

'Katherine, the fact is we can't put this matter to rest until we've got a full picture of the situation,' he says, leaning in a little. 'A full picture of the circumstances surrounding your friend's death.'

Chapter 19

1987

'We need to have a little chat.'

That's what Amanda said to me as we sat down on the sofa. Once again, everything in the room was back to normal. It even looked quite homely – more than usual. The strange smell from before was still there, but intermingled with something like bread or baking. Mum was nowhere to be seen; nor were the blankets that were previously folded on the sofa. I tried to work out what else was different, then realised the answer lay in the brown vase on the coffee table. It had been brought over from the windowsill, where it had stood empty and dusty. Now it was cleaned up and filled with orange flowers I didn't know the name of and things that looked like wheat and thistles.

'I see you like my little autumnal bouquet,' she said, brightly.

'It's . . .'

I had been about to say 'it's nice' but decided to keep my thoughts to myself until I heard what they were going to tell me.

'It's beautiful,' Dad chipped in. I looked up at him. I had never heard him use the word 'beautiful' in his life.

Over in the corner, Father Tobias said, 'It is indeed. Very seasonal.' He was sitting in the armchair, eating what looked like a mince pie. 'Isn't it, Katherine?'

I couldn't really find much to argue with, so I just nodded. Dad tapped me on the shoulder and said, 'You should reply properly, Kitty, when Father Tobias talks to you.'

I glared at him. 'He took my books.'

'But you've got lots of books here,' Father Tobias said, lifting up a stack of paperbacks from nowhere, as if by magic. I recognised some of the titles.

'You've been in my room!' I shouted, rising to my feet, but Amanda laid a firm hand on my shoulder and pulled me back down.

'I'm afraid so,' Father Tobias said. 'On your father's permission, of course. I was going from room to room, blessing them with holy water. Do you know what holy water is, Katherine?'

'Yes.'

'Tell me,' he said, smiling.

'It's water that's holy.'

There was a moment of silence, then both Father Tobias

145

and Amanda laughed. Amanda raised her hand to her face as her eyes creased up and Father Tobias's stomach moved up and down as he held on to the crust of the pie in his hand. At first, I thought Dad was going to tell me off. A look of annoyance passed over his face, but then he, too, smiled and let out a chuckle. It didn't sound real though.

'Yes, well, ask a silly question,' said Father Tobias. 'Yes, you are quite right, Katherine. Hit the nail on the head, there. It's water that has been blessed.' He took out a little glass bottle with a cork in the top, like a magician again, and held it up. It glinted in the warm yellow of the ceiling light. 'Earlier today, we told your mother we were going to bless this room. With this.' He shook the bottle and I saw the twinkle of some liquid swirling against the side. I almost thought I could hear a little splashing sound, but decided I must have been imagining it, since I was too far from the bottle to hear anything inside it. And anyway, it was too small to give off a sound even if I were right up close.

'When I said this to your mother, we were prepared for her – or rather, for something inside her – to object to the suggestion.'

I heard Dad shift from foot to foot near my side. I looked up at his face, but his direction was turned away from me, towards the crackling fire.

'I'm sure you won't be surprised to hear, Katherine, that she got quite agitated by the suggestion. Quite hysterical, some would say. And she started to say very strong, emotive and, some may argue, offensive things to me and Amanda and your father.'

I knew what he was talking about. And I wasn't sure I wanted to hear any more.

'Can I go?' I looked up at Dad again, hoping he would turn to face me. But he just stared on, as if his eyes alone were responsible for keeping the flames burning in the grate. 'Please, Dad, can I go? I want to go up to bed?'

'But it's so early, Kitty,' Amanda said. 'Stay here, just for a little while.'

I wasn't liking this. Not at all.

'I really think I should—'

'Katherine, please. We want to explain. Amanda thinks she heard the door go earlier today and saw that your coat had gone. Did you come back? Did you hear anything?'

I could feel myself going red and my eyes were starting to burn.

WE WILL TEAR OPEN HER HOLES AND FILL THEM WITH NEEDLES

I heard the words in my head so loudly, I was convinced the others must have been able to hear them too. But I shook my head, and I looked pleadingly, begging them to believe me. 'I didn't hear anything.'

Amanda returned her hand to my shoulder. 'I think you did, Kitty.'

I stopped looking at any of them and focused my eyes on the floor, trying to pretend I wasn't there. 'Please, I just want to go to bed,' I said, quietly. And the tears started to fall.

'There is a reason why we'd prefer you to play outside,

Kitty. Rather than wander about the house.' Dad was speaking now, and he came to sit next to me and Amanda on the sofa, so that I was squashed between them both. 'This . . . this process . . . this journey your mother is on. It's important. I'm sure you realise that. And we want it to work in the best possible way. But for that to happen, I think it might be a bit . . . well, a bit upsetting for you.'

I sniffed and shook my head again. 'I'm not upset,' I said, although the tear making its way slowly towards my chin might as well have been screaming *liar!* It was clear that I wasn't exactly happy. And I felt too tired to carry on hiding it.

'So, Kitty,' Dad said, 'we just wanted to explain that you didn't have to worry. Whatever you may have heard. Whatever it sounded like. We can promise that everything is OK. Or it will be OK. You just have to trust us.'

Both Dad and Amanda put their arms around me. They probably thought I didn't notice, but I could feel that their hands were touching.

'And my books,' I said, still in my small voice. 'Why have you brought my books down here?'

I looked over at Father Tobias, who let out a little laugh. 'Oh, I was just interested, my dear. That's all. I was a little worried that earlier I may have given you the impression that I disapproved of reading. Of course, that couldn't be further from the truth. Reading is a noble and important pursuit and must be encouraged in the young. But, of course, as I suggested before, there's a right time and a right place for everything, and some of the material you've been allowed to acquire may be a little, er . . .' he twisted his lips a bit, like he'd bitten into a sharp apple, 'inappropriate. Unsuitable.'

I hadn't even consciously decided to frown at him, but I was already starting to do it.

'So, with your father's permission, I have removed some titles.' He coughed, a little awkwardly.

I stiffened, drawing away from Dad's embrace. He was a traitor.

'Which ones have you stolen?'

Father Tobias looked appalled. 'Not stolen, my dear. No, I wouldn't steal. It's just been agreed . . . especially, taking into account the current situation—'

'Which books have you taken from my room?' I was half-shouting now, half-sobbing, and rose up off the sofa. Dad went to grab me, but Father Tobias raised his hand.

'It's quite all right. Let her be angry. She has a right to be.' He leaned forward and picked up the stack of books once more. 'I have given the ones I removed to your father for safe keeping. They include certain titles that cover, among other topics, ghosts haunting graveyards, reanimated corpses rising from tombs, several tales of alleged magic in the Middle East that have an unfortunate Arab slant to them, and one or two science fiction novels that imagine the aftermath of nuclear attacks on Great Britain and the United States of America.'

He paused, apparently to let this sink in. I was about to start screaming properly at him when he started up again.

149

'However,' he said, a little louder, as if he suspected what I was about to do, 'you still have numerous volumes here that I'm sure will keep you most joyfully entertained. Look at this one, Katherine: *Five Go Off in a Caravan*. That sounds like a fun adventure. And look, here: *First Term at Malory Towers*. Another, erm, classic.'

I stared daggers at him.

'I concede,' said Father Tobias, 'that the remaining books are all works by that prolific authoress, Mrs Blyton. And one by Mrs Christie, too. *The Mysterious Affair at Styles*. Did you enjoy the other one of hers you took off with you into the woods? Amanda found it on the mat near the front door.'

I nodded. 'Yes,' I said.

'Did Miss Marple save the day, as usual?' he said, chuckling.

'No. There wasn't anyone called Miss Marple in it.' I was trying to keep my voice very steady and calm. I looked him right in the eye as I continued. 'It was about *witches*.'

I saw him flinch a little as I said the last word. Encouraged by this, I pressed on. 'And the things they can do to people. How they can make bad things happen.'

He now looked rather troubled, and peered down at the book in his hand. 'Maybe,' he said slowly, 'I should re-evaluate my opinion of Mrs Christie and her output.' He set *The Mysterious Affair at Styles* down on the table. 'Well, if you're enthusiastic about witches, I'm sure you'll enjoy this one.' He held up the last book in the pile. I looked at the front. *The Lion, the Witch and the Wardrobe*.

'I've read it,' I said, flatly.

'I'm very glad to hear it,' he smiled. 'It's a masterpiece. And an excellent analysis of good and evil. Right and wrong. Important things, I'm sure you'll agree.'

I said nothing. I was expecting Father Tobias to lead on to the magazine I'd found under the bed. If he found a few collections of ghost stories unacceptable, I was rather interested to see how he'd cope with the pictures in that publication. But his search in my room seemed not to have involved the chest of drawers, and he pressed on with a smile and cough. 'Right, well,' he said, tapping the sides of the books now stacked on the coffee table so that they were in a neat tower. 'That leaves just one last thing to ask you,' he said, standing up and dusting off crumbs from his black clothes.

'What?' I asked, interested in spite of myself.

'Would you like a mince pie?'

I stared at him, confused.

'A bit early in the year, I know, but your mother seemed keen on the idea. And Amanda here was kind enough to go out and get the ingredients.'

I looked up at Amanda and then back at Father Tobias. 'Where are they?' I eventually asked.

'Why, in the kitchen of course,' he said, beaming again. He reached out an arm and opened the door that connected to the kitchen. And behind it was a sight that left me speechless.

Mum was inside. She was fully dressed in black trousers, a white top and a light pink cardigan, and over the top of them she was wearing an apron. She was standing there, holding a tray lined with pies – mince pies, I presumed – and her hands were covered with dark blue oven gloves.

'Hello, Kitty,' she said, with a smile. 'It's so lovely to see you. I've not been well, you see. But I wanted to make up for it. I've been baking, as you can see.'

Her voice was warm and soft, as it used to be. Before it got scratchy. Before it became rough and strained and sounded like she was on the edge of tears the whole time. But there was also something strange about it. Something not quite right.

'Why don't you come in here and help me finish off the final batch,' she said. 'They need dusting with icing.' She gave me another of her big, happy smiles and set down the tray of pies on the table.

I looked around at Father Tobias, Amanda and, finally, at Dad. And I was alarmed to see he looked like he was about to cry.

'Go in, love,' he said, quietly.

Mum was holding out her hand now, beckoning me in.

'Next I'm going to make some gingerbread,' she said. 'Like we used to. You can help put the smiles on the faces. You're good at that.'

I nodded. Dad gave me a very small push on the shoulder, and my feet started to move, carrying me into the kitchen.

'You used to eat so much gingerbread. And sweets. Remember what I used to call you?' she said, as I drew nearer. 'My little Gretel.'

I nodded again. She was right. That is what she used to call me. But instead of comforting me, and making me happy that my mum seemed to be back, it just made me feel worried. More worried than I'd ever been before. And I couldn't quite work out why.

Chapter 20

The next two days were very odd. It was as if I'd slipped into one of the videos I used to have of old Disney films, where families lived happily ever after. Mum seemed not just better, but even better than she was before. The night we made mince pies was like one from way back before her crying stage, her shouting stage, her silent stage. Back before she used to scream warnings at us all that the devil would not be happy with our activities and that we'd best not use knives and forks for our supper because 'shiny things will attract him out of his resting place'. We had come to always live under the same fear that she had – fear of 'Him'. Fear of 'Him' arriving, or causing her pain.

On the third morning of this new-old Mum, I was still

feeling worried. She made us scrambled eggs on toast, the way she had done the previous morning, and the one before that. Even though she spoke with smiles and laughs and patted me on the head the way she used to, I couldn't help feeling like there was something strange going on, and I didn't like it. I went to my room, took out some of my felt tips and an old notebook I'd previously used to make up names for beetles, and ripped out a blank page. On it, I wrote down a list of all the reasons I was still worried about Mum.

Problems With Mum

- *Although she smiles, her eyes look fake, like glass*
- *Although she seems happy, it's as if she's actually unhappy underneath – or maybe not even there at all*
- *Although she seems to be enjoying baking and cooking and doing washing again, it's as if she's acting in a play*
- *When I try to speak to her on her own for too long, Amanda or Dad always appear from nowhere*
- *Whenever I try to ask her if she's better now or say 'how are you today?', Amanda changes the subject or Dad tells me to go out and play*
- *Her hand shakes when she turns door handles. Very slightly. Like she's scared what might be behind them, even if it's just the bathroom or the lounge.*
- *She doesn't seem to want to go outside at all, not when I asked if she'd come to see the little bridge over the stream. She just seemed not to hear me.*

That last one had made me happy to start with. I was pleased she hadn't started screaming about the stream being poisoned. But Dad had glared at me and told me that I mustn't ever take Mum outside until he specifically said it was OK. He had whispered this to me and looked cross. Thinking about it later on made me cross, too, and I had avoided him for the rest of the day. I found myself wishing I had told him he was being unfair, and that Mum would probably like to see the forest looking all autumny-orange, now the sun was out and the rain had stopped. But I had told him none of this. I had just glared at him.

Amanda stayed in the cottage the whole time, apart from moments when she nipped off in her car to the nearest town to buy us more food, particularly baking ingredients – baking was an activity she and Dad encouraged. Maybe because they liked to know where Mum and I were. Amanda slept on the sofa – actually slept there, it seems, rather than just pretending to. With Mum talking and acting less odd, Dad and Amanda hadn't been having any late-night chats. He and Mum had continued to share a bed without any emotional flare-ups or him having to leave the room in the middle of the night.

'Oh, I'll be hanging around for a bit,' Amanda said, whenever I said things like 'Are you still here?' Dad told me off for being rude, but I thought it was a perfectly fair question. Why was she still here? Father Tobias hadn't come for a few days, and if she was only here to make Mum better, why hadn't she now packed away the pillow and blankets and gone back to wherever she had come from? Only some whispered conversations from her and

Dad had offered any real information, and they usually seemed to be filled with phrases like 'no sign of regression' and 'more normal every day'. I assumed this was about Mum. And I also had to assume they, too, had noticed the weirder parts of how she was acting. Otherwise they wouldn't need to whisper in the hallway while Mum and I were busy mixing up the ingredients for cherry bakewells. I didn't think she was 'more normal every day'. She wasn't shrieking any more, but whatever she was now, it didn't feel normal to me.

It was on the fourth day of the new Mum that something would happen to make everyone act more worried again.

It started with something that instantly made me panic: the front door was open, gently swaying in the breeze. I closed it, then walked back down the hallway to go and alert Dad. As I passed the tiny cupboard under the stairs, I heard a scraping sound, then something harsher, like a snip of some scissors. I was sure it had come from inside. I tried to pull open the door, but it wouldn't move. Then I heard something that immediately made me step back.

'Shhhh. Please. Shhhhh!'

I looked around, wondering if someone was telling me to be quiet from inside the lounge, but I knew really where it was coming from. It was coming from inside the cupboard.

'I'm not allowed . . . Shhhh! Please. Don't . . .'

And then there was silence. I was waiting, unsure what to do, when the door opened very quickly, making a loud grating sound. Mum stepped out, stooping so she didn't hit her head. She must have been all bunched up in there, and a dead spider was dangling from her hair. As soon as she saw me, her face instantly changed into a smile, one of her warm let's-bake-gingerbread smiles. But I'd seen her face in the seconds before she changed. It had been a face of fear.

'Dearest love, why are you standing here in the dark hallway?'

'Erm,' I didn't know what to say at first, so I tried to ask her a question. 'Who were you talking to?'

For a very short second, I thought she was going to cry, but then she beamed even wider and said, 'Talking to? No, no, sweetness, I was just looking for a dustpan and brush.' She ruffled my hair and laughed, as if I had told her a silly joke, and then walked towards the kitchen. 'Come on, dearest, let's make a chocolate traybake.' I looked back at the door of the now-closed cupboard, and for a moment had an urge to look inside and see what had made the strange snipping noise I'd heard. But Mum called me from the kitchen and I walked straight on.

I spent the whole time I was melting the chocolate and preparing the flour thinking about what I had heard, whilst the golden late-autumn sun shone through the window onto the back of my neck. It wasn't anywhere near as bad as other things I had heard Mum say. But that was when she wasn't well. Now she was better. Or she was supposed to be. I decided to add it to my list when I got back upstairs.

'Come on darling, you're away with the fairies today.

If you've measured the flour, let's add the sugar.' Mum passed me the bowl of white powder. I nodded and carried on.

I didn't write it in my notebook, what I had heard earlier. But I did tell Dad.

I heard him coming up the stairs with Mum late – hours after I'd gone to bed. I set aside the book I was reading and tiptoed to the door. I could hear them saying goodnight to Amanda on the stairs. Mum never seemed to properly speak to Amanda. She wasn't rude to her; it was more like she wasn't aware she existed. She smiled and did things like give her cups of tea, but she didn't seem to *notice* her. Not really.

'I'm just going to brush my teeth while you change into your pyjamas, dear,' she said to Dad on the landing.

'OK,' Dad murmured. I heard his steps go towards their bedroom, but before they faded away I opened my door quietly and whispered 'Dad!'

He jumped – actually jumped. It was like he'd been expecting something to startle him, and now it had happened it was more of a shock than he'd ever imagined. He looked at me with a confused, slightly angry face. 'Kitty!' he hissed. 'Why are you awake? We sent you up to bed ages ago.'

I ignored his cross words. 'Can I talk to you?'

Dad flicked his eyes towards the bathroom door. We could both hear Mum brushing her teeth enthusiastically.

'Can't it wait until morning? You can talk to your mum and me at breakfast.'

'It's about Mum,' I said. 'I want to talk to you. Please.'

He cast another look over at the door. And then nodded. 'All right. But it must be quick.'

He came into my room. I went over to the bed and sat in the middle, cross-legged; he sat down on the edge.

'Come on, Kitty,' he said, quietly.

I took a deep breath. 'Well, it was when you were talking to Amanda outside. Earlier today. I heard a voice. Coming from inside the cupboard under the stairs.'

His face stayed still. I waited to see if he was going to say anything, but he didn't, so I carried on.

'And the voice was Mum. She was saying things. Strange things. Upsetting things. Saying "please" a lot. Like . . . like she used to.'

Dad raised a hand to his face and rubbed his eyes, then moved his fingers to the bit between his nose and his eyes and pinched a little. He did this when he was feeling stressed.

'OK. Did she say anything else?'

I was cross with myself now for not writing it down, as I struggled to properly remember the words. 'I think . . . I think she said something like "I'm not allowed". Something like that. And there was shushing. Like she was telling someone to be quiet.'

Dad wasn't looking at me now. He was looking at the wall, but I got the feeling he was actually looking a long way away. Into a different world, maybe. Or a different time.

'Thanks, Kitty,' he said at last. 'Thanks for telling me. I thought this was too good to be true.' He sighed deeply and rubbed his face now with both hands. His tiredness made me feel exhausted all of a sudden. 'I'm sorry if I haven't been . . . been very good at coping with this. I've been a bit out of my depth. But then, I think I always have been in the dad department.'

I wasn't quite sure what he meant by this. He still wasn't looking at me, but I could see, by the narrow slice of light coming from the landing, that there was a tear slowly crawling down his cheek.

'Maybe if I'd been older when your mum and I had you . . . I think I was too young. And your mum, being a bit older and wiser – she was so much better at this than me. And what with her not being herself . . . I never thought it would be this hard. She'd have done it much better, if it were the other way around.'

The end of his sentence made me think back to what I'd said – about how I'd wished it had been Mum who'd stayed normal. And when I saw the tear on his face, making its way down his nose to his chin, I wished I'd never said it at all. I hadn't seen him cry like this before. Maybe once or twice in anger. But not like this. Slow and quiet. It made me feel bad, and scared, and strange, all at the same time.

Then the light snapped on and both of us looked up. Mum was standing in the doorway. She had changed into her night things and was wearing her snuggly pink dressing gown. Her big smile used to make me feel safe. Safe, warm, happy and comfortable. But it didn't any more.

'Well, well, well, is this a pyjama party I wasn't aware of?' She asked this in a sing-song sort of voice and then came to sit on the bed. If she noticed Dad's tears, she didn't say anything. Instead, she reached for the book at the side of the bed near the wall where I'd shoved it out of the way. She held it up close to her face and her eyes roved along the cover.

'Goodness me, I haven't seen this in a long time. *The Lion, the Witch and the Wardrobe*. I think Father Tobias would approve,' she said, with a little laugh. She handed it back to me and I took it, looking at her, trying to work out what the laugh had meant. Was she laughing at Father Tobias's disapproval of my other books? It was the first time I had ever heard her say his name or properly recognise that he existed.

'Just watch out for the White Witch,' she said, still in her jolly, bright voice. 'She tempts Edmund in with sweeties, don't you remember?'

I nodded. 'Yes. And he gets tricked by her.'

She smiled even wider, as if I'd just answered a very difficult question on a maths test. 'Indeed he does. He's a traitor. He betrays his own family. He conspires against them.'

I didn't know why, but I found I couldn't look at her. It was like her smile had become too bright, like I was staring into the sun.

'And when he regrets his actions, when he realises what he has done, it's too late. The White Witch knows everything. And she wants to punish him.'

I nodded at my duvet, still looking away.

'I think that's enough,' Dad said. There was something new in his face. It was different to his tired, stressed face from a moment ago. Mum ignored him.

'Because she has spies everywhere. *Everywhere*.' She

emphasised the last word, then leaned in, put her arms around me and kissed me on the top of my head. 'And they're always listening,' she whispered, then drew away from me.

'Even some of the trees are on her side,' I said under my breath. I thought of the trees outside. The creaking, scratchy, barky, woody forest: so many trees, stretching for miles and miles. And Adah. Standing amidst them. Telling me about the woman named Jadis who lived in this house.

'What was that, dearest love?' Mum said, looking intently at me.

'Nothing,' I said, very softly, trying to avoid her eyes.

'Well,' Mum said, and put out a hand in front of Dad, which he took. She pulled him to his feet. 'Have glorious dreams of sweet little nothings, Kitty Cat.' She flashed me another wide smile, then led Dad by the hand from the room. It was like they'd swapped roles: her as the adult, him as the child. They left me sitting amidst my duvet and pillows, trying to understand what was happening whilst trying to forget it all at the same time.

Chapter 21

The next day was bad. Really, really bad.

I woke early and watched the rain fall outside. I had known, deep down, that the sun wouldn't last for ever. I'd only really seen the good weather from indoors – I hadn't gone outside at all, since Mum seemed to be better. The tapping of the water on the glass and the splashes as it ran down the side of the house woke me from a dream about trees coming alive, commanded by a figure made up entirely of beams of sunlight. It worried me.

I knew something was wrong when I went downstairs later on in the morning to find Amanda sitting alone in the kitchen. She was eating a piece of toast in silence and looking more agitated than normal. Maybe even angry.

'Where's Mum? Where's Dad?' I asked as I walked in.

'Good question,' she said, setting down the crust of the bread. 'Do you want some toast?'

'They're missing?' I half shouted at her, enraged she could be thinking about toast when there was clearly something horrible going on.

She'd clutched her chest when I'd shouted and looked at me now with an exasperated face. 'Good grief, calm down, Kitty. They're not missing. They're . . . erm . . . in the bedroom. Upstairs.'

I looked over at the clock on the wall. 'But . . . it's much later. I've been reading and counting raindrops for ages. I thought they'd have finished breakfast—'

'Yes, I would have thought so too,' Amanda said, cutting me off.

'Have you been to check . . . have you been upstairs? Have you—'

'Yes, yes, yes,' Amanda said, brushing her hand across the air in my direction. 'It seems they're otherwise engaged.'

Now I began to see what she was getting at. And I didn't like it. I really didn't like it.

'I'm going upstairs to find them,' I said, pushing the chair that I hadn't even sat down on back under the table.

'Kitty, just sit down,' Amanda said, almost choking on a piece of crust she'd just started to chew on.

I left her coughing in the kitchen, went into the hallway and started climbing the stairs. Upon reaching the landing I lost some of my confidence. I wasn't sure I wanted to disturb Mum and Dad. They could get cross. Blame me for being silly. I stood still, staring at their door for quite a while, and was about to turn away and go back downstairs when I heard a voice. Dad's voice.

'Christ . . . please . . . we can talk about this sensibly . . . and I promise I'll listen . . .'

He sounded upset. His voice was strained, as if he was talking while holding his breath. Then I heard something else. Something that made the back of my neck go all prickly.

'Snip. Snip. Snip.' A light, sing-song voice, then a tinkling laugh. It was Mum. But it sounded strange – stranger than she'd been all this week.

And then I heard Dad say 'please' again, and it sounded like he was crying.

I couldn't help it. From my spot on the landing I called out, 'Dad? Are you coming down for breakfast?'

Complete silence followed for what felt like a lifetime. Then, eventually: 'Kitty . . . please . . . go . . . and . . . get . . . Amanda.'

I was hoping for something that would comfort me – maybe that he would call out that things were all OK. This wasn't comforting at all, and as I moved tentatively closer to the door, I felt goosebumps rush along my arms.

'Why?' I called out.

'Fuck—' I heard Dad draw in a very quick gasp of breath. 'Please, Kitty . . . Now. Do it . . . now.'

It was like he was struggling to talk.

Confused, I made my way back downstairs and into the kitchen. Amanda looked up as I entered. 'I told you to stay here, Kitty,' she said, with a glare.

'He said you need to come.' The words were breathless

and rushed, and she looked at me as if I'd said something foreign.

'Me?' She stared at me in consternation for a moment, then started moving things around on the table, clearing her plate away and putting some of the remaining bits of toast in the bin.

'Yes. He said please go and get Amanda. Except he said it like there's . . .'

I paused, not really knowing how to finish.

'Like there's . . . ?' she prompted.

'Like there's something wrong. Very wrong.' I said the last bit firmly, trying to tell her with my eyes that she should put the washing-up liquid bottle down this very moment and come and check with me upstairs.

She looked a bit worried now. Her hands hovered, as if she was not quite sure of her balance or surroundings, then she set the plate and plastic bottle down and took a breath. 'OK. Come on then. Lead the way.'

At the top of the stairs, she stopped me. She shot a hand out so that it touched the wall, blocking my way further onto the landing.

'I think you should perhaps wait here, Kitty.'

I was annoyed at this – it was me who convinced her to come up here, after all – but I, too, had heard it; the strange, high-pitched moan. And then the words. Words said in pain and fear.

'Please . . . Marjory . . . Please . . .'

Amanda started to walk slowly towards the door at the far end of the landing, the one leading to the master bedroom. I did as I was told and hovered around the top of the stairs, watching her. She reached out a slow hand for the door knob and turned. The door made a loud crack as it started to open and I heard the voice inside the room getting more panicky. More scared.

'No . . . please . . . don't let her . . .'

And then I saw Amanda freeze in the doorway and say the word 'Fuck' to herself. I could just make out her face in the cold morning light coming from the bedroom's windows. She looked horrified.

I couldn't bear not knowing any more. I walked as silently as possible to the open door and peered round. Amanda didn't seem to notice me. All her attention was focused on what was happening on the bed. And I could see why.

'Please . . . get her off me . . .'

Dad was lying on his back. He was completely naked, his thin body stretched out so that it covered the whole duvet underneath him. But that wasn't what was shocking. It was what Mum was doing that made Amanda throw her hands up to her mouth in horror.

'Christ . . . Amanda . . . please . . . do something . . .'

Mum was lying on her side, next to Dad, but part of the way down his body. And in her hands were a pair of large, rusty, sharp-looking secateurs. I had seen them leaning up against the back wall of the house, next to the old terracotta pots and dead plants. Mum had them now. And between the blades of the secateurs was Dad's . . .

'Stay completely still,' said Amanda, holding out a hand in the air, as if this in itself would help calm the situation. Her smooth, commanding demeanour was slipping. I could hear her voice wavering. She wasn't sure what to do. And she knew it.

'I'm . . . I'm fucking trying . . .' said Dad. He winced as he spoke.

I looked down at Mum, and with a jolt to my stomach I realised she was smiling. A big, wide smile, teeth bared, like some mad vampire. And her eyes – it was as if they'd come *alive*. Like at any moment they would crawl out, away from her face, and make their glistening way across the bed towards me.

'Marjory, listen to me. I need you to let go of the handles . . . very slowly, OK. And give me your hand.'

Mum did nothing of the sort. What she did do made Dad scream.

'Fucking Christ!' He shrieked the words louder than I'd ever heard him shout before. His voice had gone all scratching and screechy. Mum's hands had gripped the handles of the secateurs harder, bringing them together a tiny bit, and now I could see a trickle of blood – very small, but bright red – making its way down the rusty handle and onto Dad's skin.

'It's OK, it's OK, it's just a small surface scratch,' Amanda said. 'It's all going to be fine.' She didn't sound like she believed her own words, and I didn't think Dad did either.

'She's gone . . . She's fucking insane!'

'Shut up a minute,' Amanda said, moving closer to the bed and crouching down. 'Marjory, do you fancy coming to do some baking in the kitchen with me? We could bake gingerbread? I bought some fresh ginger yesterday. And some icing sugar. We could give them funny faces.

Or Santa hats. That would be fun, wouldn't it?' She was trying to smile – a warm smile, not the weird one like Mum's – but it didn't work. It didn't make Mum let go of the handles. But it did make her talk.

'He tried to put it in us. Tried to defile us with it. Tried to plant his seed within us to spread his base, mortal desires.'

She was talking in a low, rasping voice, similar to the one I'd heard shouting from inside the lounge, except this time it was talking quietly and slowly. In some ways it was even more unsettling.

'Kitty, please go back downstairs,' Amanda said, very quietly.

'Get her out of here!' cried Dad. He was actually crying now – I could see tears slipping down his face.

'Stay calm. Please, Kitty, do as I say. Now.' She managed to get a little bit of strength into her voice on the 'now' – enough to make me back out of the room. Once I was on the landing I stood there for a few seconds, then when I heard Dad make a sharp intake of breath, I ran away from the room, scared to hear any more of what was happening.

Just as I was running down the stairs, I heard the front door close and the figure of Father Tobias came into view. He was wearing a large overcoat, along with his religious clothes, and was rubbing his hands together and blowing on them. 'Very pleased to be out of the cold,' he said to me, smiling. I didn't smile back. 'Are you OK, Katherine?' he said, taking a step towards me. 'Is there anything the matter? You're as white as a sheet.'

Before I could speak, another noise from Dad cut into the silence between us. I couldn't hear what he said, but I suspected there were some strong, angry words amidst lots of hissing and short breathing.

'What's going on?' Father Tobias asked me, looking concerned. He moved towards the staircase and glanced up past me, towards the dark landing. 'Where is your father? And your mother?'

I took a few deep breaths, then said, 'Dad's in his bed. Mum's in there too. She's . . . '

Father Tobias tilted his head to one side. He looked rather like a bird, trying to work out if the thing it was about to eat was edible or not. 'She's what, Katherine?'

'I . . . she's . . . she's got his . . . thing . . . in a pair of garden scissors . . . seca—'

'Secateurs?' His face changed from concerned to horrified. 'Where's Amanda?'

I lifted my eyes to the ceiling. 'Trying to stop her. From cutting it off.'

Without letting another second pass, Father Tobias moved me firmly out of the way with both hands and strode past me, stomping loudly, up the stairs and towards the landing. I heard some commotion when he entered the room. More shouting. And then screaming. Mum's screams.

'BACK OFF. BACK OFF. CUNT.'

I heard Father Tobias replying in loud words. Something about 'God's might', but I couldn't really hear. Part of me just wanted to run away, back into the forest. Find Adah. Go and visit Levi in the woods. Read stories about Bambi.

But I couldn't bear the thought of coming back home and not knowing what I'd find. What horror would be waiting for me.

'WE TAKE OFF THE WEAPON OF HIS SIN AND FORCE HIM TO EAT IT.'

I ran up the stairs.

'Maybe we could both try to pull her off him . . . by force?' That was Amanda, sounding even more panicked now.

'And risk castrating him in the process?' Father Tobias barked. 'We need to talk her down.'

'P . . . p . . . please,' Dad wailed. 'Just . . . get . . . her . . . off . . .'

I was back outside the door and pushed it so that it swung open.

'Kitty, get out!' shrieked Amanda at me.

'Kitty!'

For a moment, I thought the second Kitty was from Amanda again, only softer. But then I realised, with a rush of surprise, that it had actually come from Mum.

'Kitty. Dearest. What's wrong?' Her voice was warm and soft, and as I peered round the door and into the room, I saw that she was smiling. But a nice smile this time. Not that unnerving, teeth-filled one she was doing a matter of minutes ago. And just like that, she let go of the handles of the secateurs. They fell away from her, and from Dad. He let out a gasp when he saw that he was free from them. He sat up and brought his hands, trembling, to between his legs, as if checking he was still all there.

'Fuck. Fucking, fucking hell.'

'It's all fine,' Father Tobias said, calmly. 'It looks like she's barely wounded you. Just a small cut, by the looks of it.' He was looking over at Dad, but had to step out of the way when Mum came towards him, her arms outstretched, clearly aiming for me. I saw Amanda take a step forward, looking worried, but none of them stopped her as she took me in her arms. She smelled of lavender shampoo. She must have just washed her hair before all this. 'What's wrong, dearest Kitty, my love? Did you have a nightmare?' She pulled back so she could look into my face.

'Yes,' I nodded. 'A nightmare. Yes.'

'Oh dear. Let's go and bake something delicious. Really, really delicious. That will sort everything out. And there's no need to worry about nightmares. They're here one minute, and then gone in a flash the next.'

And then she took me by the hand and led me, gently, from the room.

'That they certainly are,' I heard Father Tobias murmur as my mother closed the door behind her, leaving the three of them in the room as we started our journey down the stairs.

Chapter 22

Dad sat on the sofa for the rest of the day with a strange, far-away look on his face, like he had seen a ghost. Mum and I, meanwhile, baked gingerbread, then used up the rest of the mincemeat to make a batch of six mince pies, then, finally, moved on to an apple crumble with a fresh load of cooking apples Amanda had bought.

'That smells delicious,' Father Tobias said, watching us cook from a seat at the table, regularly sampling bits that we gave him.

Mum seemed to have completely forgotten the hysteria she had caused that morning. She hadn't said a word to Dad and he hadn't spoken to her. Amanda sat next to him for most of the day, occasionally rubbing his arm or bringing him some tea. He refused lunch, and later in the afternoon, when it started to get dark, he left the lounge suddenly. Seconds later, the sound of the door slamming reverberated through the house.

Father Tobias poked his head round the doorway of the kitchen into the lounge. Amanda looked up at him and said, 'I think he's just gone for a drive. Clear his head.'

He nodded and came back into the kitchen. 'Is it apple crumble time?' he said, sitting back down at the table. 'Can I have a sample?'

'Of course!' Mum said, sounding completely delighted, as if Father Tobias's interest in our cooking was something new and interesting. I watched him reach his chubby fingers towards the bowl being brought to him. Flecks of crumble dropped down onto his dog collar as he took a large, greedy spoonful.

'Divine,' he said thickly, through his munching.

Amanda wandered in, wrapping her cardigan around her, as if she were cold.

'There are a lot of calories in that,' she nodded to the bowl of appley, crumbly mush.

He waved aside her words with a flap of his hand. 'Tosh. Come and sit down. Marjory's cooking is going from strength to strength.'

'Mum's always been good at cooking,' I said. I felt as if I needed to be on her side, to defend her. To let them know that what happened this morning wasn't the real Mum. That we shouldn't let it upset anything for ever. But I got the feeling the reason Amanda and Father Tobias were sticking so close by was to watch her. To keep an eye on her in case she did anything like that again. In case, maybe, she did anything to me.

I didn't know how long passed until Dad got back, but all of a sudden I heard the sound of the door, then a creak. Dad came into view holding a bag of chips.

'Goodness, you must have driven for miles to get those,' Amanda remarked.

'I've got some for everyone.' He jostled two wrapped parcels under his arm.

'Crumble and chips! What a splendid tea,' remarked Father Tobias.

'How nourishing,' Amanda said, sounding a little disapproving. I thought about reminding her of the endless toast she'd been munching since we arrived, but thought it might get the meal off to a bad start.

Dad set the chips down on the table while Amanda fetched a bowl. Together they scooped as many as they could into it, then found a second because the first couldn't hold them all. Vinegar and salt were hunted for and found and then we were all sitting down, looking at the chips, waiting for Mum, who was preparing some cupcake batter at the kitchen counter.

'Marjory, do you fancy some chips?' Father Tobias said, matching the happy tone he'd kept up all day. 'Or some of your delightful crumble?'

'What?' she said, turning around. 'Chips? Where did these come from?'

There were a few seconds of silence before Father Tobias chirped up again. 'Why, your dear husband went out to get them for us. Come and have some while they're still hot and fresh.'

Mum looked puzzled and I saw a flicker of something cross her face. Irritation? Annoyance that her crumble was being pushed out by this impostor?

'Chips. Righty-ho then.' She dusted off her apron and sat down. She looked at the heaped bowls, hard and stern, as if they were strangers at the feast, and we watched her watching the chips. Eventually, Amanda reached out for the large spoon she'd put on the table, scooped up a portion and deposited them onto her plate. She offered the spoon to Dad and he followed her lead, and then I and Father Tobias did, all the way until Mum. She ignored the offer of the spoon from Father Tobias and gave a little shake of her head. She was no longer smiling. He put the spoon back down and I noticed his eyes flicking towards Amanda. She looked at him too, then back down at her plate, which she started to pick at with a fork.

'Isn't this lovely?' Amanda said, sounding fake-happy.

Nobody replied.

'Kitty,' she continued, 'why don't you tell us about your little friend? She must be missing you – you've been cooped up inside the house for the past few days.'

I let out my breath slowly. It probably sounded like a sigh, but it wasn't really – I was just creating some more time before I had to answer. I thought of Adah, probably wandering around the forest, puzzled about why her new friend hadn't come out to find her, and I was surprised how sad it made me feel. I'd been so caught up in Mum's change for the better (and then for the worse), that I'd not spared her much of a thought.

'Adah,' I said. 'Her name is Adah. And she isn't my only friend.'

Amanda arranged her face into something she probably thought looked like encouraging interest, but I thought it just made her look a bit stupid. 'Oh really? Who else have you befriended in the woods? Are we talking about a human friendship, or have you found one of your nice animal friends to—'

'I don't have any nice animal friends.' I cut across her, folding my arms, showing I was not pleased with the direction the conversation was going. 'I don't think Dad likes me keeping them as pets, so what's the point in trying to—'

'OK, Kitty,' Dad said, warningly, which surprised me a bit, as he'd been entirely silent since he'd walked in with the chips. It was almost like he was back to his normal-weird self, rather than the strange new-weird person he'd become where he looked like someone who had just woken from a nightmare.

'Anyway,' I continued, 'my new friend is called Levi.' I said this more firmly than I felt it, since I hadn't really considered Levi a friend up until this point. I'd tried not to think much about the last time I saw him. 'He lives on an estate, apparently,' I added.

Amanda nodded. 'Yes, there is a rather destitute estate on the edge of town. But most of the kids from there make do with their scraggly little common. They have swings and benches covered in graffiti. They don't often venture into the woods.'

'Why not?' Dad asked, reaching for the salt and spreading way too much of it over his mound of chips.

'Well, there's . . . there's quite a bit of chatter about the forest not being . . . I rather think people in the nearby towns are a bit afraid of it. Local superstition, you know. I think it harks back to centuries-old rumours about witches and what-not—'

Father Tobias made a throat-clearing sound and I saw Amanda look at him. His eyes moved over to Mum, who had now helped herself to some chips and was busy arranging them into two neat stacks on her plate. Amanda's face went slightly red, and she too made a throat-clearing noise. 'Anyway, Kitty, carry on about your other new friend. What is her name?'

I rolled my eyes, '*He*. I said *he*. His name is Levi. He's got a little cabin.'

'Really?' Amanda said, picking up a chip and popping it into her mouth. 'All of his own?'

'Well, I think he's sort of . . . taken it.'

'Commandeered it, has he?' Father Tobias said cheerfully. 'Well, you know what they say, possession is nine tenths and all that.'

I didn't have a clue what he was talking about, so I just carried on. 'He has things in there, books and magazines.'

'And where is this cabin?' Dad asked.

'It's just down along the stream. You get to a little bridge, then over the bridge there's a pathway deeper into the woods, although it curves round a bit back towards the river, and then a little walk up from the water there's his cabin.'

'Sounds rather idyllic,' said Amanda.

'What sorts of books and magazines has he got in there?' Father Tobias asked, looking interested, but I saw something in his eyes that I didn't like.

'Are you thinking of taking them like you took mine?' I said it to him quietly, but Dad looked up as if I'd screamed in his face.

'Kitty, that's very bad manners,' he said in his you'd-better-watch-it voice.

'No, no, no,' Father Tobias said, doing his waving hand again to make Dad settle down. 'I'm just curious, that's all.'

I had started to feel a bit cross, and a little part of me wanted to push against Father Tobias's wavy hand and 'only being curious' nonsense. I did not like him. And I didn't like Amanda much, either. And I certainly didn't like what had been happening to Mum since they got here.

'Oh, they're just nothing,' I said, reaching for more chips. 'Just magazines of naked ladies doing things with their bits. And Levi looks at them while playing with his thingy.'

I was after some kind of display of shock and outrage as a result of this, and I certainly got it. Amanda let her fork clatter down; Father Tobias's eyes widened so much I thought they were going to pop out of his head.

'You've . . . you've . . . you've seen this? Actually *seen* him do this?' he said in a hoarse, slightly shaky voice.

Dad turned properly round to face me. 'Kitty, when was this?'

180

I just shrugged, rather enjoying how silly they all looked. 'I don't know. A few days ago, I suppose.'

'And he showed you his . . . he exposed himself to you?'

I didn't know whether to mention that Adah and I had only seen Levi do this because we'd spied on him through the cracks in the cabin's walls, and that actually he had only read us a storybook. But I decided this would ruin everything I'd done up until now, so I just said: 'We saw his thingy and then stuff came out of it. It went onto the wall.'

I heard Father Tobias take in a big gasp, as if he'd never heard anything like this before, and then he started making a coughing sound and went red as if he were choking.

Then several things happened at once. Both Dad and Amanda got up to help him; Dad patted him on the back while Amanda tried to loosen his collar. 'He needs some water!' Amanda shouted, and Dad rushed to the sink and filled up a chipped mug and brought it to him. Father Tobias let out three big, larger-than-life coughs, stood up as if stretching his legs, then sat back down, taking the glass of water from Dad's hands and raising it to his lips.

'Oh . . . oh my word,' he said, croakily, taking a few more sips of water, along with a few more little coughs. 'Thank you . . . I'm sorry. So sorry.'

'Are you all right?' Amanda asked, rubbing his back as he drank some more of the water.

He nodded, looking worried and smaller than he had before.

'We need to talk about what you've told us, Kitty,' Dad said, looking back to me. 'It is very serious.'

I said nothing. I just watched them all looking worried and serious, then I looked over at Mum. Only I couldn't. Because Mum wasn't there.

'Dad,' I said, looking up at his face. He'd already turned back to Father Tobias, so I called him again.

'What, Kitty?' he snapped.

I pointed at Mum's empty seat.

Panic flickered through his face as if it were lighting him up from inside. 'Where is she?' he shouted. Amanda ran to the doorway into the lounge and peered through. 'She's not in there,' she said.

'Marjory!' Dad yelled, marching round the table and out into the hallway. I heard him running up the stairs, banging open doors, then running back down again. 'She's not up there,' he said.

Amanda came back into the kitchen. She froze still when she got near the counter.

'The door is open. Hurry, the front door is open!' Dad shouted from the hallway.

'Come back in here,' Amanda said loudly in response.

'I said the front door is—'

'I know,' she called back. 'But I need you to come back in here right now.'

Father Tobias, who had stood up when Dad had started shouting, walked round the table over to where Amanda was standing. 'What is it?' he said, at almost exactly the same moment as Dad.

Amanda pointed, just as I had pointed to Mum's empty

182

chair moments ago. But she was pointing to the drying rack, where there were now stacks of our baking bowls, washed up and ready to be put away.

'A knife is missing.'

Father Tobias looked baffled. 'What?'

Dad moved quickly. He rattled the drying rack, disturbing the bowls so that they clinked and clattered. He looked back at Amanda. 'How do you know?'

'Because I saw it there when I got the plates and stuff for the chips. It was just there, resting up against the bowls. And now it's gone.'

Chapter 23

January 2020

They allow me to have a cup of tea. I'd started crying properly when they mentioned Adah's death, and eventually DC Malik took pity on me and said he'd go and get me a warm drink. I didn't know cops were allowed to be this kind to people they suspected of being involved in a crime, but DI Cousins doesn't object as the paper cup of murky grey-brown liquid is gently placed into my hands. I sip it carefully, trying not to scald my lips. DC Malik takes his seat again and I hear DI Cousins sniff a little and shuffle her folders, apparently keen to get on. After letting me take a few more sips, she says, 'Right, Katherine. Let's get back on track, shall we?'

She probably thinks her tone is kind, but it just sounds

scratchy and strained, the voice of a woman with a lot to do and too many frustrating interviews with suspects and witnesses under her belt to find me especially interesting.

'Yes, OK,' I say in a small voice, wiping the last of my tears from my chin and setting the cup down on the desk. 'The main thing you need to understand – the thing I want to make clear – is that all this happened so long ago. I was very young, and even I can't be sure what I saw. Or what I did. That's why I tried to write it down. That was the reason for sitting down and trying to map out everything that happened. Or at least, that's how it started. Everything gets blurred the more I try to remember. The whole process was . . . it was extremely hard.'

Silence greets this at first, followed by another sniff of impatience from DI Cousins.

'The problem is, Katherine,' DC Malik says slowly, 'the coroner's court has to determine a manner of death. That manner could be murder, or manslaughter, or death by misadventure. Accidental death, maybe. In some rare cases, manslaughter might be committed by someone with diminished responsibility, because of their age, mental state, or circumstances surrounding the incident. But because we have these categories, it's important we gather as much information as we can to make sure the right conclusion has been made. At the moment, with the information that was gathered at the time, Adah's death is regarded as accidental. But we're obliged to reassess this in light of what you've revealed. Do you see what I'm saying?'

I meet his eyes and nod. 'You're saying it's important I talk now.'

'Exactly,' he says, also nodding, his eyebrows raised in encouragement, as if expecting me to take the prompt and begin again.

'It's impossible to be one hundred per cent about a lot of what happened. It was a living nightmare. I know that sounds silly or like I'm exaggerating, but it really was. I've been in and out of therapy and counselling of various kinds throughout my life. I even voluntarily allowed myself to be institutionalised for a month in the 1990s. I genuinely believe the things I witnessed in that cottage in the woods and the area surrounding it damaged me irrevocably. I became deeply disturbed by some particular instances that I've found impossible to get out of my head ever since.'

DI Cousins had been staring down at one of her sheets of paper while I was talking, but she looks up now and fixes her dark eyes on mine. 'Is one of these instances the night you describe where your mother leaves the house with the knife?'

I meet her gaze and nod slowly. 'Yes. The night she took the knife. And what she did with it out in the woods.'

Chapter 24

1987

I wasn't allowed to go and search the forest with the others. Once they'd decided Mum wasn't in the house, they all went out into the darkness with torches. I was told to stay inside with the door locked. I thought about what I should do if Mum came back with the knife and wanted to be let in. But I didn't ask about it as I wasn't convinced any of them would know the answer.

The night was cold and blustery. Rain started to arrive with occasional loud slaps on the dirty glass of the windows. I felt chilly, so I did what Mum used to do sometimes when I was very little; I turned on the oven, opened its door and let the warmth spread through the kitchen. I got a chair and sat in front of it now, feeling my shivers change to goosebumps, the rest of my body unbunching, the heat flowing to the tips of my fingers and toes and making me less scared. But I was still scared. Very.

It felt like they were out there for hours. I thought about going to bed, settling down to sleep, shutting everything out, waiting until the morning to discover if I still had a mum or if she'd harmed any of the adults that pretended to care for me. But before I could drag myself from my warm seat, I heard the scratchy scrape of the door opening, followed by the sound of it banging against the wall as people flowed into the house.

'Get him in the lounge. On the coffee table! Hurry!'

That was Amanda's voice.

'Quick!' she said again.

'He's heavier than he looks.' That was Dad. What was he talking about?

Then I heard the sound. The sound of rasping, gasping breaths. And crying. The cries were from a man. Or a boy.

And so I went to the doorway of the lounge. And saw the horrible sight. An image of horror I would never forget.

Dad was lowering something onto the coffee table. The table legs trembled as they took the weight of whatever it was. Or whoever it was.

'Fucking . . . fucking . . . crazy . . . bitch.' These words came from the figure lying on the table in gasps and sobs and a flail of hands, slipping and sliding through something that looked a lot like—

'BLOOD!' Even though she wasn't in view, this was unmistakably Mum, wailing her high-pitched, panicky wail. She ran out from behind Father Tobias as he walked in, wiping his face with a handkerchief.

'Amanda, keep hold of her,' Dad shouted. 'Take her upstairs, for God's sake. Have you still got the knife?'

'I . . . I threw it in the stream,' Amanda stuttered.

'You did *what*?' Dad looked around, but the writhing body on the coffee table grabbed his arm and croaked, 'Hospital . . . I think . . . I need . . . to go—'

'No you don't,' Dad said and pushed him, rather roughly I thought, down onto the table. And that was when I realised who it was. His once bright-blond hair was now a murky dark colour – wet and covered in dirt and leaves – but it was him. It was Levi. He was wearing his track-suit bottoms and t-shirt, only the t-shirt was splashed with red, and at the front it looked more like ribbons than something you could actually wear.

'BLOOD,' Mum shrieked again. 'HE WILL BE PLEASED. HE WILL BE PLEASED. HE IS COMING. HE IS RISING—'

'No he fucking isn't,' Dad said, turning round, looking almost as wild as Mum. 'Get her upstairs so I can deal with this,' he roared at Amanda, who looked quite frightened herself, then did as he'd instructed and dragged Mum through the other door into the hallway. She didn't put up much of a struggle. I heard them go up the stairs in loud clomps, then Dad said, 'I knew I should have packed a goddamn first aid kit.' He knelt down and said to the quivering Levi, 'It really isn't as bad as you think – stop

189

making such a fuss.' Then he looked up and saw me, standing at the doorway to the kitchen.

'Christ Kitty, how long have you been standing there?'

I didn't reply.

'I think Kitty should go to bed,' Father Tobias said. His face was bright red, and even though it was chilly, especially after the door had been open, he was fanning himself with his handkerchief and sat down on the sofa with a thump. 'All this is rather taking its toll on me, I must confess.'

'Kitty, go back into the kitchen and get me some tea towels – definitely the clean ones in the drawer – and a bowl of hot soapy water. And some scissors.'

I stayed silent for a bit longer. Then I nodded and went to do as I was told.

'Don't burn yourself,' Dad called after me as he heard me filling up the kettle.

I had the soapy water and kitchen towels ready for him in less than three minutes. I felt quite proud of how well I'd done this little job, but Dad said nothing when I went into the lounge with them – he just took them from me whilst tapping Levi's face.

'Fuck . . . stay awake. Oi, don't go to sleep. Shit!'

'He's not dying,' Father Tobias said limply from the sofa, 'it's just the shock.'

'Levi?' I said as I got closer to him. His eyes were droopy, like he was very tired, but he kept muttering things. Almost like talking in his sleep. At my voice, though, his eyelids flickered open a little. 'Where am I?'

'You're in my cottage, Levi. The little cottage in the woods.'

He looked confused. 'Witch's Cottage?' he said, then sniffed a few times, as if he'd got an itchy nose. 'Everything . . . hurts . . . she fucking slashed me.' His words were slurring together and I looked up at Dad, worried, then looked down again at his chest and had to stop myself from shouting out. Three large, straight slits in his chest gaped before me, coursing down his chest to his tummy, blood dripping from the edges.

I only discovered I had started crying when I tasted the salt of the tears on my lips.

Dad was now talking to Father Tobias, asking him for some help, but he gave up after a few words. The older man was apparently feeling 'a bit woozy' at the sight of the blood and had half-collapsed onto the armchair.

'Jesus Christ,' Dad muttered. 'Kitty, I need you to be a big, grown-up girl and just hold his head for me while I take his t-shirt off.'

I nodded, and put my hands under Levi's head where he told me to. Dad set about snipping off his messed-up top, dropping the bloody folds of material onto the floor.

'What you doing? It . . . it really hurts . . .' Levi murmured.

'It will be OK,' Dad said.

Amanda appeared in the room and came over to the coffee table. She looked exhausted.

'Marjory's asleep,' she said, with a sigh. 'Went straight out like a light, more or less. Some more muttering about the blood. And how "he's rising". But she didn't "rise", so to speak. She just lay down. She's breathing steadily.'

Dad didn't comment on any of this, and instead just said, 'I need you to drive to the nearest chemist and get supplies—'

'But . . . I really think casualty would be the best—'

'No! Just get some bandages. Disinfectant. I'll do what I can with what I have here for now, but it's not going to be enough.'

Amanda looked stunned, her eyes fixed on Levi, her hands on her face, eyes wide. She must have been seeing the wounds properly for the first time. Then she took her hands away from her cheeks and clapped them loudly, making me and Dad jump.

'There's no need! I should have some in my car.'

With that, she walked quickly out of the room. Dad looked at the space where she'd just been standing, apparently surprised, then turned back to Levi and started dabbing at the drips of blood down the side of his chest, soaking the kitchen towels in the bowl first, then dabbing some more. After each soak, the bowl's water turned a darker shade of browny-red.

Amanda came back with a dark green box clasped in her hands.

'Here,' she said, offering it out. Dad took it, snapped it open and started going through the little compartments. After removing a flat, white pack of something, he found what looked like wet wipes and continued dabbing at Levi's cuts. Levi responded loudly.

'Ahhhh fucking . . . what . . . ?' He started writhing again and even managed to lean up a little, but Dad pushed him back down.

'I'm cleaning your wounds; stay still. The alcohol might sting a bit.'

Amanda crouched down now. 'Look, he's covered in dirt, and it's in the wounds. We're not going to be able to do this properly. I say we take him to the hospital and just say we found him—'

'For the *very* last time – we are not going to the hospital. Do you want to jeopardise everything we're doing here? I've trusted you on all of this so far. You said you were sure we could avoid sending her away somewhere, to some *institution*. If people find out that she's capable of this, do you think we'd stand a chance? She wouldn't just get put on a hospital ward, she might end up in prison for God's sake!'

'OK, OK. But . . . What about his parents?' Amanda's voice was getting tight and stressed. 'They'll ask questions. And what's to stop him going to the police anyway?'

'He doesn't have any parents.' I found myself saying it in a small voice, almost more to myself than Amanda. 'Just a foster family who've stopped caring for him. They're having their own baby now. They let Levi sleep in his shed and don't bother looking for him.'

After I'd said this, a wave of anxiety flooded through me. For some reason, I feared giving this information meant I'd chosen a side. A side that wasn't Levi's. I'd betrayed his trust – or any trust that existed between him, Adah and me.

'And as for the police, leave that to me,' Dad said. 'I think I know a way to make it worth his while not to talk. Plus, a little reminder of the risks he runs if he decides to. As we heard from Kitty earlier, if messing about with little girls is his thing, I doubt he'll want to talk to any cops.'

Amanda seemed to be thinking, her face stern in concentration. Eventually she sighed again and ran her hands through her short hair. 'Well, we at least need to clean him up properly. He's going to get an infection, otherwise. Don't use any more of those until we've got him washed. We'll have to take him to the shower.'

I expected Dad to object to this, but he just paused for a moment with his eyes closed, thinking, then gave a short, sharp nod.

'Agreed. OK, Kitty. Bed.'

I stayed where I was.

'Kitty, leave, now.'

'He's my friend.' I said it quietly, but he and Amanda heard it all right. I saw the look they shared.

'He's not your friend. What's happened here isn't right, but what he did to you wasn't right either.'

I didn't understand what he meant at first, then I remembered. The fuss at dinner. The fuss that started all this. Then I realised – this was my fault. All my fault. If I hadn't been silly. If I hadn't tried to make Dad embarrassed and cross, or tried to upset Amanda, none of this—

'Kitty, upstairs. Now.'

Tears fell from my eyes as I ran, leaving the horror behind me in the lounge, taking the steps as fast as I could manage. I slammed the door shut behind me once I was in, then, thinking better of it, pulled it open a crack and sank down. I may not have been allowed to stay with him, but I was definitely not going to let anything else happen to Levi.

I sat on the floor for what must have been five or ten minutes, then I heard them coming up the stairs.

'Take his other arm,' hissed Dad. 'He's a dead weight.'

'Fine, you go backwards – I'll make sure he doesn't fall back down the stairs. Christ, if only he wasn't so stoned – then he'd probably be able to walk for himself.'

'If he wasn't fucking stoned out his head, he'd probably have run off and called the bloody police himself,' whispered Dad loudly in response.

I heard them shuffle onto the main part of the landing, and then risked a peek out. They were holding Levi between them, his arms flung over their shoulders, his head lolling down, although now he drew close I could tell he wasn't asleep. He was making a constant, strange moan, halfway between a grunt and a whine, and gave little shakes of his head every few seconds.

'Get him into the bathroom,' Amanda whispered. Dad backed up to the door and reversed himself inside and Amanda followed, with Levi between them.

I scurried out onto the landing. Staying very, very still, trying not to let the floorboards creak, I watched them through the open bathroom door. Dad was laying Levi down in the tiny bathroom and Amanda was gathering up the faded pink shower curtain and pushing it out of the way. 'He's got another wound on his knee,' she said, 'where he tripped on the bridge and fell into the stream.'

I felt my heart start to beat rapidly. He'd been in the

stream. Into the Poison Stream. And something bad – something terrible – had actually happened.

'OK. You go and get the first aid box, and some clean towels from on top of the washing machine. I'll get the rest of his stuff off and get the water on.'

I saw Amanda nod. 'Not scalding water though. Test the temperature first. Gentle warm.'

I heard Dad huff a little, then before I could move, Amanda came out onto the landing and saw me standing there. She hesitated for a second, gave me a weird look, and continued right past me to walk hurriedly down the stairs.

Turning back to the bathroom, I saw Dad struggling to get Levi in a manageable position. He finally got him lying down lengthways, as if ready to enjoy a relaxing bath, his head tilted back, then he started to pull down his tracksuit. There was more blood underneath. All around his right knee there was a whole load of it. He must have scraped himself during the struggle. I couldn't make out the wound properly in the low yellow of the bathroom light, but it must be a proper gash to cause that much bleeding. His underpants were ripped at the side, like his t-shirt. Mum must have slashed him all the way down his body. Dad chucked his tracksuit bottoms aside and then moved him a bit roughly to the side so that he could pull down his underwear too.

'Ehhh . . . fucking . . . fucking pervert,' Levi murmured.

Dad pulled the ripped material free from each of his legs and dropped it on top of the trackies, then, suddenly, put his hand on the boy's throat.

'No,' he said in a half whisper that managed to be both strong and quiet at the same time. '*You're* the fucking pervert. And part of me would like nothing more than to give the knife back to her and let her finish the job.'

Levi started to shake now. It began as a shiver in his face, his eyes opening, looking terrified, then the trembling seemed to ripple through his whole body until he couldn't remain still. And then he started to cry. 'I'm not . . . I haven't done . . . Please . . . just let me—'

'Shut up,' Dad hissed in his face. He let go of the boy's neck and then, with the other hand, turned on the shower. It must have been cold, as Levi let out a shriek and pulled his arms over him, causing more blood to ooze out from the slashes on his chest.

Amanda came running up the stairs, the dark green box in her hand, along with a little packet. She sent one frightened-looking glance my way, then strode into the bathroom. 'What's going on?' she demanded. 'I said to make sure it was warm water.' She pushed past Dad and fiddled about with the taps. After holding the shower head over her hand for a bit, she seemed satisfied and handed it back to Dad. 'Gently run this over the wounds. Damn it, I should have brought a glass up.'

'There's one in the bedroom,' Dad said, distractedly.

'I *really* would prefer not to have Marjory waking up and trying to join in with all the fun,' she replied. She was starting to sound more cross than worried.

'I've got a cup in my room,' I said in a tiny voice that I didn't really expect them to hear, but both of them turned to face me.

'I told you to go to bed, Kitty,' Dad started, but Amanda held up a hand to cut him off.

'That would be very useful, Kitty. Could you go and get it, please?'

I nodded and walked back into my room, picked up the cup of water I had on the windowsill and walked backs towards the bathroom.

'Here,' I said, holding it out, not quite stepping over the line where the old, wispy landing carpet met the bathroom floor.

'Thank you, Kitty.' Amanda took the cup and filled it with some of the water from the shower head. She then picked up the little packet she'd brought upstairs and popped out two of something from it. They were pills.

'Here. It's paracetamol with codeine. It will help with the pain,' she said to Levi. He tried to lean up again and this time he managed it, and Amanda helped him swallow each tablet, one after another.

'Good boy.' Then she turned to Dad. 'You ought to wash his hair too.'

'Why the fuck would I want to do that?'

'I'll do it,' she said, impatiently. They switched places, she soaking Levi's hair so all the bits of twigs and dirt washed away. 'I daren't use shampoo – don't want it getting in those cuts and irritating them – so this will have to do.'

'We better use clean towels,' Dad said, looking around him. 'These are at least two days old.'

I didn't wait to be told. I left the bathroom and ran downstairs. There was a pile of folded, clean towels on top of the old, clunky washing machine near the back door. It had already broken twice and Dad had nearly electrocuted himself trying to fix it the last time. But it was still going, just about. I picked up two of the new towels from the stack and went back into the hallway. Just as I set my first foot on the stairs, I heard a voice say something I couldn't quite catch.

'Hello?'

I turned and looked through into the lounge. It was Father Tobias. He was still looking around him, as if he didn't know where he was. 'What . . . oh . . . it's you . . . dearest Annabelle.'

I stayed still, unsure why he was getting my name wrong. He usually called me Katherine, to my annoyance; but at least that was actually my name. Annabelle didn't sound anything like it.

'I'm not Annabelle. I'm Kitty,' I said, simply.

He looked me in the eyes and smiled, then made a strange lunge forward with his hand. I took a step back straight away, clasping the towels to me. He looked surprised and hurt by my movement.

'Annabelle? Why are you so afraid of me?'

He started to cry. Big, glistening tears started to fall down his red face and into his white-and-black collar.

'I need to go upstairs now,' I said. Seeing him cry made me want to cry again, and I didn't like it. I really didn't like it.

I left the warmth and light of the lounge and went back into the chilly darkness of the hallway to start my journey up the stairs.

'That's fantastic, Kitty. Thank you,' Amanda said in a businesslike way when I handed the towels over to her. Dad was lifting Levi out of the bath, one of his limp arms thrown over Dad's shoulders, making Dad's shirt damp at the back. As he helped him step out onto the wet bathroom floor, I saw Levi's thin chest crease and the large slashes in the flesh come properly into view. Now that they had been cleaned and the blood washed away, they looked very different; like slits in dead meat, thin flaps of skin parted by thin red lines. I could also see that they were not quite as bad as I had first thought. There wasn't any bone visible, nor those muscles or ribs I'd seen in drawings of the human body. They didn't seem deep enough for that. Strangely, though, I didn't find Levi's nakedness nearly as interesting as I had when Adah and I were spying on him through the gaps in the shed's back wall. Here, with Dad supporting him and Amanda dabbing him dry gently with a towel, it reminded me of when I and some friends from playschool would run naked in and out of the paddling pool in the garden, not really caring what the others could see. Levi being older made it different, but not as different as I thought it would.

I was expecting Dad to turn round at any second and be angry I was watching, but his mind didn't seem to be on me, for the moment at least.

Now they had both got him dry, Amanda washed her hands thoroughly by the sink, then took a little tube from the dark green box. She squeezed some white cream out of it onto her hand. 'This is just an antiseptic ointment,' she said. 'Stay still. It might sting a bit, but it will help stop infection.'

She very gently touched some of the cream to the wounds. Levi flinched, but didn't struggle. He was leaning against Dad and looked awake, but not properly. At least he'd stopped moaning and swearing now. Amanda started to open a roll of bandages and began to wrap them slowly around his body so that, bit by bit, they started to cover up the slits in his skin. She kept them in place with a bit of tape, and a large sticky plaster in the centre.

'That's the best I can do,' she said, to herself more than to Dad, who was watching her every move. 'I'll put a plaster on this gash on his knee. We'll have to look at that again closer in the morning.' She did as she said, taking another sticky plaster out of its wrapping and putting it over his hurt knee. Levi gave a little sniff as she did so, but still said nothing.

'Let's get his clothes back on him,' Dad said, 'then we'll take him downstairs. He can sleep on the sofa. I'll keep an eye on him.'

I puzzled for a second about where Amanda was going to sleep if Levi had the sofa and Dad stayed up watching him. They didn't seem to have thought this through, but I dared not say anything in case they started telling me to leave again. It was almost like they'd forgotten I existed.

Amanda was picking up his ripped and bloodstained grey tracksuit. 'We can't let him put these back on. He'll have to wear something of yours.'

'What?' said Dad, looking horrified.

'Do you have a better idea?'

'I don't think they'd fit him.'

Amanda tutted. 'He's hardly a tiny little child. He must be, what, sixteen? You're not *that* different in size.'

Dad's face twisted, as if he was trying to think of a reason to argue, but apparently he failed.

'Fine,' he said, sounding cross. 'He can have a pair of my pants and a t-shirt, but I'm not wasting any of my jeans on him.'

'Christ,' Amanda said under her breath. 'OK. Just don't wake Marjory.'

'Do you think I'm stupid?'

Amanda didn't answer, she just took Levi from Dad's hands, laying her palms on his shoulders. 'Here, sit down on the side of the bath,' she said.

Dad moved past me, laying a hand on my shoulder as he left the bathroom. I waited for him to tell me to leave, but he didn't – it was like he'd given up fighting.

I looked back at Levi. He was shivering slightly, so Amanda picked up one of the towels and wrapped it round him, covering some of his nakedness. Dad returned in less than a minute, holding some white underpants and a grey t-shirt of the kind he normally used for sleeping.

'The white will show up the blood stains if his cuts get on them,' Amanda said.

'Well I'm not going to get them back, am I, so it hardly fucking matters.'

He put his hands on Levi's shoulders, pulled him up and then turned him around, so that he was facing the bath and the wall. The towel dropped down, and Levi stood there as Dad guided his feet through the leg holes of the briefs and pulled them up onto him, Amanda holding down the large plaster on his knee to make sure it didn't get disturbed. Then Dad dropped the t-shirt around Levi's head and both together, Dad and Amanda pulled his arms through the sleeves and gently smoothed the fabric down.

'I can't believe we're bothering with all this after what he's—'

'We don't know what he's done,' Amanda said, stopping him before he could finish. I saw her eyes flick towards me for a second. 'But we do know what Marjory's done. And like you said, I would prefer she didn't end up in prison or some institution or for the police to start asking us questions about what's going on, OK? Unless you want all that?'

'Of course I don't,' Dad snapped in response, forgetting to keep his voice quiet. He turned Levi round again and looked at him. 'Right. I think you need to sleep. You still look stoned out your head.'

Amanda straightened up, her knees clicking a little as she stretched. 'The cannabis probably helped with the pain,' she said.

'I wouldn't know,' Dad said, scratchily. 'I'm not a drug-using pervert.' He gave Levi a little nudge. 'Can you walk?'

The boy nodded.

'Great. We're going back downstairs.'

'Take it slowly,' Amanda said.

I stepped out of their way as they went, but my hope

of remaining in their company was ruined when Dad said, 'Bed now, Kitty. Please. Just . . . just go to bed.'

Something in his voice meant I didn't want to stand my ground this time, so I turned and went back towards my room, pausing to watch him and Amanda help Levi walk from the bathroom and, one slow step at a time, down the stairs.

Chapter 25

The night went very slowly. I kept waking up and then going back to sleep, but not a proper sleep – a strange, sort-of sleep that made me feel like I had a temperature. Eventually I gave up and put my light on. I tried to read *The Lion, the Witch and the Wardrobe* for a little bit, but none of the words on the page seemed to make much sense.

I got up and went to look out onto the landing. There was complete silence throughout the house – all I could hear was the occasional patter when the rain grew stronger, or a bird rustled nearby.

I tiptoed down the stairs, trying not to make them creak; the few that did happen to let out a low noise didn't cause anyone to shout or run out to stop me. Eventually, I got to the door of the lounge. It was pulled to, but wasn't fully closed. I pushed at it, very, very gently, and peered through the darkness.

Amanda was lying back, asleep on the armchair near the door. Dad was on the floor, slumped up against the chair, his face leaning on her legs. Both of them were completely still. I looked over at the sofa and saw a light figure stretched out lengthways, the cream-coloured blanket Amanda usually kept folded up at the end now covering Levi's body.

I walked, very carefully, over to Levi and looked down at his face. As if he could sense me, his eyelids started to flicker. He opened them both, slowly and dreamily.

'Kitty?' he whispered. 'Is that you?'

'Yes, Levi,' I whispered. 'It's me.'

'I got hurt, Kitty. I got cut.'

I nodded. 'I know. It was my mum.' I didn't know why I was telling him this, but his eyes were making me feel bad. Perhaps I thought I could make things just a little bit better by being as good and honest as possible.

'Why did she hurt me?' he said. I looked down and saw that there were tears in his eyes. One fell quickly, down the side of his face and into the pillow he was resting on.

'I . . . I . . .' I couldn't bring myself to say it. I couldn't say anything at all. It was too much.

'I'm scared, Kitty,' he whispered, and I nodded and felt the tears slide from my eyes.

'I am too,' I whispered. After a few seconds, I brushed

my tears away with my fingers and said quietly, 'Will your parents be cross? That you didn't come home?'

He gave a tiny shake of his head. 'They don't care. I sleep in my cabin for days and they don't notice.' Just as I'd told Dad.

In that moment, I wished Levi did have people who cared for him. People who would run through every inch of forest and come hammering on the doors with flaming torches and pitchforks, demanding he be set free. I glanced over at Dad. Did he care about me, still, I wondered? Or did he just care about Mum, now? Had all his caring been so used up by her that, one day, he'd stop caring about me at all? And I'd be like Adah and Levi, wandering the woods without anyone expecting me home.

'I care, Levi,' I said.

He looked at me, blinking a little, then said, 'Maybe Adah was right about the river.'

I let the words sit between us for a bit, growing to something terrifying and huge in the darkness; then I asked, even though I knew the answer, what he meant by them.

'She always said that I shouldn't touch the river . . . that bad things would happen.'

'She said that to me too,' I whispered.

I heard him draw in a breath. 'I touched the river. I've been swimming in it. Do you think . . . do you think . . . ?'

Rather than saying something, I did something instead. I didn't think much about it – I just reached down, took up his hand and gave it a gentle squeeze. More tears slipped from his eyes. He didn't say anything. Just looked at me.

207

'I should go back up to bed now,' I whispered. 'They might wake up and get angry. I'll see you in the morning.'

He nodded slightly, but I could tell he was already falling asleep again. Maybe he wouldn't even remember I had been there in the morning. I turned and walked as silently as I could back through the living room and into the hallway.

As I was going up the stairs, though, I missed the third step and my foot fell down flat onto the second with a loud slam. Instantly I heard someone give a gasp from the living room. And then I heard Dad.

'What the fuck was that?'

He must have startled Amanda awake too, because seconds later I heard, 'What . . . what's going on?'

'I thought I heard . . . never mind. I thought he was running out on us.'

'He's still there.'

'I know . . . I think I was dreaming. Dreaming that he escaped.'

'He's not our prisoner,' said Amanda, softly. 'Although we might have to prepare for a bit of a fight in the morning. The cannabis will have worn off by then. He'll be more lucid. And I doubt he'll be happy.'

'I think I've got an idea of how to settle it all. We'll see.'

A slight pause, then Amanda said, 'You know . . . we're reaching the end of the road with what we can do for Marjory.' She sniffed.

A deep breath in from Dad followed this, then, 'Don't say that.'

'I mean it,' Amanda continued, still talking very quietly

so that I had to strain to hear. 'We're either going to have to admit defeat or . . . well . . .'

'Well what?'

Another pause. I heard a slight creaking, which must have been one of them turning to face the other.

'I mean, we might have to . . . step it up a level. Take things a bit further. Try some things that might seem more extreme. But I think they could work. I'm confident we could see results if . . . if you were less squeamish . . . more open to the whole thing.'

Another sniff and silence from Dad.

'Perhaps now isn't the time to talk about this,' she said. 'Look, we'll swap places – you sleep on the chair for a bit. Your back must be killing you down there.'

'It's fine,' he said stiffly.

Amanda sighed, then they both returned to their silence.

I waited in the darkness of the stairs for what must have been over three minutes, hoping that that would be enough for them to fall back to sleep. After that, I couldn't hold my position any longer, so I half-crawled my way up the stairs and onto the landing, managing to get there with only the tiniest little creaks and groans from the wood beneath me. I shut my door properly this time when I got back into my room.

'Police!'

I heard the shout come from down in the lounge and it woke me up. There was some talking – loud talking – but I couldn't make out the words. After that there was more shouting: 'I said I want the fucking cops!'

Levi had awoken properly, by the sounds of it. And, like my dad predicted, he didn't seem to be very happy about what we'd done.

I pulled on my dressing gown over my pyjamas and ran downstairs to the lounge. Amanda had her hand on Levi's arm, apparently trying to calm him down. He was standing in the middle of the room, still wearing Dad's underpants and t-shirt, trying to bat Amanda's hand away. I saw him wince with the movement and Amanda half pushed, half helped him sit back down.

'You shouldn't exert yourself,' she said, tutting. 'Your cuts aren't as deep as they could have been, but I really would advise keeping still so the skin can heal over.'

He didn't seem calmed by this – if anything it made him angrier. 'Who the fuck even *are* you? What *is* this place?'

I walked in properly at this point, and Levi stopped and looked at me. 'Kitty?'

'Levi,' I said, quietly.

'So . . .' He seemed lost for words. Confused. He looked back at Amanda and then at Dad, who was standing in the corner by the TV, his arms folded awkwardly.

'So what?' I said in response.

'So . . . it wasn't a dream. You really are here?'

'Yes,' I nodded. 'I came to see you last night. Don't you remember?'

'I . . .' He rubbed his head and looked around him, as if seeing the room for the first time. 'I thought it was a dream. So you really do live in the Witch's Cottage.'

Dad stepped forward at this. 'Witch's Cottage? What

210

nonsense is this? I think we've heard enough.' He rifled through his pocket and brought out a wodge of something. Even though it was folded, I could make out the outline of the queen's face on the notes. It was a handful of money. And he was holding it out to Levi.

'Here. This is what we're giving you. No more talk about police, no more shouting, no more fuss.'

Levi took the money silently. Turned it over in his hand so the banknotes unfurled like dried leaves. 'What . . . what do I do with it?'

Dad made a sound of disbelief, like a cough with his tongue. 'You can go and blow it all on more drugs, or save it for something actually worthwhile; I *really* couldn't care less.'

Levi looked up at him, then down at the money again, then over at me, as if to see what I thought about all of this. I didn't say anything. I didn't know what to think.

'The main condition is that you don't bother us, or my daughter, again.'

He looked properly confused now. 'What . . . why . . .' His glance went from me to Dad and back to me.

'I don't know what sick things you've been up to in that funny little cabin of yours. Maybe there's a reasonable explanation for it, but from what I've heard it all sounds very . . .'

'Inappropriate,' Amanda chipped in, nodding like she was some kind of expert in inappropriate things.

'Yes, inappropriate. And between that and the drugs, I doubt you'd like the police involved in this any more than we would,' Dad said, nodding too.

Levi fixed me with a hard stare. 'What you been saying? You been saying I've touched you or something?' He turned back to Dad. 'All I did was read them a fucking story.'

Dad held up his hand. 'I don't want to hear any more. Amanda here is going to drive you to the nearest shops where she will purchase you some new clothes. You can choose them, so long as they're reasonably priced. Nothing outrageous. She'll then drop you home.'

Amanda straightened up, ready for her task.

Levi had returned to looking at me. Tears seemed to be forming deep in the corners of his eyes and I found that, not for the first time, I could not look at him properly.

'Come on, it's time to go.'

Levi sniffed and got up. 'And what about the mad bat who tried to kill me?'

Dad shifted where he was standing. 'Let's just say that she's not very well and is being dealt with.'

'Should be locked up, not allowed to run around the woods with fucking knives—'

'Yes, we're well aware of how unfortunate the whole thing was,' Dad said, prodding Levi in the back so that he started to walk towards the door.

I was left standing alone in the lounge. I stood, listening to the burbling buzz of Levi's protestations and Dad's efforts to get him out of the house. When I felt the rush of cold air from the open front door, I went over to the doorway. Amanda had gone out and was getting into her car. The engine revved as she started it. Dad was crouching down doing up Levi's shoelaces. It all looked very strange, Levi wearing shoes but no socks and no trousers.

'Would you like my dressing gown, Levi? To keep you warm?' I tried to say it as loudly and normally as I could, but it still came out small and teary. My tears fell properly when Levi didn't reply. He just walked out towards the car without even a glance back at me.

'Don't be ridiculous, Kitty,' Dad said, frowning at me. 'It wouldn't even fit him. Now go and get dressed.'

I didn't go straight away. I watched Levi get into the front seat of the car, next to Amanda behind the wheel, wincing as he slid in. Then the door closed and she reversed the car into the road through the trees and drove away.

Dad watched them go too, and then closed the front door. He looked down at me and at first I thought he was going to say something. Something important. Then he closed his mouth and eyes, and when he opened them both again, all he said was, 'Do as you're told, Kitty. I'll make us some breakfast. Now go upstairs and get dressed.'

And so I did.

Chapter 26

Father Tobias came back before long. I was sitting at the kitchen table when I heard his car arrive, then the sound of him clattering through the hallway. He talked to Dad for a bit, then came through into the kitchen and smiled at me.

'Good morning, Katherine. What are you eating?'

I looked up at him. The red, tear-stained face I saw last night had gone; he was eyeing up the mince pie I was gnawing at.

Before I could reply, Dad stepped in. 'Would you care for a pie? I realise it's not exactly traditional breakfast material, but we seem to be overrun with pies, cakes and god knows what else.'

Dad was doing his posh voice again. *Traditional breakfast material.* I was not convinced by it.

'Why were you upset last night?'

I asked the question, sort of knowing that Father Tobias wouldn't like it. I heard Dad falter whilst reaching for some Tupperware. He looked round at me.

'Don't ask Father Tobias intrusive questions, Kitty,' he said, sharply. Father Tobias, on the other hand, did one of his waving motions with his hand, as if to say don't worry about it, and his smile widened.

'Oh it's quite all right. I, er, I had a bit of a nightmare. I do apologise if I unsettled you, Katherine. But grown-ups get nightmares just as much as young ones like yourself, you know. Sometimes, because we've experienced so much more of the world, the nightmares can be a lot worse.'

With these last words he settled his gaze more on the table than at me, as if dragged away from the kitchen and into some other world that only he could see. Dad turned back to us and set the square plastic tub of mince pies down on the table with a thud.

'Here we go,' he said. 'Tuck in. I'll get you a plate.'

'No need, no need,' Father Tobias said, dipping his hand into the tub and pulling out the largest, most generously stuffed pie from the ones in front of him. 'I catch the crumbs with my other hand. Always have.'

Dad nodded, though I could tell he wasn't really listening. He had his mind-elsewhere face on. That's what Mum used to call it when she saw him looking like that – his mind had gone elsewhere.

Eventually, he said, 'Kitty, we need you to stay in your room today and promise not to come out.'

I was about to make a fuss; about to say I was tired of all these strange things happening and nobody properly doing anything about them, but then Father Tobias said, 'I've brought with me some more books for you, Katherine. I realise you've probably already gone through all those other paperbacks you had, so I thought you could do with some more, to keep you occupied.'

I gave him a concentrated frown. 'Are you giving me back the ones you stole?'

He pulled a bit of a funny face. 'No, Katherine, that wouldn't be appropriate. And I didn't steal them. Your dad is looking after them. No, these books are some more detective mysteries from Mrs Christie. I spoke to your father about the content and he's aware they do feature murder and criminality as a central theme, but I have assured him this is offset by the strong moral focus of her books: the guilty party is always brought to justice. Evil isn't allowed to flourish in any form and is always met with punishment.'

He had clearly forgotten about the witches, I thought to myself. He tapped his hand on the table, as if to say that the matter is all dealt with, then bent down to retrieve a carrier bag from the floor. He passed it over to me and I peered inside. There were indeed about six or seven paperbacks in there. They looked brand new, their covers crisp and smooth, unlike the lined, dog-eared ones I kept on my little chest of drawers upstairs.

'So, how about you run along and see if you can polish one off before dinner time?'

I didn't move straight away. I waited for Dad to look up. After a few seconds he finally focused his eyes properly on me and said, 'Go on, hop it, Kitty.'

Once at the door, I turned around and asked, 'And if I wanted to talk . . . about last night . . . If I had . . . some questions?'

Neither Dad nor Father Tobias said anything to this at first, but I saw them look at each other. Then Dad said, 'I really don't think we need to go over all that. Not . . . not right now.' I noticed he wasn't looking at me when he said this. He was avoiding my eyes. I didn't reply to him. I just turned around and walked away, clattering up the stairs as I went.

In my bedroom, I unpacked the bag of books Father Tobias had given me and lined them up. They were indeed all by Agatha Christie – six of them in all: *Crooked House, Endless Night, Hallowe'en Party, Peril at End House, Ordeal by Innocence,* and *Evil Under the Sun.* I spent some time looking over the covers, enjoying the illustrations and the bold font. I especially liked *Endless Night.* I decided to go with *Peril at End House,* because the back of it sounded most interesting.

Whilst reading, I didn't really notice the rest of the world. I often went into something Mum used to call my 'book trance', where everything surrounding me became another place and time to the one I was living in within the pages. It was like I was underwater, or lost at sea, and it would take an earthquake or avalanche to remind me there was a real world outside. I barely noticed the sound

217

of Amanda knocking on my door, telling me there was some lunch on a tray outside. I vaguely remembered her doing it later on in the afternoon when my stomach started rumbling. On the tray was cheese on toast, three mince pies and a slice of apple pie. I brought it into my room and ate everything bit by bit while holding *Peril at End House* in my other hand. The cheese on the toast was no longer at its soft-melting best, but it still tasted good. So did the pies, although I saved one for later in case tea didn't appear.

By the time the light was growing dim and my legs were starting to ache, I came to the end of the book and put it down. I liked it better than the last one I'd read, the one about the old ladies who might be witches, and it had more of an obvious connection to what Father Tobias had said about mysteries and detectives – even if I still didn't know who Miss Marple was.

I lay back on my bed, the characters of the book still swimming around my head. The woman who appeared to be in great danger, having escaped a number of attempts on her life. The house where she lived, away from the main town, large and intimidating at night. And the surprising twist at the end that showed you that the very worst people don't always look like the monsters you expect to find lurking in the shadows.

While these thoughts floated through me, I started to become aware I was drifting off to sleep, my tiredness probably down to everything that had happened the night before. At least sleep is something I'm allowed to do, I thought to myself, telling the sleepy part of my brain that it had permission to take me off into the darkness. They'd come to get me if they needed me.

But they didn't come. Night time arrived, and if someone came to check on me, I didn't hear them. When I awoke, in the almost-pitch darkness, I wondered how long I'd slept for. It felt like hours, but a glance out of the window told me it was still well and truly night time. It had started to rain again – large droplets were hammering onto the glass and I could hear the little streams they made trickle down the side of the building.

I got out of bed, feeling a little cold as the skin of my ankles and wrists came out from under the duvet. I must have pulled it over myself during my sleep, because I didn't remember being under it. The door opened with the tiniest of creaks and I tiptoed out, very slowly, onto the landing and listened. I could hear voices, loud voices, coming from the lounge. And there was that smell again – a weird, slightly perfume-like smell, as if they were burning flowers in there, or those weird dried colourful bits some people had in bowls on their tables.

I started creeping down the stairs to get closer. The sound of the lounge door opening made me stand dead still. It was Amanda, saying, 'Honestly, it's probably best if I'm not here . . .'

Someone inside – Father Tobias, I thought – told her she should come back in, but she left out of the front door, letting it clatter behind her. She didn't see me. She was in too much of a rush, and although I couldn't see her face in the darkness, I could tell by the way her voice was shaking that she was upset. A scream erupted from the lounge then. It was Mum, it had to be; it was a shriek I now knew very well, the sound she made when she was at her worst. Then I heard that voice. And I couldn't help but fall to my knees, crouching halfway up the stairs, scared by the strange, deep, twisting sound of it.

'GIVE IT TO ME. I WILL NOT LEAVE HER UNTIL YOU HAVE SPILLED YOUR SEED INTO HER CUNT. UNTIL I FEEL HER FILL WITH YOUR WICKED DESIRES. DO IT. DO IT.'

Then there was more screaming.

Years later, I'd still wonder why I stayed. Why I didn't just go back upstairs and close the door to the horrors unfolding before me. Nearly every part of me was pulling me back, away from whatever was happening, inches away from where I stood. *Nearly* every part. But a small part wanted to see – wanted to see if it was really Mum making that horrible sound. I tiptoed down the stairs as if I was floating, feeling the perfume-like scent get stronger, mingled with a lingering chill from when Amanda had gone outside. I reached the door and peered through carefully, keeping as quiet and slow as I could.

It was as dark as could be, with only the light from the almost burnt-out fire making it possible to see the chair in the middle, the two people standing around it, and the writhing, struggling shape within the chair. Screaming.

'We don't have to do this,' Father Tobias said. He was facing Mum in the chair, but it seemed like he was talking to Dad.

'It was you who said we're running out of options.'

I saw the shape of Father Tobias's head nod. 'Fine. I can either stay and say the words, or I can leave you both. I could go outside to find Amanda. I think she's distressed.'

I heard Dad breathing quickly. Saw him scrunch up his fists, as if he was worried, or nervous. Mum's screams had dialled down to a low burble now and as Dad shifted, I could see her face going from wide eyes and open mouth to slit-like eyes and a weird, scary smile.

'DO IT.' The voice rumbled out of her, like distant thunder. She was looking at Dad.

'Is it more likely to work if you say the incantations?' Dad said.

There was a moment of silence, then Father Tobias said, 'I cannot promise. This is untested territory.'

'If you had to guess?'

Father Tobias paused again, then nodded. 'Then I would have said yes. It is probably more likely.'

Dad raised his hands up to his face and rubbed his eyes with the palms of his hands. The shadows on the walls from the flickering firelight made him look like some kind of monster, his fingers poking out from the top of his head like claws or wiry antlers.

'Stay, then,' he said.

Mum started to scream again. A mixture of words, stretched far away from their normal sound and meaning.

They both had their backs to the door by this point. With a rush of bravery I didn't think I would ever have again, I scurried as quietly as I could from the doorway and made for the coffee table. It had been pushed back so that it was sandwiched between the sofa and the back wall. One of the blankets Amanda had been using for sleeping – the one that had been given to Levi the night before – was on top of it, flopping down, so the space underneath was like a hidden den. Crouched underneath, I thought I'd made it without being spotted. But then Mum's screams stopped, and the horrible voice returned.

'I SEE AN IMP. IT WATCHES. IT HIDES.'

I watched from under the folds in the blanket. Mum was staring right at me. And the scary smile was spreading over her face once again.

Dad and Father Tobias, however, didn't seem to be paying much attention to what she was saying. They were too busy having their own conversation.

'Let's get this over and done with,' Dad said. And then he took off his t-shirt.

Father Tobias shifted a bit. He seemed uncomfortable. 'Are you sure you feel . . . capable? I mean . . . able . . .'

'Well, we'll see, won't we? I have to try.' He unbuckled his belt, unzipped his jeans and started to take those off too.

I didn't want to understand what was going on. The things Mum had been saying, when I heard her from the hallway, now seemed even more horrible, even more nasty, and watching Dad now stepping forward towards Mum, and Father Tobias starting to say words I didn't understand in a low voice, I started to feel very, very sick.

'JOIN US. JOIN US. DO IT. DO IT.' Mum was shouting the words now, then laughing, big, loud laughs, like a scratching cackle – as if the lounge was full of witches and they were all laughing and laughing and wouldn't stop. Father Tobias's nonsense words got louder – they almost sounded like a poem in another language, and they flowed together like some strange song that I'd never heard before. I watched without properly seeing. Dad in front of Mum, hunched forwards. He lifted her legs from the ground and she wrapped them round him. I saw him rocking forwards, the back of his legs looking tense and tight, like an animal straining at the leash. It went on for ages, or what felt like ages, Father Tobias walking around them, still saying his words, pausing only a few times to draw a breath, letting a few seconds of silence go by when all there was to hear was the crackling of the fire, the grunting of Dad, and the continuous laughter and shrieks from Mum.

I found I could not watch any more. I took hold of the blanket hanging down in front of me and pressed it to my face. I smelled its washing-powder scent. Its slightly scratchy feel on my face. I focused on these things. I tried not to look. Not to listen. Wishing I had never come down here at all.

It all seemed to come to an end when I heard Dad let out a loud breath-filled noise, like he'd just put down something heavy he had been carrying. I didn't move, but I did let the folds of the blanket hang loose between my fingers, letting in a crack of light. A slice of strangeness that I couldn't make sense of at the time. Dad stepping back from the chair. Father Tobias flicking something small and glinting in his hand, with droplets of water falling from its tip each time he passed it through the air. And Mum just sitting there, nightdress bunched up around her waist, legs apart, face completely still. She wasn't moving, or making a sound. It was like she had died, even though I could see her shoulders rise slightly with each slow breath she took.

After a few moments, Dad spoke.

'Did it work?'

Father Tobias stayed silent as he walked all the way around Mum, flicking more of the liquid at her. Then he turned round to Dad and said, in a quiet voice, 'I think so. I can't be one hundred per cent sure. But she's not responding to the holy water. It's the first time she's remained impassive to it.'

'And that's a good sign?' Dad asked. He was staring at Mum like he was afraid she would pounce at any moment.

'Oh, I think so,' said Father Tobias, and tapped a hand on Dad's shoulder. 'Come on. Get dressed, and we'll help get Marjory into bed. I'm hoping we'll see further positive results in the morning.'

Dad bent down and started pulling on his clothes, all the time watching Mum. She still didn't stir. She didn't do anything. She was like a limp doll.

Once Dad was fully dressed again, he and Father Tobias each took one of Mum's arms and pulled her out of the chair. She didn't resist them, or try to scratch at their skin and say terrible words. She didn't look as if she was in the right mood to help them, either. Instead, she just stumbled and leaned against them, like she had no bones left inside her. It took them a little while to get her out of the lounge. I listened very carefully, hearing them go up the stairs, a thud at a time. Once I was very sure that they were in the big main bedroom above the lounge, I crawled out from my hiding place and ran out of the room. I made it up the stairs OK, but on the landing I heard a creak to my right and saw Father Tobias coming out of Mum's room.

'Katherine. What are you doing?'

He sounded surprised and ever so slightly disappointed, like I was an old friend who had let him down. I looked at the floor.

'Just . . . needed to go to the loo.'

I heard another creak and looked up to see Dad coming out of the room.

'Kitty? What—'

'It's all perfectly fine.' Father Tobias raised a hand. 'Katherine was just going to the bathroom.'

Dad looked at me, his eyes full of worry. 'Is that right, Kitty?'

I gave a short nod. 'That's right.'

'Very well, then.' Father Tobias smiled. 'We were just checking if your mother was OK, Kitty. And she is. Better than she's been for a long while.'

I wasn't really sure how I should react, so I just said, 'Umm . . . that's nice.'

Then I walked past them both and went into the bathroom, closing the door behind me. I was pretty sure they were both downstairs now; probably going to find Amanda. But as I cried, I tried to make sure the noise of the tap running covered the sound of my sobs. Just in case.

Chapter 27

Loud, shrieking screams. Mum's screams. They made me jolt upright in my bed. I didn't know how long I had been asleep, but my eyes still felt slightly wet from my tears, so it couldn't have been too long. Then there was some clattering around and I heard Dad talking hurriedly and running down the stairs, then back up again, followed by a slower, heavy thud. He had gone to get Father Tobias, I thought to myself as I pulled on my dressing gown and went out onto the landing.

'Go back to bed, Katherine,' Father Tobias said to me, sharper and sterner than usual. I didn't obey him. Instead, I watched as he and Dad gathered round the bed in the main room, Mum's body hidden by the part-open door.

'I think we should just let her work through it,' Father Tobias said loudly to Dad over the screams. 'There's nothing much that can be done, short of forcibly sedating her.'

'I thought we were supposed to be over this. I thought the whole point—'

But Dad broke off, as the screams stopped as suddenly as they had started. Silence throbbed around us all. Then a deep voice sounded from Mum's room. A voice I'd heard before; except this time, it wasn't shouting. It was talking in a low volume but clearly; firm, definite, terrible.

'A CHILD. BRING ME THE CHILD.'

It might have been my imagination, but I thought I saw Dad's face going even whiter than normal. He looked up at me, standing on the landing, and our eyes met.

'Kitty, go to bed right now,' he said, his voice hoarse and raspy, as if he needed a drink of water.

I stared at them, and slowly Father Tobias turned his head to look at me too, just as another loud shout emanated from the bed.

'BRING. ME. THE CHILD.'

I was still standing there, transfixed. Even though I couldn't see the mouth saying the words, I knew that they came from the body that used to be my mum – my kind, fun, warm mum, who used to take me to the shops and make sandcastles on the beach.

'BRING. ME. THE CHILD.'

Father Tobias turned the rest of his body round so he could face me properly. 'Kitty, come here.'

227

'No,' Dad hissed, clasping the upper part of Father Tobias's arm. 'I will not have her involved.'

Father Tobias didn't shake him off or respond. He just carried on looking at me.

'Katherine. Please come here.'

This time Dad didn't argue. He moved his hand from Father Tobias's arm to his face, rubbing his cheeks, as if he was very unsure about everything.

'I just need you to come in here,' Father Tobias said, reaching out his hand as if he wanted to take mine. I paused. Then walked. Two steps. Three steps. Five steps. Then I was there. And he had my hand, leading me into the room, around the door, and in front of the bed.

Mum was lying there, in her old pink nightie. She looked different to how she'd looked over the past few days. Her skin was grey and her hair was losing its colour too. Even though she'd been baking pies and cakes, her face seemed thinner and I could see the jut of her jaw beneath her skin.

'Marjory. We've brought you Katherine. You said you wanted to see her.'

Her face remained still for about three seconds. Then it spread into the smile I had seen downstairs. That horrible, toothy smile that wasn't like Mum at all.

'MARJORY DOESN'T WANT HER HERE. SHE'S BEGGING HER TO GO.'

The voice was low and strong. She wasn't shouting, but her tone had a deep resonance to it, like bombs exploding a long way off. I heard Dad take in a sharp breath.

'You just asked Katherine to be brought to you. And here she is,' Father Tobias continued, talking as calmly as if we were all having a picnic.

'SHE'S FRIGHTENED.'

'Who is?' Father Tobias asked pleasantly.

'MARJORY. FRIGHTENED WHAT SINS THIS LITTLE GIRL MIGHT BE EXPOSED TO. OR MIGHT WANT TO COMMIT.'

'What do you mean, Marjory?' As he said this, Father Tobias put a hand on my shoulder, holding me still. He had probably seen that I was starting to shake, although whether this was because of the cold or something else, I didn't know.

'THAT LITTLE GIRL SHOULD JOIN ME. I WILL SHOW HER THINGS.'

The horrible smile spread across Mum's face again. And I felt sick.

'Please can I go?' I whispered.

'No, stay here, Kitty,' Father Tobias said, calmly but firmly.

'I don't think—' Dad started to say, but Father Tobias held up a hand to silence him. 'Please. Let's just see what else Marjory has to say.'

'I . . . I think I know where this is going. This is about what she said before,' Dad said. He was tripping over his words, his hands now going up past his face, clutching at his hair as if trying not to start screaming himself.

'Please control yourself,' Father Tobias said, a little sternly. 'Katherine's going to come to no harm here.'

'THAT LITTLE CUNT IS WHAT WE'VE ASKED

FOR. IT'S WHAT WE'VE WANTED. FOR SO LONG. MARJORY IS SCREAMING INSIDE HERE. BEGGING US TO LET HER LITTLE GIRL GO. BUT WE WILL TAKE HER. WE WILL HAVE WHAT IS OURS.'

I felt Father Tobias straighten up. 'Well, I think we've heard quite enough now. Go back to your room, Katherine. This doesn't appear to be getting us very far.' His tired, lined face was scrunched, like he was put out about something, or someone, though I'm not sure if it was me, Dad or Mum.

I heard him exchange some muttered words with Dad as I padded softly back to my room, but I didn't quite catch them. I was in a daze when I sat down on my bed. This had been the longest night of my life. It felt like it would never end. And just as I thought this, I heard the birds start to sing. Louder and louder, as if they were gathering near my window. And I knew morning would come eventually, like it always did.

It was Amanda who woke me. This was unusual, but she'd brought me some toast, so I didn't feel too cross about it. I bit into one of the slices greedily.

'How are you today, Kitty?'

Of all the questions she could have asked me, it was the one I really didn't know how to answer. But she didn't seem too interested in waiting for a proper response, and pressed on.

'I understand there was a bit of a . . . there was . . . some excitement during the night.'

Excitement? I was puzzled by this choice of word. 'What excitement?' I asked.

She stared at me, eyes open, encouraging me to remember, or to talk about something she seemed sure I knew about. 'You know, last night. About what happened. With your mum.'

I felt the little hairs on my arms prickle and a tingly feeling creep up my neck. She was talking about what happened in the lounge. But she couldn't know that I was there. She hadn't been there herself. Or had she seen me, through the window? She'd gone outside. I remembered her leaving. The cold air coming in from the door.

'Kitty?'

The low burning fire. The flicker of the light. The darkness underneath the coffee table. The smell of washing powder on the clean blanket.

'Kitty, are you all right?'

It took an effort to pull my mind away from that awful place. I looked at her, blinking quickly in case my tears slipped over and down my face. 'What?'

'I was talking about what happened in Mum's bedroom. Father Tobias just told me about it?'

These two sentences weren't questions, but she said them as if they were. I nodded in response and she seemed a bit happier.

'Good, I'm pleased we're on the same page.' She gave me a smile. 'I want you to remember, Kitty, that your mother is . . . she's a bit . . . a bit poorly.'

I didn't know why she was telling me this as if it were news, but I had a suspicion she thought she was being kind.

231

'And what she said . . . well, it isn't to be taken to heart.'

I nodded again, and she seemed to like that. Her smile returned. 'Good. I'm pleased you understand.'

It was only now that I realised the tray she'd brought the toast on also had a cup of tea on it. She picked it up and took a little sip from it. 'So,' she said, wiping her mouth discreetly with the back of her hand, 'this leads me on to something that might cheer you up.'

I narrowed my eyes. It was her happy, sing-songy tone that had started to worry me. It was like she was trying to get me onside for something. And, based on what had been happening over the past few days, I thought it was unlikely I was going to like it.

'I was wondering if you'd like to invite your little friend – Adah, isn't it? – to tea? Would you enjoy that?'

This took me completely by surprise. 'Why?' I asked.

Amanda took another sip of her tea and smiled again. 'Oh, we just thought it would be a nice thing. A nice thing for you, after a few days of . . . unpleasantness. It's time to put that sort of stuff behind us, and I think this would be the perfect way to move forward. A nice little tea for you and Adah.'

The idea of inviting in someone else when Mum could start screaming at any moment seemed a strange way of dealing with the situation. What if more 'unpleasantness' happened when Adah was here? What if something awful happened to her, like it did to Levi?

Amanda seemed to guess what I was thinking. She set her tea down and clasped her hands together. 'Don't worry about a thing, Kitty. It will all be fine. Father Tobias and your dad will stay with your mum upstairs and I'll sort out the food for you and Adah. We'll have a very merry time, I'm sure.'

Again, there was something that sounded wrong about her voice. Like a performance. Like she was trying to be kind to me whilst not telling me something very important, something that would make all this make a bit more sense, if only she'd say it. But she didn't say it. She just got up to leave.

'That's all sorted then,' she said. 'Shall we say five o'clock? I might even be able to get that old television working in the lounge and put on a Disney video for the two of you? Would you like that?'

I nodded. It was all I could really do. She seemed so set on it all, I felt it would be worse to argue.

'Excellent,' she beamed. 'I'll go downstairs and start planning what to cook for this evening, and you can run along to find your little friend. You could go and play with her in the woods during the day. Actually, shall I run you a nice warm bath before you go? Or would you like one when you get back?'

I nodded again. 'When I come back,' I said, and she smiled and left, closing the door softly behind her.

I got dressed slowly, thinking about what she'd said. I could ask Adah for tea, I supposed. But a little part of my mind was telling me not to do what Amanda wanted. I found it strange that they'd all been discussing me having tea with a friend after everything that had happened last night.

I felt myself shiver. I didn't want to think about last night. I could feel it upsetting me.

I pulled on my shoes, which were normally by the front door, but seemed to have found their way upstairs, and left my room, deciding to see what Adah thought about the teatime invitation. If she wanted to come, she could come. If she'd rather stay away, I couldn't really do anything about that.

I headed down the stairs, opened the front door, and set off into the trees, only vaguely aware of Amanda standing in the hallway behind me. Watching me go.

Chapter 28

January 2020

'We accept, Katherine, you must have been in a particularly fragile state during this ordeal.' Although these words sound understanding, I see DI Cousins's eyes glance at her watch as she says them. My time is limited, it seems. Or maybe it isn't. Maybe they have to stay here however long this takes. This plays to the rebellious streak inside me. Maybe I could just keep them going round in rings, lamenting my lack of firm recollection, and wait for them to lose patience and send me home. Or place me under arrest.

'Nobody's doubting that,' DC Malik chips in when I don't respond straight away.

'I'm still struggling to understand one key thing,' DI

Cousins says. 'If you find them upsetting to remember and difficult to speak about, why did you decide to publish a book about these events? Surely you must have known it would bring the skeletons out of the cupboard? I appreciate you say it may have been therapeutic to write it all down, but to actually *publish* it? This suggests you wanted to go public with the truth. Or your version of it. But the truth, as we know, isn't just a matter of perception in this case. As we've discovered from our own research and from talking to others involved, and of course from the video, there seems to be a wide gulf between what you allege to have happened and what actually may have occurred.'

I look down at the table when she says this last bit. I know what she's getting at, and I don't feel ready to go there. It's a dark, black hole in my mind which hides everything that is dark and evil – but even though I can't see what's within, I can hear the sounds, the whispers, the ghosts of the past tugging on me, pulling me; and the sound of them terrifies me to the core.

'Enough tiptoeing around the issue, Katherine,' DI Cousins says, her voice now strong and steely. 'Please tell us, in plain, honest, clear English, exactly what happened on the day Adah died.'

Chapter 29

1987

It may just have been because I hadn't been outside much over the past few days, but as I walked along through the woods, I was convinced the trees seemed to be growing closer together. Even though more leaves had fallen along the ground, so that they stretched out in front of me like a golden-green carpet, the branches appeared to have got thicker, blocking out more sunlight. It wasn't raining, but the air felt damp and my breath rose in little clouds as I walked.

There was no telling if I'd actually find Adah. I had sort of come across her by accident on the couple of times I'd seen her before, but just wandering through the woods hoping to bump into her seemed a bit silly.

After a while, I reached the little bridge that went across the stream, and for a second I thought I could see Adah standing on it. But it was a branch – a big thick one, leaning on its side. It must have fallen from one of the overhanging trees during the wind and rain.

I did a little loop round, sticking to the bits of the forest I now felt I knew, and found myself along the winding path that led to the bushes and thicket – the area that hid the little hut from view. Levi's little hut. I was slightly scared to go near it, the memories of my earlier visit flickering through my mind. Part of me wanted to see him, to talk to him, see if he was OK, but another part of me wanted to forget there was ever a boy called Levi, and that I ever knew him.

The shed was empty. I discovered this after I had got my courage up to open the door. I half expected to find Levi lying there on the old cushions and duvet reading his Bambi book, but there was nobody there.

But there was something else. Something that wasn't there before.

Blood.

I almost stepped on it as I went to walk inside, before I saw it – a long dark trail, and some odd drops here and there. The duvet looked the most dramatic; a dark red-brown mark stained the centre. He must have been sitting on it when Mum . . .

I walked out of the shed quickly and closed the door.

'What are you doing in there?'

I swung round, alarmed to have been caught out (caught out doing what, though? I wasn't quite sure), but I relaxed a bit when I saw who it was. Adah was standing in front of me, holding a little white paper bag, pinching her mouth a bit, apparently sucking on something.

'Oh, it's you,' I said.

'Correct!' she replied, brightly. 'It's me. Do you want a toffee?'

I nodded and took one, popping it into my mouth and hoping it would mean I didn't have to answer her question. But she said it again almost straight away.

'So, what were you doing in there? Looking for Levi?'

I thought for a few seconds, then nodded.

'Well, you won't find him in there. He's gone.'

I froze. 'What do you mean, *gone*? He's not . . . he's not . . .'

Adah looked at me like I was crazy. 'He's not *dead*. Nothing as exciting as that. I saw him yesterday. Although he *was* a bit weird. He seemed really strange – stranger than normal. I saw him wearing these different clothes – new clothes, nicer ones than his tatty old t-shirts. He said he had bought his motorbike or scooter or something, the one he'd wanted for ages. A guy in the garage had been teaching him to use it just for fun. Probably didn't think he'd ever be able to buy it. But now he has, suddenly. Don't know where he got the money from. Probably robbed a bank. Then he said he was out of here. Off for new adventures. And now I think he's gone for good. He's not been around here, anyway.'

I stared at her, and she nodded earnestly, as if to make it clear she was telling the truth.

239

We walked for a little bit in silence, then I asked her, 'Did he mention me at all?'

Adah let out a loud laugh. 'You? Why would he? Why, do you *fancy* him? I fancied a boy once. He had red hair and freckles. But then the girls at school said he was a gypsy and his brothers would steal our car if they got a chance. But he wasn't a gypsy and my aunt doesn't have a car, and I went off him anyway.'

I had nothing to contribute on this subject, so I stayed silent.

'So, why you asking about Levi?' she asked again, sounding irritated that I wasn't giving her full enough answers.

'I just wondered. The cabin was empty.'

I didn't know if Adah had been in there and noticed the blood, but because she hadn't mentioned it I thought it was best I didn't either.

We spent a few hours in the forest not doing much – throwing sticks into the stream and watching them float along; playing a jumping game that Adah was quite a master at but I struggled with. I couldn't get my feet to land in the right order in the circles she'd drawn in the dirt.

When we finished, tired and with mud on our shoes, we started walking in the direction of the house. It was then I realised I hadn't asked Adah the very thing I'd come out here to ask her. 'Would you like to come for tea?'

I saw her turn to me, immediately interested. 'At the Witch's Cottage?'

I nodded. 'At my house, yes.'

She pulled a face. 'Is it *your* house now? I thought you were just staying there.'

I shrugged. 'I don't know. Does it matter?'

She shook her head. 'No. I just wondered. Wouldn't your dad mind? I thought you said your mum was poorly or something?'

I wasn't sure how to step around this. Adah had a good memory. 'Well, the woman who is staying with us . . . my dad's friend . . . It was her idea to invite you. My mum will be in her room.'

Adah thought about this for a few moments, then asked, 'Is that her way of saying sorry for keeping you from me for weeks and weeks and weeks?'

I made a noise of impatience. 'It hasn't been weeks and weeks and weeks! Nowhere near!'

'Well it's felt like it.'

Part of me liked the fact Adah had noticed my disappearance. I'd never been one for friends; I usually preferred to stay by myself a lot of the time at school. But it was like the closeness I'd felt with her, holding hands in the wood shed, hadn't been just something I'd imagined.

'So, do you want to come?'

Adah huffed. 'Of course! Much better than stale old cereal for tea at home. Unless we're having cereal at yours?'

I laughed. 'Of course we're not. Amanda will cook us something.'

Adah nodded. 'OK then. I'll come.'

We walked on a few paces and then Adah said

something that made me stop. 'It's a shame Levi isn't here. He could have come too.'

She looked back at me when she realised I'd stopped. 'What? What's wrong?'

'Nothing,' I said, quickly. I didn't want to give her a reason to ask me any more questions, but it was too late.

'Did it, like, scare you? What I showed you. Last time. When we saw him in his hut?'

I tried not to look at her. I couldn't. It was like my head was filled with a buzzing – a whole nest of bees – and I couldn't focus on anything as the buzzing got louder and louder.

'Don't . . . I don't want to speak about it any more,' I muttered. My behaviour made her even more convinced there was something to talk about.

'What are you doing? Come on, stop messing about. You're being silly.' She tried to pull my arm.

'Promise me you won't talk about Levi!' I shouted this now, and it shocked her. As my eyes finally found her face, I saw her looking stunned.

'Why?' she demanded when she'd managed to make her mouth work again. 'Why can't I talk about him? I can talk about who I want.'

'Just don't,' I said, staring back.

She grabbed my arm again. 'Stop being stupid,' she said, as if she was an adult and I was her little child. I didn't like this. I didn't like being told I was stupid or that I didn't understand. Because I didn't understand, not really, but it made it even worse thinking about it. I pulled

242

roughly away from her and she grabbed at me again. So I pushed her. 'Stop it!' I screamed. 'Stop it!'

I wasn't sure which of us dragged the other near the water's edge. But suddenly we were there. And as I shoved Adah away, getting ready to run – to bolt back to the house and leave her out here alone – I saw her topple. Her face jerked as she realised she was about to lose her balance, and she flailed, trying to grab me again – not to pull me or hurry me up this time, but to save herself. But her hands weren't fast enough. There was a splash. And a shriek.

Blood was rushing into my head, making my ears pound and my balance go wobbly. I heard Adah gargle something. It might have been 'help!' or 'please!' but I couldn't quite work it out. And I just stood there. Very still. Watching.

Chapter 30

It was like I had woken up from a dream. The real world hit me. The expanse of water in front of me, which before had seemed narrow but now seemed like a vast ocean. For a moment, I thought I had been standing there for ages, and I panicked.

And then another thought thundered into the front of my mind. A memory of Adah telling me about her time messing around in the pool at school. And how she'd never learnt to swim.

'Don't worry!' I shouted at Adah. 'I'm coming.'

We were only a matter of steps away from the bridge, and I remembered there was a big fallen branch leaning up on the side halfway along. I raced towards it, grabbed it – it was lighter than it looked – and dragged it back across the bridge and down to the stream's edge. With horror, I saw Adah was being dragged along, slowly but surely. She couldn't swim. And she was losing her fight with the slow-moving water.

'Take it!' I shouted at her. 'Take it!'

A few grabs. Some splutters. Then she had hold of the branch. It took every effort in me to pull the branch with her clasping on until she reached the bank. She crawled onto the leaf-covered mud, pulling herself up, her hand clawing at the mixture of leaves, water and mud as she struggled to get onto the hard ground.

She was coughing and spitting out water, and when she'd straightened and rubbed her face, I could see that she was crying.

'I'm really sorry,' I said, and I took off my coat and put it round her. It seemed like the nicest thing to do. 'Do you want to come back to mine? It's not far. It's too early for tea but we can maybe watch a video and you can change into some of my clothes.'

She didn't spend any time thinking about it. She nodded, meekly. She was trembling all over, though I thought it was more from the scare than the cold.

'Or I can walk with you back to your aunt's house? I don't mind.'

It was making me feel more and more worried, the fact she hadn't said a single word since getting out of the water. She started to plod along slowly in the direction of the cottage. 'Yours,' she said, quietly. I followed her, and we walked the rest of the way back to mine in silence, broken only by the sound of drips from her soaked clothes pattering on the leaves as we went.

Chapter 31

There were things going on in the lounge. I couldn't hear any screams, but there was definitely a conversation of some sort being had. I could hear Dad's voice, raised a little as if he was about to get angry, and I could hear Amanda responding rather loudly too. 'We should have spoken about it *properly*,' she said, sounding stressed. I couldn't hear Dad's answer.

I let Adah in and she started taking off her shoes and gave me back my coat. I hung it up and kicked off my own muddied, drenched shoes. 'Let's go upstairs,' I whispered to her, and she nodded and followed. I went into my bedroom to fetch my dressing gown and pyjamas while Adah dripped on the landing.

'You can wear these,' I said to her, going back out onto the landing, holding out the pyjamas in my hands. But it wasn't just Adah standing there. Amanda was staring at me, with a wide smile on her face.

Wolfish, I thought to myself. She looked wolfish.

'Kitty, darling, you've brought back your little friend to play.' She turned to Adah. 'And why is it she's all wet? It's not raining.'

My eyes darted to Adah, who was looking at the floor, then back to Amanda. 'She tripped and fell into the stream.'

Amanda's eyes widened. 'Did she now? Well, we must get her out of those wet clothes. Come on, Adah, let's get you sorted, and then we'll warm you up with some mince pies. Would you like that?' Adah gave a little nod and Amanda led her away into the bathroom. I went to follow, but she took the dressing gown and pyjamas off me and said 'Thanks Kitty,' then closed the door, barring me from going in. I heard the noise of the bath running and Amanda asked her about temperature, so I turned to go back to my room.

'Kitty.' It was Dad. He must have climbed the stairs without me hearing him, and now he was standing almost at the top, looking out onto the landing. 'You're back quicker than . . . well, I expect you got hungry?'

I nodded. It seemed like a good excuse.

He nodded too, but as if he was thinking about something else.

'Adah's here,' I said.

'Already?' Dad looked a little alarmed. 'But it's not even four o'clock. I thought she was coming for tea.'

I did a little shrug. 'She tripped and got her clothes wet. So Amanda's running her a bath.'

He looked a little confused by this, but said, 'I see,' then turned to go back downstairs, before stopping and looking up at me. 'Well, if you want, this afternoon you can both watch some videos on the TV in the lounge if we can get it working. Amanda suggested that earlier. She brought her VCR with her the other day. I'll see if I can get it all hooked up.'

I didn't answer, but he showed no signs of caring, and just went quietly back downstairs. 'Oh, and Kitty,' he called up in a loud whisper. I went to the top of the stairs and looked down. 'Don't go into your mother's room. OK?'

I didn't know why he thought I'd want to go back in there after what happened last time, but I just gave him a nod and he seemed satisfied.

I went back to my room while Adah had her bath, and Amanda came in after a bit and started talking in a weirdly nice way again. 'Hello Kitty, Adah's just getting all dry and into those pyjamas and dressing gown. She's happy to stay for tea and watch a video or two. Why don't you run down to the lounge and pick one? I've brought a bag of them with me. I'm sure you'll find lots of nice films in there.'

I wasn't at all convinced that Amanda's idea of what made a nice film would be the same as mine, but I didn't argue. I put the book that I had been half reading back on its shelf, and followed her out onto the landing. She went into the bathroom, but nodded at me to go down the stairs.

The lounge looked completely normal, with the chairs back in their proper place, the coffee table in the centre, and the little TV on its stool. The only thing noticeably different was the VCR machine Amanda had brought, which had thick black wires snaking back round to the plug sockets.

'Amanda was kind enough to get you both some videos to watch. They're in the bag here.'

I turned round to see Dad pointing at a dark green carrier bag on the sofa. I looked through the options, taking them out one by one. *Escape to Witch Mountain*, *The Black Hole*, *The Rescuers*, *Labyrinth*, *The Aristocats* and *The Dark Crystal*.

I lined them all up on the sofa and knelt down to consider them carefully. It was something Mum and I used to do, whenever it was a rainy day or the school holidays. 'Let's have a hot chocolate and video day,' she'd say. And we'd line up the potentials and make our selection together, with her agreeing with whatever one I picked.

Amanda's choices weren't as terrible as they could have been. We'd watched *The Rescuers* at school a couple of Christmases ago, and *Escape to Witch Mountain* and *The Black Hole* looked a bit silly. I think I'd been taken to see *The Aristocats* when it came back on at the cinema a long time ago, but I didn't remember it much. Some cats playing the piano, but that was about it.

I decided on *The Dark Crystal* first, and just as I was taking it out of its plastic case, there was a sound by the door.

'Here we go. All warm and in dry clothes.' Amanda

showed Adah into the room with a hand on her shoulder. Although she wasn't smiling, Adah seemed a bit more alert now, as if the shock from her experience was starting to wear off. 'Would you like a drink, Adah?'

She nodded. 'Yes, please.'

'What would you like? We've got milk and orange squash and apple juice, or you can have some water if you prefer?' Amanda was still doing her sweet-and-kind voice, and it made me frown a bit. She seemed to notice. 'Kitty, why the stern face? Do you want a drink, too? How about I bring you both a glass of fresh cold apple juice? It really is quite a treat, having fruit juice, isn't it? I certainly don't have it at home that often! We're quite spoiling you two girls.'

She walked off through to the kitchen with a little laugh, as if she had said something funny. I turned to Adah, who was hovering in the middle of the room. I was nervous about being alone with her now, wondering if she'd bring up what had happened by the river. 'Where do you want to sit?' I asked, not properly looking at her. 'We can go on the sofa, or you can have that chair all for yourself?' I pointed at the single armchair.

When she didn't reply, I let my arm fall back to my side and allowed my eyes to meet hers.

'I really am sorry,' I said.

At first her gaze was hard and I was worried she was going to be angry with me. Then she seemed to soften, and although she didn't smile exactly, her mouth moved in a way that seemed comforting and friendly. 'Let's go on the sofa,' she said, nodding.

Feeling relieved, I cleared the cases off it and went over to put the video cassette in the machine. Then we both settled down to watch *The Dark Crystal*. The apple juice Amanda brought us was very cold, but I didn't mind. The coldness reminded me how thirsty I was and I drank it down quickly. Adah took hers in little sips. 'We never have juice at home,' she said as the movie began. 'My aunt said it costs too much. She always seems to find the money for what she wants to drink, though.'

I wasn't sure how I should react to this further insight into Adah's home life, but luckily I didn't have to say anything, as Amanda brought us mince pies, one each on a separate plate. She explained she didn't bring too many as she didn't want to spoil our tea. She was doing us sausages and chips and she'd have it ready for when the film finished. She looked at the back of the video box, probably to check how long it would be on for, then disappeared back into the kitchen.

The Dark Crystal proved to be a very strange film, and part of me felt quite unnerved by the peculiar-looking creatures within it, especially the creatures known as the Skeksis. I glanced at Adah. She was watching with glazed eyes, almost as if her mind was somewhere else.

Towards the end of the film, just as things were starting to get happier for the characters, the scent of cooking became strong. I could hear the fizzle of sausages in a pan on the stove and Amanda pottering about. As the credits were running, she came into the lounge and said, 'So then, are you both ready for some dinner?'

I nodded, and Adah said, 'Yes please, I'm very hungry.' I was relieved she sounded a bit more like her bold, loud self now. We got up and followed Amanda into the kitchen. She dished up the sausages – we got three each – and then took out a large tray of oven chips and emptied them into the frying pan the sausages had just been in.

'This is my secret trick,' she explained as she nudged them carefully with a spatula. 'Cook chips in the oven, then fry them for a minute right at the end in the fat from some meat – it makes them *delicious*.' She seemed to have forgotten her concerns about calories and nutrients she had mentioned the other day.

Dad walked into the room and went straight over to Amanda. 'That smells amazing,' he said, ignoring me and Adah.

She muttered something in response that sounded like, 'Is he here yet?' and Dad replied in a quiet voice, 'No, not yet. And Marjory's sleeping.'

'Thank goodness for that,' Amanda said, quietly. Then there was a rattle as the pan was lifted off the stove and brought over to the table. 'Right, chips!' She shovelled a large pile onto each of our plates, steam and fat hissing as she did so.

Amanda was right – the chips were delicious, soaked in the fat of the sausages; they melted in my mouth as I shoved them in. Dad would have normally told me to eat more politely, but he was staring off into the distance again while he drummed his foot on the ground over and over.

'These sausages are very tasty,' Adah said, getting through her three very quickly, then finishing off the chips with similar speed.

'I'm pleased our little tea has gone down a treat,' said Amanda, smiling at the two of us. 'So, how about we continue this little tea party into the evening?'

I saw Dad glance at her. She met his eyes for a quick second, then looked back at the two of us sitting there.

'I'm sure you don't want to run around and play in the dark after all this food. How about you stay a bit later, Adah? You and Kitty can watch another video. I'll drop you back afterwards so you don't have to walk home alone.'

I wasn't sure about this, but Adah beamed and said, 'Yes! Yes please, that would be great.'

'Won't your aunt mind?' I asked, but she shook her head straight away.

'She won't even notice,' she said.

'Splendid!' Amanda clapped her hands together with apparent joy.

I didn't know what was going on, but I could tell there was something happening that I wasn't being told about. I looked at Amanda and then at Dad. He was now eating a chip very, very slowly, his eyes on the table.

'Have you chosen another video, Kitty? Or did you both want to get the bag out and have a rummage?'

I shrugged. 'I don't mind. I did see another one earlier that looked good – I think it was called *Labyrinth*.'

'Oh that's quite a new one,' Adah said. 'I saw the posters up near the garage when it was at the cinema.'

'Did you go to see it, Adah?' Amanda said, moving in to take our plates.

'No, my aunt doesn't like the cinema. She tried to take me once to see something with dogs in it, but the people who worked there wouldn't let her take in her bottles.'

'Well . . . quite.' Amanda set down the plates on the side and said, 'Why don't you two run along and get the film started. Your dad can get it all running if you need help.' She looked over at Dad and smiled.

Dad was still in his daze, but seemed to realise she'd said something about him. 'Sorry, what?'

'I think we'll be fine,' Adah said. She got up first and walked through into the lounge. I stayed at the table.

'Go on, Kitty.' Amanda nodded her head towards the doorway into the lounge.

I got up, my chair scraping across the floor, and looked over at Dad, sitting there, still staring off into nothing.

'Dad?' I said in a small voice. His eyes floated towards me.

'Yes, Kitty?'

I looked over at Amanda, putting plates into the sink with a clatter. I saw her tilt her head to the side slightly. She was listening.

'Nothing,' I said finally. He didn't push me to tell him what I was going to say. I didn't really know myself what I was going to say, not really. I just knew that something was wrong. Something strange was happening, and I didn't like it.

'I'll bring you both a nice warm drink while you're

watching the film,' Amanda said from the sink. 'Hop along now.'

I left the kitchen. Back in the lounge, Adah had already got the tape of *Labyrinth* into the machine and it was about to begin. I took a seat next to her and started to watch.

Amanda did as she promised. I wasn't sure how far into *Labyrinth* we were, but it was up to a bit where there was a swamp and a fox-human type creature. A lot of it was quite similar to *The Dark Crystal* – unsettling animals that looked real but weren't, in a strange world a bit like ours but not like ours at the same time.

'Here we are,' she said, holding a tray on top of which were two mugs, steaming a little, bringing in a sweet, comforting scent. 'Hot chocolate. *And* I have some marsh-mallows to go on top. How about that?'

Adah seemed very excited by the idea. 'Yes please!' She took the mug from Amanda's red-nail-varnished fingers, nodding when she was told to be careful because it was very hot.

'And for you, Kitty.' She handed me my mug. I didn't say anything. For a moment, I thought she was going to tell me to say thank you or at least look a bit happier, but she didn't, and soon Adah and I were alone again, sipping at our hot chocolates, watching as an army of goblins tried to disrupt the efforts of the heroes.

'It's like a dream,' Adah said, as she drank more of her hot chocolate, leaning in to watch the unusual creatures move across the screen.

'It is,' I agreed. I looked down at my marshmallows, melting in the hot liquid, leaving white and pink trails around the edge of the mug.

Adah leaned back with a little sigh. She finished off her drink and put the mug down on the floor. I didn't want to finish mine. Maybe it was all the fatty food, or the sweetness of the marshmallows, or the strange videos we'd been watching, or maybe a mixture of all three, but I was starting to feel a bit sick. I placed the mug down on the floor like Adah and snuggled back into the cushions.

'I dreamt I was in another land, once,' Adah said, sleepily, to my left. 'Another land where things were all good and safe.' She yawned a big wide yawn, and brought her hands up to her face, nestling into them. Seeing her yawn made me feel sleepy, so I copied her and was amazed how quickly being still and quiet like this gave way to sleep.

For the time that followed, I couldn't really work out if I was dreaming or if it was the film. I was being taken into a maze by someone, or something, and they were leading me down a dark pathway towards . . . what was it? I couldn't be sure. It looked a little like the stairs here in the cottage. But I couldn't walk up them, so whoever was taking me lifted me up, and it was like I was flying. Flying towards something soft, something a little cold against my snug warm sleepiness. It wasn't a bad feeling. It felt nice. Like I was drifting among clouds. Drifting. Drifting.

But the clouds didn't last. When I heard the sound of a door opening downstairs, I realised I had been dreaming, and that I was actually upstairs in my bed. And, from the dull clunk I heard somewhere off in the distance, I could tell someone had just been let into the house.

Then I heard it. A man's voice. Father Tobias's voice.

'Is the girl here?'

Chapter 32

My legs and arms felt slow and heavy. It was like someone had taken all the energy out of me. But I wanted to get up. I needed to get up. I forced myself to walk slowly and carefully through the doorway of my room and out onto the landing, making sure to remain silent and out of sight of the conversation happening in the hallway. I heard a shuffle, as if someone had just come through from the lounge.

'She's completely out of it. But we should start soon. Immediately, I'd say.'

That was Amanda. Was she talking about me, I wondered? But I wasn't 'out of it', I was there, awake and trying to work out what was going on. I thought about asking them, then I remembered that I had fallen asleep on the sofa, not in my bed. And I hadn't been alone. I'd been with Adah. Had she gone home? Had I missed her leaving?

And then, with a really horrible feeling, I realised what they were talking about. They weren't talking about me. They were talking about Adah. She was still there. In the lounge.

'Where's Marjory?' Father Tobias asked.

'In the kitchen,' Amanda said. 'Nathan thought it best for her to remain separate from the girl before we start. She's not talking or moving. She's been refusing to eat today, too. But she's said it again a few times. Muttering about needing a "creature of innocence". Maybe she's gone quiet now because she knows she's getting what she wants.'

I heard a heavy sigh from Father Tobias. 'I'm grateful for the effort you've put in to this. I really think this could be a breakthrough.'

Amanda sniffed a bit, and didn't say anything for a moment. Then she said, 'Let's . . . let's just get started. I don't want her waking up in the middle of something terrifying.'

I leaned forwards a tiny fraction over the banisters and saw them both disappear through the lounge door. It was open very slightly, allowing a beam of light to give a yellow glow to the dark hallway. I was worried that my heavy, sleepy legs would make the stairs creak too much as I walked down, one step after the other, but I managed to make it, and paused for a moment once I had reached the bottom, listening. It sounded like there was furniture being moved in the lounge. I thought about the way they had it set up before – the night I stayed in and watched from under the coffee table. If they were moving the furniture, to make a space, and Adah was there, what did that mean?

The thought of what might happen to her made me feel instantly unwell, as if I had caught flu just by standing there and already had a temperature. I put my arms out and slid against the wall, dragging myself along until I was right by the lounge door. And through the small crack that had been left open, I could see inside.

She was there. Adah. And she was no longer on the sofa. She was on one of the chairs from the kitchen. Like how Mum had been on that horrible night. She was tied up, her head drooping forwards. Completely out of it, as Amanda had said earlier.

That strange smell was spreading out from under the door again, and then I saw Father Tobias walk into sight, wafting a stick around in the air, smoke rising up from it. 'Turn off the lights,' he said, and someone tapped the switch. Everything went darker, and the only light remaining was the flicker of the fire. 'Close the door,' he said again.

My view into the lounge vanished as the door was closed shut, but then it appeared again, thinner than before, but still there. The metal latch hadn't stuck in place, making the door bounce back a little. I could still see in. Just.

Then there was a scream. And I knew straight away that it was Mum. 'THE CHILD. THE CHILD.'

I felt my breathing quicken, and then the doorway on the other side of the lounge, leading to the kitchen, opened up. In walked Mum. Dad was behind, half pushing her, half supporting her, and she was shrieking, her head thrown back, her hair, now straggly and a little bit grey, spread across her face. I really wanted someone to pull it back for her, brush it away, make it nice like it used to be – back when she was the old Mum.

She started to scream words that didn't make sense now. Then Father Tobias began his weird half-song, half-speech in another language that I didn't understand. And Mum stopped screaming and allowed herself to be seated in a chair right behind Adah's. Dad came into view, holding ropes similar to the ones Adah was tied with, and began wrapping them around Mum so she, too, was tied to the chair. I kept thinking she was going to stop them, scream something awful at them, but she didn't. She had gone quiet by this point. But that smile was back – a wide smile, with her head tilted down, and her teeth showing. It was like she was hungry.

Then she spoke. And her voice, low and horrible, gave me goosebumps.

'The child. A perfect body. A creature of innocence.'

I saw the hand of Father Tobias point quickly. Dad stepped in and slowly turned Adah's chair so that she was facing Mum.

Father Tobias carried on speaking his strange words, and Mum started to scream again, wrestling against the ropes, trying to reach out. Trying to get to Adah. The scream was a mixture of words, but there were three I could properly make out. Three that were said clearly enough to be separate from the rest. 'SHE IS MINE.'

And then something very strange happened. As quickly as she had begun, Mum stopped suddenly. She went limp, like a ragdoll, her hair falling back over her face, her eyes closed. Then someone else started to scream. It wasn't Father Tobias, or Dad, or Amanda. It was Adah. She was screaming and screaming and rocking back and forth in her chair, her head going up and down, her shoulders trying to wriggle from the ropes, as if desperate to break herself free. I saw Amanda rush over to her, but Father Tobias cried out, 'Wait!'

'We can't – she needs to get out of here! Now!' Amanda shouted at him. Adah had begun to shake very fast, her body trembling and juddering. I couldn't see her face, but I imagined her teeth were clenched and her eyes screwed up, just like her fists. And then, as quickly as she had begun, she stopped. The silence almost made me jump. Her body went limp, her head went heavy, just like Mum's had, and Amanda was lifting her from the chair, with Dad helping. She wasn't making a sound.

'I . . . I don't think she's breathing,' Amanda said in a trembling voice. 'Quick, she's not breathing.'

'I'm sure she's fine,' Dad said. 'She must have just fainted or . . . I don't know, had a seizure maybe?'

'She's not breathing!' Amanda repeated again, this time with an even louder shriek.

'Stop getting hysterical,' Dad said, but his voice too had become loud and shaky. He bent down over Adah, putting his fingers to her neck and then tapping her face. 'Can you wake up for me?' he asked her. 'Come on, I need you to wake up now.' She didn't respond. She didn't even move.

Amanda had started to pace, saying 'Oh my god. Oh my god' over and over, her hands holding the sides of her head. 'Please, Nathan. She needs to go to hospital. *Now*.'

Dad took Adah out of the chair and laid her down on the floor. Amanda hurried to his side. He started pushing her chest up and down with two hands. I couldn't properly see, with Amanda and Dad crouched around her and Father Tobias standing in the way of the firelight. It felt like they were there for ages, and some of their mutters I didn't catch, but when Dad said, 'Call an ambulance,' I heard the words clear and strong.

'No,' Father Tobias said in a harsh, loud voice.

They carried on, fussing around Adah's little body. Because it was just a little body, now. I didn't know how I knew that she wasn't properly there any more. No longer inside her small frame. But I did know. I could feel that Adah wasn't in that room. I could tell the panic in their voices was real, and that something terrible had happened.

I left the hallway. Went back up to my room. Fell under the duvet. I didn't know what came first, the dreams or the sleep. But it felt like the dreams started before I'd properly drifted off. Dreams of people screaming and crying, pleading and whimpering, with terrible things happening in the corners of hundreds of rooms I couldn't quite see. And in the distance, a creature, with long black claws, leading Adah by the hand away from me, into the centre of a maze.

Chapter 33

'Kitty.'

I woke at once, gasping as I sat up. It was Dad. He was on the end of my bed, looking at me. He looked sad and tired, even more than usual, and his eyes were red, like he'd been rubbing them.

'We're going home.'

I had given up hope I would hear those words. I didn't know how long we had been there by this point, but it felt like for ever. 'Home? Like, as in . . . ?'

'Proper home,' he said. He gave me a little smile, but his eyes had more sadness in them than happiness. 'Amanda and Father Tobias have been helping me pack up the house downstairs. Nearly everything is cleared away now. It will be like we were never here.'

It was a strange thing to say, that last bit. I almost asked him to explain it, but there was another question I wanted answered first.

'And Mum? What about Mum?'

He took a slow, deep breath.

'She's better now. She's very tired and has been through a lot. But we're hoping she'll be back to normal within a week or so.'

'Back to normal?'

He wasn't properly looking at me. His eyes were on my shoulders. 'Yes. Or thereabouts.'

'But . . .' I was struggling to get my thoughts in order. Things weren't fitting, like puzzle pieces being forced into the wrong slots. 'Mum got better before, and then she wasn't better . . . she started getting bad again . . . She went back to being . . .' I found I couldn't finish the sentence.

Dad brought his hands to his face and slid them down his eyes to his nose. He didn't say anything at first, then he said, 'Well that's just a risk we'll—' He stopped himself and sighed. 'It will all be OK, Kitty. Can you get your stuff together? All your books and clothes and duvet and things? We'll be leaving very soon.'

He got up and walked slowly out of the room.

I wanted to ask him what had happened during the night. What happened after I left the door to the lounge and ran back to my room, trying my best to pretend what I thought was happening wasn't really. And as I got up

266

and started taking my books off the top of the chest of drawers, I only had one sound in my ears. The sound of Adah's screams. Confused, frightened, and surrounded by strange things she didn't understand. And nor did I.

Downstairs, the lounge was back to its usual arrangement, but a lot of our things had gone. The rug and blankets, cushions, Amanda's video machine – all had been taken away. The kitchen was looking bare too, although there was a plate remaining in the centre of the table. On it were two little bakewell tarts. I half expected to see Mum standing in front of them, telling me she'd baked them for me, with an instruction to get my apron on and make a new batch with her – this time with even more cherries. But she wasn't there. And neither was Adah.

I craned my neck out towards the hallway, and then turned to glance into the living room. Still no Adah.

I was about to leave the kitchen when I noticed something on the floor. A little pile of something. Clothes. I nudged them with my foot and saw that they were jeans, a t-shirt, some socks and a dark green jumper. I recognised them immediately as Dad's. And they were covered in dirt. There were patches of soil and mud all over them, especially on the knees of the jeans, as if someone had been sitting or kneeling on the ground outside. As if he had been doing something outside, in the forest, in the mud.

Then Dad came into the kitchen and made me jump.

'Have you packed up your things?' he asked. He saw what I'd been looking at on the floor. 'I thought I'd packed these,' he said, gathering them up quickly, pulling a folded plastic bag from his pocket and stuffing them in. 'Let's get going, Kitty. Time to say goodbye.'

I looked up at him, confused. 'Goodbye?'

'Yes, goodbye.' He seemed impatient. 'To Amanda and Father Tobias.'

My stomach churned and twisted. I didn't know my place in all of this; I didn't know what I had done and what I had helped to happen. But I did know one thing. I said it to Dad, in no uncertain terms, with my head raised a little. 'I don't want to say goodbye to them.'

I heard Dad let out a short breath. 'Come on, Kitty, we're leaving. Please, just do as you're told.'

I shook my head. 'I don't like them and I'm not talking to them. Ever again.'

He had his angry face on now. 'Kitty, of all the days to test my patience, you're picking the wrong one.'

My arms remained folded. He lunged forward towards me and grabbed my shoulder. 'Come on! Get in the car.'

'Get off me!' I shrieked.

I heard footsteps and Amanda walked through from the lounge. 'Kitty, dearest, what's all this racket?' She had her leather jacket on again, although didn't seem to have found the time to do her lipstick and nail varnish this morning. The sight of her made me want to scream. And so I did. But not just one, loud sound. I screamed words.

'Where is Adah?'

Something collapsed in her face, taking with it any colour or appearance of control. Her eyes widened, her lip trembled, and then, after giving me one horrified glance, she left without saying another word.

268

'Come on, Kitty,' Dad said, pushing me, almost carrying me, forcing me to walk out of the kitchen, through the lounge, the hallway and out the front door.

Father Tobias was standing outside, although he no longer had his normal black-and-white church clothes on. He was wearing an old-person's jumper, dark brown and patterned, and a thick, dark red coat. Dad handed something to him, and from the little jingle, it sounded like keys. Father Tobias nodded, and then looked over at me. He didn't say anything, but I did. I screamed it again. The same words, leaving my body with a rush and exploding into the air around us. 'Where's Adah?'

'In the car, now!' Dad bellowed. I saw him throw a glance at Father Tobias, before pushing me into the back seat, amidst all the stuff. It took me a second or two to realise Mum was there already. She was asleep, her head pressed against the car window, her breath misting up a little patch.

I realised I had started to cry, and Dad told me to be quiet, please, for the sake of everyone, would I just be quiet, and although I tried, I couldn't properly say words any more. I couldn't shout like I wanted to shout; I couldn't ask again where Adah was; what they had done to her. I could only cry, and writhe about in my seat, looking around at the trees through the windows as the car started to move.

My last memory of the cottage – that terrible, terrible place – was of Amanda, picking up something long and thin that had been leaning up against the wall. It was a shovel. She put it in a large bin bag that Father Tobias was holding open. Then he dropped it into the boot of his car.

My view was hidden as we turned round a corner. And I found that I was all cried out, so I let the hum of the engine and the pale light through the trees fill my head. And before long, I was asleep too.

Chapter 34

January 2020

DI Cousins places something on the table in front of me. I recognise it in an instant. It's my book. *The Poison Stream.* Its intricately designed jacket, featuring a swirling illustration of a forest with a winding stream of water going through it, still both excites me and horrifies me each time I see it.

'Your description of Adah's death makes for very interesting reading, Katherine,' she says, her hand resting on the cover. 'Very disturbing reading, many would say.'

I take in a deep breath. 'The whole experience was disturbing.'

'The thing is, Katherine,' DC Malik says, 'the fact you decided to fictionalise what happened – arguably the most important part of the book – puts you in a difficult situation.'

I stare back at him. 'A difficult situation? I was clear from the start that this was a novel. That's why I published it as such. Yes, I started writing it as a memoir, but I knew difficult questions would be raised if I said it was all exactly as it happened, so I just published it as fiction. I explained all this to my father. We had a bit of a row about it before Christmas. But of course he's not exactly thrilled about what I've done. It doesn't exactly make him look very good.'

DI Cousins doesn't respond straight away to this, but instead flicks a page over in her folder. 'You've said in two interviews, one in a magazine and another on a literary website, that it was "inspired by key events" in your childhood.'

I can't help but shrug a little. 'Well, that's true.'

'I'll tell you what I think,' DI Cousins says. 'I think you thought rewriting history would make you feel a little better about what happened, and in the process scare anyone who happened to read it who knew the truth into silence. Meanwhile, you can sit and watch the royalties roll in. Is that more or less on track, Katherine? You've monetised your childhood but don't have the guts to be honest about what actually happened?'

'Monetised!' I gape. 'Seriously? Do you really think that's why I did it?'

'*You* tell us,' said DI Cousins. 'Because, from what we've gathered speaking to another key player in all of this, a lot of your book could fairly be summed up as a bundle of lies.'

'It isn't,' I say, quietly and firmly. I'm gripping my chair now, not in distress but in anger.

'Then what is it, Katherine?' DI Cousins says.

I look up and feel my eyes flash with a rush of emotion. 'It's revenge.'

Chapter 35

November 2019

Two months earlier

The Churchill Gardens estate was seen as a beacon for new-age London, once upon a time, full of hopes and dreams for a capital still recovering from the Blitz. Its thirty-two blocks, some of them Grade II listed, stand within walking distance of both Buckingham Palace and the Houses of Parliament, yet remain the homes of relatively ordinary people going about their daily lives, with the eye-wateringly expensive houses of Pimlico and Belgravia within shouting distance. The whole area is a fascinating mixture of classes, backgrounds and lifestyles.

Within this mixture lives my father. And his second wife, Amanda.

I decide to get off at Sloane Square station and use the

short walk past Chelsea Barracks – now gleaming penthouses and multimillion-pound apartments – to gather my thoughts and decide how to play this. It is quite likely my father will try to guilt me into an apology. I haven't seen him since *The Poison Stream* was published, and if it hadn't been for his persistent attempts to get in contact, I wouldn't be here at all. His text message threatening to turn up at my flat was the final straw. The thought of my little haven of a flat being stained with his presence is too much for me to stomach. Which was why I agreed to come to his neck of the woods. All the way on the District line to Zone 1. Even though there are only about fifteen miles between us, it's enough for us to live perfectly separate lives.

I've been hoping Amanda would be out, but the 'we'll be in and waiting' at the end of his last email put paid to that. It doesn't really matter much. She's no match for me any more. In truth, I don't think she ever really was. I just need to make sure I hold my nerve.

I'm dying for a cigarette. Discovering my handbag empty, and regretting not picking up the new pack on the kitchen countertop before I left, I take a detour to stop off at a small Sainsbury's Local. I purchase a pack of Lambert & Butler King Size and pause outside to light up.

'Need any help, love? Want a light?' It's a young man, watching me struggling to light my cigarette. I hate it when male strangers call me 'Love' but right now I'm so desperate for a smoke, he could have shouted anything and I'd have let him light me up. I look him up and down – he's got a builder's outfit on, with the logo of a construction company on it. 'Having a nice day, love?' he asks.

The question startles me. The fact he's spoken to me at all feels oddly inappropriate.

'None of your business,' I reply, and turn to leave.

He stops leaning up against the window of the shop and starts to walk with me.

'Are you following me?' I say, baffled by his behaviour.

'Nah, I work there,' he says, pointing at an expanse of space cordoned off by a dark green wall, bestowed with the logo for the property development site. The sense of smugness about it makes me gag.

'How much would I have to spend to buy one of those flats? The ones you're building?' I ask him, out of interest.

He laughs. 'Millions, I think. Millions and millions. I heard prices start at five. For the cheap ones.'

'Christ,' I say, shaking my head. I leave the young man behind me as I walk off. At the junction at the end of the road, I think of the day Dad, Mum and I came to London to see the tourist landmarks. I can still vaguely remember it, although the memories are weak and poorly defined. The terrorist attack that took place on that day, where I'm standing right now, took the lives of two people and injured many soldiers approaching the then-functioning soldiers' barracks. It didn't have as big an effect on me as some may have expected – too many things happened later in my childhood – but I've come to appreciate, as I've got older, how it may have had a bigger impact on my mother. What should have been a nice day out with the family turned into panic, filled with sirens and running and screaming. A horrible situation to experience for anyone, especially someone of a naturally nervous disposition. She was always the type of person who feared the worst, whose sense of 'badness' and 'evil' was always hyper-reactive. That day may well have served as stark, terrifying proof for her that the world can be a wicked place, where people really do do terrible things.

I choose to continue my walk by going through this last stretch of Belgravia and over the bridge across the railway tracks into Pimlico. Within minutes I'm heading onto Lupus Street and I see the towers of flats rising up, dwarfing the posh townhouses that surround them. He's in there, somewhere, I think to myself. In there with *her*. They've been living here in Pimlico for about ten years now, with me only visiting on one occasion, about five years ago, when I gave in to my dad's pleas and agreed to meet up with him for a cup of tea on the anniversary of Mum's death. Mercifully, I hadn't been present on the night she'd taken her own life, but Dad had. She'd been sent home from whatever facility she was in because they'd run out of space. She hadn't been deemed well, just the 'least unwell' person there, and so she needed to go home and await reassessment. She hanged herself with the rope from her dressing gown, a piece of material so old and flimsy it apparently broke as she swayed and writhed and choked. But the damage had been done.

Fifteen years on, the anniversary meetup with my father hadn't gone well. Even without Amanda present, we'd still managed to start fighting; I screamed all the words I'd saved up since our previous row.

I ring the buzzer at the entrance, stepping round a group of boys nearby. They've got bikes, but they've left them on the pavement in a big metallic pile, blocking the walkway, while they crouch on the floor hacking apart an old football with what looks like a kitchen knife. One of them is smoking and a strong scent of cannabis finds its way over to me. I ring the buzzer again, unnerved by the sight of them, and finally the door buzzes and I can get in.

They're on the fourth floor, and the lift looks a little dodgy, so I walk up the narrow flights of stairs, which wouldn't look out of place in an old hospital. I feel my legs protest at the harsh incline as I pass each floor, the lingering smell of the drugs still strong.

I locate the correct door after a few false starts and knock loudly. It's opened instantly. And there he is. Standing before me. It's rather extraordinary how much a man can age in five years.

'Hello Dad.'

He takes a quick intake of breath, looks at me, hard, then says, 'Hello, Kitty.'

I can't breathe. I take a step back, away from him, then step forward again. He's walking away now, down into the flat, but I can't bring myself to step inside. After finding the journey from the underground station relatively easy, I'm rather amazed how quickly my own resolve and sense of determination can crumble.

He's out of sight now. He must have gone into the kitchen or living room. I force myself to inhale and breathe calmly, then step inside.

There's certainly no scent of illegal drugs in this place. I can smell something cooking – maybe bread, something baked and inviting – along with freshly made coffee. It's warm and comforting – the opposite of how I currently feel. They've made a home here. Him and her. They may have weed-addled youths on bikes with knives outside their door, and the building itself is hardly a looker, but it's surprisingly nice inside. Nicer than they have any right to.

'We're through here,' I hear Dad call, so I follow the sound of his voice and then see him, standing in a lounge complete with armchairs, faux fireplace, large television – and her. Amanda, sitting on the large two-seater sofa. She's already staring directly at me the moment I walk in and greets me with a simple, 'Hello, Katherine.'

I stare at her for a bit, taking her in. She, too, has aged in the last five years, but not as much as my dad. And it looks like she's making a bit more of an effort, too – she obviously has had her hair dyed, for one thing, and it looks impressively natural. And the bright red lipstick is still there, although her mouth isn't forming a wide smile today. It's pursed and tense, geared for a fight.

Because I can smell coffee, and I see Amanda is already drinking from a mug, I automatically presume Dad's prepared some for my arrival; but he sits down without offering. 'I wondered if you would come,' he says, sitting straight-backed next to Amanda, who is sipping at her drink.

'I said I would.' I swing my arms a little, not sure what to do with them, and eventually he nods at the seat opposite and says, 'Go on, sit.'

Annoyed with myself that I waited for permission, I look away from them both and my gaze falls on the coffee table between us, its surface bare. Except for one thing. I glance up at Dad and see that his gaze has also settled on the book in the centre of the coffee table.

'Please could you tell me why you did this?'

The copy he has still looks quite new, although a few tell-tale lines in the spine tell me it's been read. Every time I see it in physical form, I feel a wash of disorientation. Seeing my dreams, my nightmares, my memories, crafted into something so definite – so physical – always makes me feel a bit shaky. It was probably the fusion of catharsis and hate that did it. Working through my issues by putting them onto the page, only to shoot them through with a strong dose of anger and resentment. When I'd first seen the finished book out in the wild – in a Waitrose in Upminster – I'd sat down on the floor and started to cry. It caused a bit of a stir; the store supervisors were unsure what to do with the sobbing woman by the small books bay. I'd heard an announcement amidst the fuss about 'cleanup needed in aisle four' and wondered if they were referring to me. Did I need to be cleaned up, like a smashed bottle of merlot? Swept into a dustpan and sent out with the rubbish? It had taken me a while to get myself together and be helped slowly to the in-store café for a complimentary hot chocolate. I'm still not sure if they believed my sobs of 'it's my book . . . my book', or if they just thought I was insane.

I turn my head to Dad now, who is waiting for an answer to his question. I knew he'd ask it, and I had my line prepared, but it still takes me a few moments to get the words in order. 'It was an act of self-therapy.'

Amanda lets out a harsh laugh of disbelief. 'Oh come off it,' she says.

Dad lays a hand gently on her knee, and she closes her mouth, biting back whatever else she was about to say.

'It was,' I say firmly. 'It was necessary.'

Dad puts his head in his hands. I hadn't expected him to get emotional this early on, but here it is, happening.

'Katherine . . . I don't know how you expected us to react to this . . . this . . . to what you've done. But you must surely understand that we're hurt. And angry.'

I shrug. 'Well, what's new about that?'

Amanda shakes her head and half smirks, half grimaces. She's always hated me. Even when she was nice to me, when we were first introduced at the cottage all those many years ago, I'm sure she was just pretending. And over the years, all need for pretence has gone. I think it was at my mother's funeral twenty years ago when it all came to a head – when our loathing for each other crystallised into an intensity so combustible, it couldn't be contained any longer. We'd been by the graveside, watching them lower the coffin in. I didn't have a clue why we were burying her rather than cremating her. Dad probably had some bonkers rationale for it – I never asked.

It was my fault that the fight had erupted. I couldn't help myself. As we all turned to walk away, the cold December air torturing our skin, I'd said to them both, 'Well, at least you got what you wanted.' Even now I'm older and wiser, the memory of Amanda's fury still startles me. It was the very definition of the word 'incensed'. I haven't seen anything quite like it, before or since. Not even at their wedding, years later – the last time I saw her. I'd made up my mind not to go, then got slightly drunk the night before, staggered onto an early-morning train the next day without bothering to get changed into anything nice, turned up at the chilly old church in Putney just as the last guests were sitting down, and sat in the front row ('Budge up! Thanks!'). I had proceeded to enthusiastically eat a large sharing bag of Galaxy Counters, rustling the packaging the whole way through the vows, meeting the mortified looks from Dad and Amanda with a blank face.

Dad returns now to his straight-backed position, his hands clasped together in his lap. 'You mentioned in an *Evening Standard* magazine article that the book was the story of your own childhood. That the *inspiration* for it is autobiographical.' He says 'inspiration' like it's a dirty word.

'Well, that's true. It is.'

He raises a fist, slams it down on his lap and winces. It must have hurt. But the look of pain is mingled with something else – pure fury. He's struggling to hold it in. 'It's a lie, Katherine. A lie.'

I don't say anything. I have a feeling it's best to let his anger burn out.

'A wicked, *nasty* lie,' says Amanda.

'I just don't know what prompted you to do such a thing,' Dad continues. 'I mean, there are things in here that are . . . well . . . abhorrent.'

'Things I *saw*,' I hiss at him. 'Things I saw and never forgot. Things a child should never have to see.'

'Well whose fault is that?' says Amanda, bitterly. 'I have

to say, some of this garbage was rather enlightening. What a poisonous little busybody you were as a child. According to your own words, you disobeyed our instructions to stay away. Do you think we *wanted* you to see what you . . . claim to have seen? Don't you think we took measures and precautions to avoid unnecessary exposure to anything too disturbing?'

This makes something snap inside me. 'Well it didn't fucking work, did it?' I'm borderline shouting, heat rising in my cheeks. 'No one took any care of me. Nobody bothered to explain what was happening. It was only natural to be curious about what was going on. Your "measures" and "precautions" amounted to banishing me to my room or telling me to roam an unknown, sprawling forest on my own for hours on end.'

She waves her hand as if I'm talking nonsense. 'It was a different time,' she says, rolling her eyes in exasperation, like she's dealing with an insufferably stupid child. 'Back then kids went off to play and just came back for tea. It was simple, it was normal, it was just what kids did.'

I gape at her. 'Around neighbourhoods they *knew*. Not in a strange, intimidating forest. I think you'd have to go back to caveman times to find a community who'd think that was acceptable.'

Dad's got his face in his hands again. 'Kitty, please—'

'And can you stop calling me that. I've told you before. I'm not a child any more.'

He ignores this and carries on. 'We did what we thought was best for your mother. She was unwell. She needed help.'

I lean forward now, keen for him not to miss a single word. 'She needed proper *psychiatric* help. Not amateurs playing dress up, hosting fake, dangerous "exorcisms".'

Amanda stands up suddenly at this and goes over to the window. The late-afternoon light is fading now into that grey dusk November usually brings at around 4.30. I can see the glistening dance of lights along the Thames, and the impressive, domineering presence of Battersea Power Station on the other side of the river.

'We *were* psychologists,' Amanda said. 'The whole thing would have formed an integral basis of our thesis if . . . if things hadn't got out of control.'

'Out of control?' I look at her in consternation, although she's still got her back to me. 'It was unethical. Abusive. Criminal.'

She whips around now to face me. 'Criminal? Are you *sure* you want to go down that road? You'd know all about criminal, wouldn't you? And we helped you, we supported you, we stood by you to make sure the truth wouldn't ever come out. We had you and your mother's best interests at heart.'

'You and that buffoon you worked with allowed *him*,' I point at my father, who is avoiding my gaze, 'to rape her while she was tied to a chair in a state of psychosis.'

I see the tears falling down Dad's face now. 'It wasn't like . . . it wasn't like how you wrote it.'

'*Nothing* in that book happened how she wrote it!' Amanda shouts.

'She was tied to a chair and you . . . you . . .' I struggle to finish the sentence.

Dad wipes away his tears and sighs. 'She wanted to have sex. She'd been trying to get me to do it for days and Dennis – Father Tobias – he seemed to think going along with it might help. She was never *tied* to a chair. She could have got up at any time she pleased, but she didn't, did she? She loved it. Laughing all the way through. But I really am sorry you had to witness it, Katherine. If we'd known, it would have explained so much of what happened.'

'You had a chance to do things *properly*. You weren't stupid. You knew you could have sought help through legitimate means.'

'Do you know what her GP said to us when we tried to get her help? He said he thought that her work at the local travel agents' three times a week had sent her into a permanent state of stress, typical of career women who tried to juggle families and jobs, and that she should probably just stay at home. He blamed the rise of feminism for the alleged increasing rates of women having break-downs and he said the female mind just couldn't cope with it. Then he gave her some pills which she flatly refused to take and that was that.'

I have my hands balled into fists listening to this. 'You could have pursued other avenues of help. You could have stood your ground, demanded she be seen by psychiatrists.'

'And have her hauled up in some institution, crawling up the walls. I've seen those places. I saw when I was just nineteen what they did to my mother. I wasn't going to do that to Marjory.'

I let out a sharp laugh. 'But it did happen to her, didn't

it? All of it. Just later, once you two had fucked her up more than she was already. I remember what it was like after we got back home. She started to forget who we were. She'd withdrawn so far within herself after what you'd done, she forgot her own world, her own existence.'

As I say this, I have a vivid flashback to the final day at home before Dad sought proper psychiatric intervention. It was probably just over a year, maybe two, since our time in the forest. I'd come home from school to find the windows of the lounge smashed, dripping with blood from where she'd crawled out of them. The police had found her near the Dartford Crossing, hammering on car bonnets, trying to climb up to shout at the terrified passengers within. That was when Dad gave in. He'd collapsed on the floor by the stairs and sobbed. And so began my mum's stint on psychiatric wards, only to be sent home some years later, not better, not cured. Just with suicide in mind.

'I was just trying to care for her,' Dad says to me now. 'I just wanted to do what was best.'

'And were you caring for her and thinking of her best interests when you went off shagging other women?'

He shifted in his seat, his mouth clenched. 'There weren't other *women*.'

'Just *her* then?' I don't bother diluting the nastiness in my voice, the hatred that's starting to rise to the surface.

I see Dad glance over at Amanda, who is still looking out of the window with her arms folded.

'Amanda came to me at a time in my life when I didn't know if I could carry on. She offered me tenderness and comfort. She understood that I loved your mother, but over time she and I found our own love too.'

'She *used you*. That's all she was doing. Used you to get near her . . . her specimen. Her case study.'

Amanda whips around. 'If that were true, if all those vile lies were true, why would I still be here now? Why would I have stuck through everything with your family – all your dramatics when you were young, every disaster that's come our way? I've stayed and I've been grateful to be married to a man as kind and understanding as your father.'

'Maybe,' I say, anger shaking my voice, 'it was always your plan to send her off to some asylum once you'd had your fun and games, and claim her husband as your prize.'

Amanda gapes at me, her face pure, white-hot fury.

I get up before she can speak again, feeling a sudden need to leave. Back out on the street away from both of them. 'I can't do this,' I mutter, gathering up my bag from where I'd dropped it on the carpet.

'Not so fast,' Amanda says. 'We haven't even got started on the real reason we agreed to meet. What we *actually* need to talk about here.'

I stand still where I am, half turned, ready to walk out the room. I know what she means.

'You painted *us* as murderers, Katherine.' Dad says it quietly, sadly, a galaxy of pain threaded through the words. 'And you've been telling everyone that it's true.'

I can feel my tears starting now. 'I haven't. I've made it clear the book is first and foremost fiction. And nobody knows who you all are, anyway. We have different surnames now. We don't live together. And it's not like you have high and mighty reputations that can be damaged as a result of it.'

'It matters to us,' Dad says. 'Just . . . tell us why?'

I sniff loudly, trying to find a tissue in my pocket. 'It felt . . . just.'

'Just?' Amanda's face has gone white, her eyes wide. 'It's the opposite of just. After everything we did for you. Making sure you could live a normal life; paying for your education away from the whole mess you created; making sure nobody ever found out the truth of what happened out there; protecting you from every difficult question—'

'I saw the look on your face that day,' I cut in. 'I knew you were planning something. I knew you were going to do something to her.'

'You spiteful, hypocritical little bitch,' Amanda hisses at me.

Dad gets up and stands in front of Amanda, as if she might run at me. 'Enough.' He looks at me, hard and unblinking, his eyes still wet with tears. 'Katherine, we beg you: do another interview with some magazine, or post something online saying you made the *whole thing* up. It will be better for everyone. I don't think you realise the danger you're in. People might make the connection between what you wrote and . . .'

He doesn't finish, but he doesn't need to. 'The ending I wrote,' I say, trying to keep my voice slow and calm, 'is representative of what you put me through. I know it isn't entirely accurate. But it gets across the magnitude of the experience. And,' I wrestle with how to say this, but there's

288

no good way to put it, 'it worked better. Narratively speaking. It felt like a good climax to the story.'

'A good climax?' Amanda shrieks. 'Is that what you call it? It's nothing but vicious *lies.* Lies from a girl who's never got over her own mother's suicide and can never forgive herself she wasn't there to save her.'

'How could I have been?' I shout at her, crying properly now. 'When you'd packed me off to that awful school, barely able to speak, barely able to comprehend everything that had happened during those weeks!'

It's too much. I've had it. I can't handle any more. I pull my bag and coat close to me and walk out of the lounge and back down towards the front door, wishing I'd never come. I should have just let Dad turn up at my flat and try to hammer down the door. I could have just hidden under my duvet and pretended he didn't exist.

Back outside on the pavement, the remnants of the dissected football remain – bits of material and fluff drifting along in the cold winter wind. Somewhere out on the main road there are blue lights flashing, and as I walk towards them, I see there's police tape across the other side of the road, near a primary school. I cross over to see what's going on and a police officer walks into view. 'I'm sorry, I'm going to have to stop you – there's been an incident. Are you a resident around here? Do you need access to one of the flats?'

I shake my head. 'No, no I'm just . . . visiting someone. Have visited. I'm going home.'

She nods distractedly and walks over to someone on

the other side of the street, where the police tape continues. They're filming on their mobile phone.

I walk along the sectioned-off area, keeping slightly back, until I see what has caused all the excitement. A body is lying on the ground, with paramedics crouching round it. Another paramedic is running back to the ambulance parked nearby. The body is a girl. She has colourful red waves of hair, and a pale, young face. And there's blood. Lots of it.

I feel dizzy all of a sudden and, seeing a bench in a patch of public garden space a little walk away, I go over to sit down. It's freezing and the bench, though dry, feels like a slab of ice. I take my cigarettes out, but after a whole minute of scrabbling about in my bag, I can't find my lighter. So I just sit there, feeling the cruel wind dry the tears on my face, while more police vans and people in forensics gear arrive with briefcases and gather around the crime scene. The girl looks so young. Probably only eighteen or nineteen.

A life gone. A life wasted.

I grow so cold, sitting on that bench, that I get to the point where I no longer notice my trembling, or the numbing feeling spreading across my skin. Or the police officer coming over to speak to me.

'Hello, can I speak to you for a moment?'

I look up at her.

'We're talking to people who may have witnessed the violent incident over there,' she nodded back at the crime scene. 'Did you happen to see what happened?'

'No, sorry,' I croak. 'I came along after . . . sorry, I can't quite think about things . . . very clearly . . . right now.'

The police officer says nothing to this. But she does sit down next to me.

'Do you think I committed the murder?' I ask.

'No,' she says. 'We've arrested the person we believe to be responsible. But I'm interested as to why you're sat here watching a crime scene from a bench on a cold evening like this.'

I sigh. 'I wrote a book about my childhood and now my parents hate me. Well, parent, singular. My mum's dead.'

Whatever she was expecting me to say, it wasn't this. Even though I'm not looking at her, I see out of my peripheral vision that she's tilted her head a little.

'You're not upset because you witnessed what happened across the road?'

I shake my head. 'No. Just about me. My life. Things that happened. And things that didn't happen.'

The police officer stands up. Places to go, people to see, it seems. Can't waste too much of the taxpayer's money talking to screwed-up writers on benches. 'It's very cold. I don't think you should sit here for much longer. Does anyone live nearby that I can call for you?'

I'm tempted to laugh at this, but manage to contain myself. Nothing about this is very funny, anyway.

'I'll be fine. I'm going home now.' I get up off the bench and make a show of zipping up my coat properly and checking I've got my bag and scarf.

'Well, so long as you're OK,' the cop says, then she starts walking away back towards the crime scene.

I take one more look at the activity on the corner of the street. Then I walk away, back through the estate towards Lupus Street and up through Pimlico towards Victoria Station. I just need to get home. Rest. Sleep. Forget.

Just as I'm about to cross the road to the entrance of the London Underground, my phone sounds with a text. It's from Dad. I glance at the lock-screen preview of the message.

Because you stormed off I didn't get a chance to tell you that . . .

I open up the home screen and tap on the message in full. I read every word. And then I'm sick all over the street, right outside the entrance to the musical *Wicked*, groups of people waiting for ticket returns dodging round me, looks of repulsion on their faces. If only they knew what I'd done. They'd understand my reaction then. In fact, they'd probably be surprised I hadn't thrown myself under a bus on my way up Wilton Road.

Stumbling over to the boarded-up entrance of a closed-down Argos, I huddle in the doorway and read the message again. Every single word is like a knife to my heart.

Because you stormed off I didn't get a chance to tell you that Adah's aunt has been in touch. I don't know how she tracked us down, but she sent me a letter. She's read your book. She wants to talk to you. She says her number is 0722124475. She lives in Glasgow now. Please get in touch with her. Try to explain why you did this – for her sake, even if you can't for us.

Chapter 36

Three days pass. I barely leave my flat – a tiny little place near Dagenham Heathway tube station. I just manage one trip to the little independent off-licence at the corner of my road, its harsh fluorescent light causing my head to pound. Ever since I read Dad's text, things have been getting gradually worse. It's like I'm properly unwell. My temperature has been up and down and I've developed a strange, scratchy cough. I know this is a response to my mental state rather than a virus, but I still choose to stay inside and burrow under my duvet, like an animal in hibernation.

Leading up to the publication of my book, my colleagues at the local newspaper were saying to me things like 'You must be on top of the world' and 'Are you still pinching yourself this is happening?' or even 'You can get the office treats next time, now that you're a rich author'. That one did make me laugh, though not in the way they'd intended. I'd used the relatively small advance I'd got to pay off some credit card debts and invest in a new hoover and tumble dryer, rather than yachts and Ferraris. I'd taken a couple of weeks' holiday around publication, and one of the girls thought I must be going on a celebratory cruise or something; or maybe doing 'press junkets'. The *Evening Standard* magazine interview Dad had referred to was the only bit of major press I'd done, leaving aside a few blog interviews my publicist had put together. But it had led to a boost in sales, my publishers reported, and they'd asked if I'd like to speak to another journalist, this time from the *Daily Mail*, sometime soon.

The ping of my phone pulls me out of the daydream I'd been having, wrapped in my duvet on the sofa in front of a 1970s Hammer horror film called *The Satanic Rites of Dracula*.

It's Dad.

Can you let me know you've got my previous message and you're ok. We're still very upset, but wanted to check. I imagine it was a bit of a shock when you read the message. I do love you. But this is all very difficult. Love, Dad.

A bit of a shock. That's one way of putting it, I think, as I pause the screen on a particularly over-the-top vampire snarl from Christopher Lee. I read his message through a couple of times, type 'I'm fine' and send, then scroll back and reread his previous one. I haven't done as he asked. I haven't phoned her. I've been putting it off, even though part of me knows that I shouldn't. I'm putting off the inevitable. Over these past few days, I've been scared of hearing a knock on the door, imagining an elderly woman standing outside ready to batter me to death with a copy of my own book. Or worse, just standing there and crying.

I could just go to ground, I think. Never get in touch. Ignore her calls. Take out a restraining order if she tries to pester me. The truth is, I never imagined in a million years she'd find out. Of all the thousands of books published each year, how did she manage, by sheer coincidence, to pick up this one and make the connection?

I stare at Dad's message for a few minutes more, my feelings of guilt and anxiety building to a nauseating crescendo within me. I bite the bullet and dial the number he's given me.

The call connects the moment it starts ringing at the other end. It's as if she's been sitting there, poised, phone in hand, waiting for my call.

'Hello?'

Her voice is deep and disconcertingly soft. I pause, the words catching in my throat.

'Hello?' she says again.

'Hi, er . . .' I swallow hard, trying to get myself together, 'Is that . . . is that Ms Okafor? Andrea Okafor?'

'Speaking,' comes the firm, slightly guarded reply. Maybe she thinks this is going to be a sales call and I'm about to launch into a monologue about why double glazing really is the only way to go.

'I . . . this is . . . my name's Katherine. Katherine

Marchland. I realise we've never met, but, but you may have heard of me as . . .'

'Kitty Carlson.' She says the name without any trace of emotion. 'Yes. I remember the police mentioning your name years ago. Back then. I was hoping you would call.'

I feel myself growing hot. Blood is rushing to my face. I put my fingers to my lips to take a drag on a cigarette I'm not holding – a tic I have when I'm stressed.

'I understand . . . my father – he said you'd been in touch.'

A few beats of silence pass. Then, 'I think it's better if we meet in person.'

This is a sentence I've been dreading, but I think I knew it would come. What do I do now? Evade? Refuse? Hang up?

'Of course,' I find myself saying. 'When would be best for you?'

I try to keep my voice steady, make it sound like a business meeting, but I can't help stammering a little on the 'w' sounds. I wish she wasn't being so damn calm. It would be better if she shouted. Screamed at me. Told me exactly what she thinks of me. At least then we wouldn't have this strange politeness hovering between us, both choosing words very carefully.

'The day after tomorrow would be fine. Saturday. I trust you'll be able to get to Glasgow by then.'

This stumps me. Rather stupidly, I had imagined meeting her here in London – perhaps on the South Bank in one of the restaurants. Somewhere public. How preposterous that seems now when I think about it.

'Of course,' I say, eventually. 'Of course I'll come to you.'

She doesn't say thank you. She just tells me to grab a pen and copy down an address in Dennistoun. I do as I'm told and then ask what time.

'Come to mine at four o'clock.' The line goes dead.

Busying myself quickly so as not to immediately start brooding on the conversation, I grab my laptop from the coffee table and immediately go onto Google. I find a flight to Glasgow International from London Gatwick on Saturday morning, with a return in the evening of the same day. I pay the £140 with my debit card and then sink back into my duvet, willing my mind to close down so I can sleep peacefully, saving my worries about the upcoming meeting for the whole free day stretching out before me tomorrow.

Chapter 37

The flight to Glasgow, though short, is hellish. It is pouring with rain when I wake that morning, and by the time I've got to Gatwick on the train the temperature has dropped and the rain has turned to fast-falling sleet, landing on nearly-frozen ground. While I am having a McDonald's breakfast, the sleet turns to snow, carpeting the ground outside the airport. I sit there next to the floor-to-ceiling windows, watching it fall, waiting for them to cancel my flight, but they don't. I'm not an overly nervous flyer, but I have become used to all modes of transport grinding to a halt if the word 'snow' is even mentioned, so I am a bit concerned nobody seems to be sounding alarms and evacuating the airport. As I trudge up the steps to the aircraft,

I feel like tapping someone on the shoulder and asking if they've noticed the weather and if there has been some sort of mistake.

On the plane, I'm seated next to a teenage boy who looks like he's just walked out of one of those American high school movies where they have jocks and prom queens. He appears to be on his own and takes one look in my direction, as if identifying me as 'non-threatening', before burying his head in a book entitled *The Rise of Domestic Terrorism*. What a thing to bring on a flight, I think, as I familiarise myself with the safety procedure leaflet.

I'm starving again once we touch down at Glasgow International, so I go through baggage collection and immediately locate an Upper Crust, buying a baguette so large you could probably use it as a weapon. I stare at my phone. It's 11.30 a.m. – four and a half hours to go. I've never been to Glasgow before, but I'm not in the right frame of mind to seek out the tourist landmarks. Instead, I pass the time by drifting around the city, looking in shops, buying a phone case I don't need from a street seller, then finally taking refuge in a pub with a bowl of chips and the sound of some sporting game nobody seems interested in emanating from the TVs on the wall.

At 3.20 I get in a taxi, which makes its way slowly through a new downfall of snow to Dennistoun. Some of the buildings I pass look like they could have been ripped out of the London council estates I'm so familiar with, but the street the taxi turns into – my final destination – looks more upmarket and affluent. I pay the driver and, unsure of how I'm going to make my way back to the airport in all this snow, watch him disappear off, driving carefully into the ever-thickening winter wonderland that stretches out before me.

3.55. Does it matter I'm early, I think as I stuff my hands into my coat for warmth? I should have brought gloves. But before I have much time to think about it, the door opens and a woman stands there, looking at me. She must be in her mid-sixties. Her short hair is still so deep-black I realise she must be wearing a wig. The lines on her face tell a different story. All she says is 'come in', so I do, dusting off the snow on the doormat.

The house isn't huge, but it's very tidy and clean, and although one wouldn't describe it as a home for the ultra-wealthy, there is a gentle note of money about the cream-coloured hallway and chic lounge design. I feel the same sense of surprise I had when I first heard her voice. None of this was how I had imagined it. 'Sit,' she says, when I reach the sofa, and she perches herself opposite me. 'Would you like anything to drink?' she asks, although now she's settled it seems bad to ask her to get up and make me something. Maybe that was on purpose, similar to the chilly welcome I'd been given by my own father earlier in the week. She probably doesn't want me feeling too comfortable.

'Terrible weather,' I say, a little brighter than I'd planned.

She lowers her head slightly and looks at me impassively. After a few seconds of painful silence, she gets up and walks to the bookshelf on the far side of the lounge and takes one, separate from the others, off the middle shelf. After sitting back down, her eyes focus on me. She pulls out a small pair of reading glasses from an invisible pocket, opens the book to a page number she's apparently memorised and reads aloud.

'My aunt can be so mean. Sometimes she throws bottles at my head. Glass ones. They never hit me, of course. She's too drunk to be able to aim properly. But once one smashed just above my head and one of the pieces cut me quite badly.'

I wince. She looks up from the page, staring at me over the rim of her glasses. She pauses, perhaps to see what reaction this extract might provoke in me, then speaks slowly and firmly. 'You painted me as an abusive drunkard.'

I can't hold her gaze for very long. I start fiddling with the zip of my coat. 'It's fiction,' I say in a small voice. 'I made it all up.'

She closes the book carefully. 'No you didn't. That's the problem. You fictionalised the truth. You took an incident that happened; an incident that has reverberated throughout the lives of the people involved – in some ways *ruined* the lives of the people involved – and you manipulated it.' She's still talking in her calm, firm voice. It reminds me of a newsreader on Radio 4 – traditionally middle-class English; educated, one might say, although of course such a description is unfair to the many people with an education who have retained a regional accent.

While I'm thinking about this, she reopens the book, straightens her glasses and begins reading aloud another passage: 'I'm a waste of space. I ran away once to a big city. She didn't come to look for me. I stayed away for a night. I slept in a disabled toilet in the park.' She glances up at me, then continues. 'I did wonder if the police would come looking for me, but nobody seemed to care. The next morning I felt too cold, so I went home. My aunt was in the lounge watching TV and just said "Christ, I thought I was fucking shot of you."'

She closes the book again. 'Adah did run away once. She was too much of a free spirit at times. But I *never* spoke to her like that. I *always* went looking for her. So tell me: did she actually say those things to you? Or is this part of your breathtaking use of creative licence?'

I shake my head, trying not to cry. 'It's . . . it's not actually Adah. I just . . . made her up.'

'Then why did you use her *name*?'

The last word is emphasised in a way that makes it crash down upon me. She's right. I didn't have to use her name. 'There were probably a thousand occasions when I was going to change it,' I say croakily, clearing my throat. 'I deliberated over it for a long time. But for some reason I couldn't bear the thought of calling her something else. It felt like a final insult – to strip her of her identity.'

She straightens up, and I see her fingers tense around the book, holding it tightly in her lap. 'She was stripped of her identity when she died. She no longer has an identity. The one thing I promised my sister when she herself passed away was that I would take care of her daughter. I was a mother to her. I did everything I could. Yes, I probably shouldn't have let her roam the forest alone. It was a bit different back then. But don't think a moment goes by when I don't feel guilty about her death. It's with me every second of every day.'

I hang my head. There's nothing I can say to that.

'And on the subject of her death . . .'

This is what I've been waiting for. I watch as she opens the book again, turning to the back pages. Then she stops and closes it, moving her hand to her eye to catch a tear that's rolled down. When she speaks, she's quieter, as if the words are causing her physical pain.

'If you needed to write it all down – put it all into a story in order to help you make sense of what happened – why did you have to have her die in such a strange . . . such a bizarre . . . It's horrible. *Horrible*. To make her out to be some sort of human sacrifice. A sick little detail in a warped exorcism your parents were a part of. I don't know what sort of thing you witnessed when living there, and if this book is anything to go by it was certainly far from normal, but to drag Adah's memory into something so horrific? And to do *that* to your family? I don't know how they'll ever forgive you.'

I'm crying now. I feel a tear escape from the corner of my eye and drop with a tap onto my coat sleeve. 'I'm not sure they ever will,' I say, in not much more than a whisper. 'But it's not all lies. They were doing . . . trying to do . . . an exorcism. On my mother. They didn't really believe in God, Hell, the devil – or at least I don't think they did. They thought it would have . . . I don't know . . . some sort of placebo effect on her. And it did, for a time.'

'Before she killed herself,' Andrea says.

So she knows about that. I briefly wonder how, but I'm in a hurry to get across my strong opinions of my father and stepmother. 'I do hold them responsible. I know Amanda and the man I knew as Father Tobias had backgrounds in psychology, but they weren't experts or operating ethically. She was a woman my dad was having an affair with – infatuated with – and she used him to be part of some messed-up project she wanted to try out. She probably thought she'd be able to write a thesis on it or something. What they did to my mother – the rituals . . . the ceremonies. It's no wonder she never got properly better.'

Andrea now has a tissue in her hand and has taken her glasses off to dab at her eyes. 'Your father is still with Amanda, I understand,' she says. 'She was how I found out about the book. She sent it to me. It took her a while to find me, apparently, but after a little bit of Google-assisted detective work, she did it.'

I have to stop myself exclaiming out loud. How could she have done this? Stirring and manipulating and working against me, even now, even after she's got everything she wanted; she still can't resist playing God behind the scenes. Andrea notices me tensing and continues.

'She seemed to think we could maybe form some kind of collaborative force against you, with a view to consulting lawyers.'

This makes me even more enraged. With a trembling hand I wipe my eyes, then scrabble in my pocket for a crumpled pack of Kleenex. 'She is nothing but a murderer,' I say through clenched teeth.

Andrea fixes me with her stern, steely gaze. 'No, she isn't. She didn't murder my niece, like you allege. She didn't murder your mother, although I can understand why you hold her responsible.' My skin prickles, like a current of electricity is running through it. I stare back into her eyes as she continues. 'But the truth remains that, if there is a murderer amidst this whole sordid mess, that person would have to be you. Because Adah never did come out of the water that day. As you well know.'

Chapter 38

I hold a cup of hot tea in my hand, feeling its warmth spreading through me. Andrea's house isn't cold, but I don't seem to have fully thawed since coming in from the snow. She got me the tea when I broke down in tears after what she'd said. She just rose up and went to put the kettle on while I sat there, uncomforted, worrying about what was coming.

'So,' she says, setting her own mug of tea down on the coffee table. 'I think you'll agree you owe me an explanation. I want to know the truth. The *actual* truth. I'm going to ask you some questions, and I want you to answer them properly, without thinking about how you can embellish them or remove your own culpability.'

I nod. It's all I can do.

She takes a few moments to compose herself, dabbing again at her eyes with her tissue. Then she says: 'Were you present when Adah drowned?'

I don't wait. I don't think about it. I just answer, like she's requested. 'Yes.'

I see a few more tears slip from her eyes. 'Did you watch her drown?'

I continue to stare at her, ignoring my tears forming. 'Yes.'

Andrea lets out a strange sound, halfway between a cough and a sob, as if some energy, some pent-up emotion, is making a bid for escape. It alarms me, this insight into the distress that must be bubbling beneath her otherwise calm exterior.

'Could you have saved her? Like you did in the book?'

I think of the branch on the bridge. How I'd imagined running to get it. How I thought about it at the time. How I did nothing, except stand there and watch the life leave her body. And how now, years later, I've written myself out of her death, absolved myself of the biggest sin in my life.

'I think I could have, yes.'

Andrea doesn't speak for a full minute after I say this. Then she says, 'Why did you have your dad and Amanda kill her? In the book?'

This I have an answer for, and it's one I feel no remorse in giving. 'Because they deserved it,' I say, harshly.

She doesn't move when I say the words, but I see her eyes widen ever so slightly. Then the tension goes out of her face, and she picks up her mug of tea off the coffee table. 'Maybe they do,' she says, quietly. She takes a long sip of her tea, swallows and then surveys me, as if trying to work out how to phrase her next question. 'So you do admit that you lied to the police when they asked you about Adah all those years ago?'

I shuffle uncomfortably. 'Not exactly. Well, by omission I suppose. I said I hadn't seen her for a while, and we'd played together in the woods. I even said I'd warned her not to go near the stream. But I did tell Dad and everyone that I hadn't seen her that day. So yes. That was a lie.'

Andrea takes in a deep breath and sighs. She gets up, stretches her shoulders and neck a little, and goes to put the book back on the shelf. After taking a moment to straighten an ugly and oddly out-of-place plastic figurine of an owl on one of the higher shelves, she turns back to me. 'They didn't believe her death was suspicious. They found that her shoe had hooked on to a large piece of fallen tree submerged in the water. She struggled to free herself and took in a long gasp of water and . . . never came out. Depressingly common with children. Happy one minute, the next in mortal peril.'

I nod, vaguely, but something she's said has caught my attention. 'So,' I say, 'if I had . . . if I had tried to help her . . . if I'd lowered a branch in to help her out . . . she still may not have survived.'

Andrea looks up at me quickly, and I see something flash in her eyes – anger, resentment, grief? – but it's gone in a second. Then she says, with a horrible air of finality: 'Well, I guess we'll never know, will we?'

I don't respond. I'm not sure she expects me to. After a minute or two of sitting in silence together, she stands up and stretches out a hand for my mug. I give it over, only half drunk, and I think I'm being dismissed, but then she speaks, making me fall still. 'Follow me into the kitchen,' she says, 'I've got something I want you to see.'

I look around, slightly panicked, wondering what she's got in store for me. She walks ahead and I follow, taking in the very modern-looking oven and stove. 'This is a nice place,' I say, then regret it, thinking it sounds oddly insensitive and out of place. Andrea shrugs. 'You get more for your money up here.'

'What is it you do?' I ask, realising I don't know.

'I'm an accountant.' She doesn't say it with much emotion, but the lack of elaboration shuts down the chance of any further questions. With an almost seamless movement, she takes something out of a drawer and drops it onto the kitchen table. It's a copy of the *London Evening Standard* magazine. I stare at it, and then turn to see her looking at me. 'There's an interview you gave in there.'

I nod, slowly. 'I know. I didn't realise you'd get that . . . in Glasgow.'

An irritated look flickers across her face. 'I was sent it. By your stepmother.'

I wince at the term. 'She isn't my stepmother. I don't think of her as that.'

'It was in her little parcel,' Andrea continues, ignoring my interruption. 'You talk about the book just coming to you like a strange dream, woven into moments of your childhood.'

'Yes,' I say, looking at the front cover of the magazine. It's filled with a well-known model and Instagrammer, one hand lifting up his white t-shirt as if to scratch an imaginary itch on his perfectly toned torso. He has his mouth open, laughing down the lens of the camera, a wave of blond hair flopping untidily over his forehead. The insincerity of the image here, in this strange world of grief and lies, is almost too much to bear. I turn away from the magazine and say to Andrea, 'I didn't say anything untruthful in that interview. Not really.'

'You did. By omission. As seems to be your trademark.' Her eyes are sharp on me now, and I can tell she's building to something. She folds her arms, takes a breath, and then says, 'Here's what I want you to do. I want you to write a small piece and post it on Facebook, or whatever platform you like. I've seen your Facebook page, and I'm sure that would do nicely. I'm not sure many people will care, or even see it, but that's not the point. I just want you to explain everything properly and publicly. I want you to tell the truth. The whole truth. The true story behind your book; how you came to write it. No evasion, no innuendo, no sly way of phrasing it. You paint yourself in that book as an innocent victim. You owe it to Adah to tell the world that you're not innocent. I suffered my share of hatred. The neglectful guardian, letting her child roam the forest. But it was you that did something truly terrible, no matter how young you were. And it's your turn to let it out into the open. Explain why you let her die.'

I raise a trembling hand to my face again. 'I don't know

why I did it. Really, truly, I don't. That whole autumn . . . it was like I was in a strange other world. It was all so long ago now.'

Andrea's lips grow thin and she lifts her chin up, defiant. 'Not to me. To me, it's like it was yesterday. And *this*,' she points at the magazine, 'along with that book, have made it more present than ever. You decided to send this out into the wild. Now it's your job to own it properly for what it is. A confession.'

I stay completely still, watching her. She shows no sign of softening; changing her mind; reaching some kind of compromise. I suppose, in a way, this *is* her form of compromise.

'Do you have any more interviews coming up?' she asks.

I nod. 'One with *The Mail on Sunday*'s *You* magazine this coming week.'

'Well, think about it,' she says calmly. Then she starts to walk out of the kitchen and out into the hallway. I take it I'm supposed to follow her. 'But I should mention: if you don't, things might get a bit trickier for you.'

She's got her back to me, so I can't see her face, but I notice a strange change in her voice. It sounds slightly higher, as if she's a little unsure of what she's saying. Or unsure if she wants to say it.

'What do you mean?' I ask.

We're at the front door now, and she turns back to face me. 'A kind young police officer who was a great help to me back when all this happened recently got a promotion. He's a superintendent now. And do you know, I think

311

he might just remember me. If I were to get in touch, that is.'

'I . . . you mean . . .' I stammered, feeling panic grip me.

'Just . . . do the right thing, Katherine, and all will be fine. Or as fine as it can be.'

With that, she opens the door and a huge gust of wind and snow swirls among us. She gives me a little nudge towards the open doorway. 'Go on, I don't want to let the cold in. Thank you for coming all this way.'

I step outside, the bitter cold cloaking my body with alarming immediacy. I'm about to turn around and say something to her, though I'm not sure what, but the door closes in my face. It stuns me for a second or two, then I regain my senses, knowing I need to get out of this horrendous weather. I take out my phone and book a car on my Uber app, then spend the ten-minute wait walking up and down the street in an effort to keep warm, my shoes upturning some of the virgin snow covering the pavement.

When the car arrives, the driver asks me if I really want to go to the airport in this weather. He seems doubtful about whether the planes will be taking off. I tell him I'll risk it, and he shrugs in a 'rather you than me' sort of way.

The journey is excruciatingly slow, although I still have a few hours before my flight is supposed to leave, and according to the airline's website it's still on schedule. I go through security in a sort of daze, not properly focusing on anyone or anything, just dumping my bag and phone into the trays and walking through the body scanners. I almost don't hear the airport guy telling me to take my belt off when the machine bleeps at me.

Waiting for the flight becomes more and more torturous. They've cancelled a few and are delaying others. Mine gets pushed back an hour, then an hour and a half; then finally we get called for boarding. By some miracle, the flight leaves Glasgow and its snow-strewn landscape behind, and I spend the short flight replaying Andrea's words in my head. *Now it's your job to own it properly for what it is. A confession.* But this wasn't ever meant to be a confession. This was to punish, not to absolve – to prove to Dad and Amanda that their messed-up little experiment had lasting consequences they can't escape from. And they'll never escape from them now.

Back in London, I get home and collapse onto my bed without properly undressing. I think I sleep for a few hours, but I wake up in the night strangely hot, and I go over to the open window. There was snow on the streets when I landed. Now, thick flakes are falling fast, and instead of feeling bitter and biting like it did in Glasgow, the wind here is soft and almost non-existent. The snow floats to the ground at a leisurely pace, and the Christmas lights adorning the outsides of the shops below give the whole place a wonderfully tranquil, festive feel. I feel myself calming down a little, although with this calm comes the ability to think clearly. And with that comes anger. How dare Andrea lecture me; tell me what I can and can't do; offer empty threats while throwing me out of her house?

All of it is just words. She doesn't own me or my writing, or have any say in what I tell the press. I paid her the courtesy of visiting. And now I need to carry on with what I'm doing.

Chapter 39

I don't go to work that week, even though my annual leave has come to an end. I ignore the calls from my boss and continue to sit on my couch, rising only for the bathroom, to put a new disc in my DVD player or to open the door for Dominos deliveries. I don't leave the house. I don't speak to anyone. And I don't use my social media accounts.

The interview with *The Mail on Sunday* was supposed to be over the phone, which would have suited me much better, but my publicist emails to say the journalist is now happy to do it face to face and wonders if I'd like to go for a coffee. I consider refusing, or even asking her to cancel the whole interview, but when I stand up to stretch and see the mess of my flat laid out starkly in the morning light, I know something needs to change. I can't stay in here for ever. And a trip into central London, with the chance to play the author role I was just getting used to before visiting my parents, has an appeal I can't quite shake. I can do this, I tell myself as I shower and dress, slowly and methodically. I'm OK. I'm not crying, or shivering, or doubting. I'm in control. I tell myself this over and over to the point where I very nearly believe it.

I end up meeting the journalist in a Costa in Liverpool Street. I'd imagined somewhere a bit posher, but apparently lunch at The Wolseley isn't on offer. She looks shockingly young, probably about twenty-four or twenty-five – blonde, beautiful, with flawless make-up and an overly posh accent.

'Hi, I'm Sara, it's lovely to meet you. Can I get you anything?'

After fetching me a flat white and herself an Americano, she starts talking animatedly about the book; how she *loved* it ('so strange, so *other*'). She asks the same sorts of questions that I've been asked before – how did I get into writing; how does juggling my full-time job in local advertising work amidst all this; and then, of course, the killer question: 'So tell me, what was your main inspiration for the book? You've mentioned before in another interview I read that it was partly inspired by a strange experience that happened in your childhood, and I was wondering if we could explore that a little more fully?'

I blow on my coffee, buying time. A thousand thoughts

are flashing through my head, and I'm finding it hard to stop the room from spinning. And in the midst of all the panic – in the midst of all the swirling glimpses of forest trees and screeching owls and freshly baked tarts – I hear a voice. A strangled cry; gurgling; a mouth filled with water shouting one word. 'Help.'

'Katherine?'

The sound of the running water is getting louder: starting as a trickle, growing to a roar; as if I'm standing under a waterfall, the gush of it beating down on my head.

'Katherine? Are you OK? Do you want to . . . I don't know . . . take five?'

I snap back to the here and now, the noise of the full coffee shop replacing the pounding of the water. Sara is looking at me with concern and a slight edge of impatience.

'No, I'm fine.'

She nods, pleased we're moving on. 'Splendid. Because there's something I'd really like to get your opinion on, if I could. I've been speaking to a source about a very interesting detail regarding your book; specifically a key scene towards the end. It's been suggested to me that, well, this book may actually serve as a confession of sorts. For something you may have done as a young girl. Would you care to respond to that?'

It's as if her words shatter the air around us. For a few, vertigo-inducing moments, I wonder if I've just imagined it. If my mind is playing tricks on me. I close my eyes, but when I open them, there she is, her face controlled and enquiring – clearly, she has done this many times before and is used to sitting out the inevitable rush of emotion it provokes in her victims.

I eventually manage to open my mouth to speak. 'Who . . . what . . . I don't understand.' But I do. She's spoken to Andrea.

She gives me a smile. 'I'm afraid I can't reveal that at the moment, Katherine. I'm sure you understand. I just wanted to get your take on the whole thing while I have you here.'

Again, I open my mouth to speak. Pause. Then I start. 'I can't properly tell you what happened. I've spent my life trying to work it out, and it's not the time to go into it now. But what I can say is this: I was an innocent child. I saw things I shouldn't have seen – that no child should ever see. And I don't take *any* responsibility for it. Please, make sure that's mentioned. I was upset, I was probably traumatised at times, and I lay the blame entirely at my father and stepmother's door. My conscience is entirely clear.'

The look on her face is hard to read, but I see her inch her iPhone closer to me, as if worried she might not catch every word. 'So . . . are you saying . . . that you may have been culpable in some way for the death of Adah Okafor? Because I've done some digging – just a sec.' She bends down and pulls from her bag an iPad in a purple leather cover. She flicks it open, taps away for a few seconds, then turns the screen towards me. It's a newspaper article. It looks like it's been scanned in from an old paper copy. The date is 1987.

I can't do this any more. I stand and push past Sara's

chair, ignoring her protestations of 'Oh wait, Katherine, please just sit down'. I vaguely notice people turn to look at me; at the commotion I'm causing.

When I reach the busy bustle of Liverpool Street station, I try not to think about what Sara will put in her article. I can't think about any of that now. I make my way to the Central line and change at Mile End, almost as if on autopilot, and when I finally come to, like rising up from under water, I'm on the District line passing through Barking, with only a few stops to go until I get off. What have I done? Did I sound hysterical? Will Sara ditch the interview and complain to my publicist about me? I have to admit to myself that this would probably be the best outcome from the whole thing. Whatever I said to her, it won't do me any favours having it printed, and it certainly wasn't what Andrea wants to hear.

With a steady flow of unease lapping against me, I alight at Dagenham Heathway and walk slowly to my flat, desperate for my duvet, a cigarette and then sleep.

My interview, in the female-focused supplement of *The Mail on Sunday*, doesn't turn up in the issue it's supposed to be placed in. I get an email from my publicist, saying they're apparently still working on it and it should appear at a later date. I try not to think about that, or about what Andrea may have said to her or written to her. Whatever she's done, I can only hope it's not enough for the journalist to go on, and that the story will fizzle out before it's even begun. Anyway, I've got another pressing concern to worry about.

'Hello Katherine, this is Moira from *work*.' The Essex-accented nasal tones of my boss sound out from my mobile's answerphone. I notice she emphasises the word 'work' just to labour the point. 'As I mentioned in my last email, you have been referred to HR for a disciplinary due to your unauthorised absence. I'll send you a copy of the details so you can look them over. If you've got any evidence of mitigating circumstances – a doctor's note or something like that – please bring it with you. As Sheila from HR is still recovering from that botched operation on her tonsils, the disciplinary will be headed up by me in my office at 9 a.m. sharp tomorrow.'

So much of this would be amusing if it wasn't so downright stressful. Moira acting like HR is a separate department is a joke in itself. HR is made up in its entirety by the inept Sheila, who herself is frequently off sick with whatever reason she can dream up that week, and who spends the rest of the time boring us silly with estate agent catalogues, showing us the homes she and her ex-convict boyfriend are planning to buy 'in *Romford*'. The word 'Romford' is always said in a hushed, reverent tone, as if she feels it's akin to moving to Kensington or Chelsea.

The idea of returning to work does nothing to raise my mood, but at least it gave my mind something to work on and gives me an excuse to move Andrea Okafor and her attempts to stir up trouble to the back of my mind.

I wake up the next morning telling myself everything is going to be OK. I get myself ready for work whilst listening to an audiobook of Joan Hickson reading some Miss Marple short stories by Agatha Christie – an author

I've managed to continue to enjoy in spite of my memories of reading *The Pale Horse*, cold and confused, amidst the trees in Barret Forest. Once dressed and showered, I sit quietly and calmly in my kitchen eating some marmalade on toast. I decide I'll tell Moira that I had an illness or a family emergency, and that I'm very sorry and it won't happen again. I'll carry on with my job selling advertising space in the local paper to brick makers, home decorators and small plumbing firms, and everything will go back to normal – at least in Moira's eyes. I'm aware this won't immediately make her leave me alone, and I'll probably have to go through a lot of lectures on how lucky I am to even be employed and how tough it is out there for 'people in our industry', but she's also aware that I'm more competent at my job (when I'm actually there doing it) than any of my colleagues. I can write better copy, draft better adverts and get better business for the paper than anyone else, and the only reason I haven't been promoted is because the next step up would be deputy editor. That position is occupied by Brian, the 26-year-old son of the company's owner, who mainly sits at his desk playing Angry Birds while Moira – who is technically his boss, though due to his family connections, she doesn't feel like she can manage him properly – glares daggers in the direction of his desk from across the office.

I make sure I arrive at the office a good twenty minutes early. I put my coat around my chair, my bag under the desk, and walk over to the only walled-off part of our working area, where Moira sits. She's there, sipping coffee from a mug that's seen better days, while clicking at her computer screen, trying to get it to unfreeze. 'Hi Moira,' I say, making a show of knocking lightly at her already-open door.

'Nice to see you here, Katherine,' she says, barely casting a glance my way. 'Is there something I can help you with?'

This throws me a little. 'Well . . . you said I was to come to your office . . .'

She cuts across me. 'Your disciplinary doesn't begin until 9 a.m. and according to my clock, it's 8.42.'

'Oh,' I say. 'Right. I'll go and sit down then.'

She doesn't reply, so I click about on my own computer for a bit, opening up my email and nearly fainting when I see the number of unread items in my inbox.

'Hey stranger, look who it is!' My always-bubbly colleague Danielle sits down next to me. It get on reasonably well with her, mostly because I allow her to talk at length about her teenage children's trouble with the law without interrupting her. Her son Erik has twice been arrested for antisocial behaviour – something which, for Danielle, is a sad reflection on police priorities within the Met, because they just can't handle the fact that 'boys will be boys' or see that her son is 'a good lad at heart'. Today, she's brought with her a large croissant and she proceeds to munch it with vigour, flakes of it falling between the keys of her computer's keyboard. 'You been off being a famous author?' she asks with her mouth full.

'Yes,' I say, not bothering to tell her that if I ever become famous, it's going to be for something far more serious and life wrecking. Part of me can't believe I'm even here, when just days ago I was sitting in that house in Glasgow,

322

my world tilting on its axis while Andrea stood over me. The ping of a new email jolts me out of my thoughts. It's from Moira with 'See me now' in the subject line, the rest blank. Why she couldn't have just called me over, I don't know. Everyone must know what's going on. I get up from my desk, and Danielle whispers a pastry-filled 'good luck' at me.

'Sit down,' Moira says, as soon as I've reached her door. She spends a few seconds finishing whatever she's typing, as if I'm only one of the many things on her to-do list today, and then she turns to me, glasses at the end of her nose. She only acquired these glasses a few months ago and has quickly worked out how to use them to promote her authority. She peers at me over the thick rims and says, 'I presume you've got some excuse?'

'Sorry?' I say.

She tuts. 'An excuse. For your unauthorised leave.' She roughly jerks her desktop screen around to me, causing the straining plastic to squeak unpleasantly. An Excel document is open, with all the team's names and their holiday dates highlighted in yellow. 'These are the days you requested for annual leave and which we generously gave you,' she trails her finger down the screen, 'and these days in red are all the times *after* your agreed leave when you just didn't materialise, nor could you be contacted.' She tosses her hands in the air a little, apparently to illustrate my blasé attitude to working life. 'I mean, I know you probably consider yourself a cut above us all here now that you're an *author*,' she does a little eye roll at this, as if silently saying *who isn't these days*, 'but it may surprise you to learn that life goes on, and if you wish to remain in paid employment here you need to actually, well, *turn up*.' She swivels the screen back towards herself, takes off her glasses and begins rubbing at the lenses with the sleeve of her cardigan. 'I'm sure many of your colleagues would enjoy actually writing for a living rather than drafting advertising copy for Dave's Surf and Turf Grill and local vermin control services, and if you can support yourself writing books, be my guest, but don't piss us about in the process.'

I nod. It's all I can do really. That and say, 'I'm sorry.'

She lets out an exaggerated sigh. 'Have you brought with you a doctor's note? Anything to explain your absence? A hospital form or something? I mean, the only reason we didn't report you missing was because Danielle's brother-in-law works at the local pizza place and he said he'd been delivering meat feasts to your address. But there's got to be some reason you just went off-radar?' She does another hand-flourish – a palms-up motion this time, both to signal how preposterous the situation is and her desire for some sort of explanation.

I consider telling her it would be worth reporting Danielle's brother-in-law for a serious GDPR breach, but I doubt it would go down well. Instead, I just say, simply, 'I've been unwell.'

She just blinks at me, so I continue.

'I think it was . . . norovirus.'

She stares at me for a few seconds, and then says quietly, 'Is that a joke?'

I shake my head. 'No, not at all. I was . . . vomiting. A lot. I should have emailed. I'm sorry.'

Another deadpan stare greets this. 'And the bacon-loaded pizzas were what? Medicinal?'

She's rather got me there. 'I . . . well . . . they say have a little of what you fancy . . . and I sort of fancied them . . . on occasion.'

She takes in a deep breath through her nostrils, then turns back to her computer. 'Just go and do some bloody work, Katherine. This will go down as a formal warning on your employee record.'

I don't wait to be told again. Relieved, I take my seat back at my desk, quite proud of myself for not crying.

'Christ, how was it?' Danielle whispers, even though she must have been able to hear every single word that had been said.

'Fine,' I say, expanding my email inbox program and starting to scroll through the list. I open up Gmail, too, and keep it to a bottom corner of the screen so I can keep an eye on any book news that might come in.

A new message arrives in my Gmail account just as I'm clicking delete on all of Sheila's *Where are you?* messages in Outlook from a week ago. It's from my editor Ivanka at Matthews House Publishers, with my publicist and agent CCed in. I open it up fully on the screen and start to read. She starts off by saying she doesn't want to alarm me, but a video has been posted on YouTube – a video of me – and she wonders if I've seen it. She says that a trade publication and another industry website have been in touch for a comment, asking if I'd like to offer some kind of statement about it. Apparently they'd been sent the link by an anonymous source. Baffled, I skim through the rest of the email until I find the blue hyper-link I'm looking for. YouTube opens up on my computer screen in a new tab. And suddenly I cannot breathe.

It's me. And I'm sitting in Andrea's lounge. And she's sitting on the sofa in front of me. Holding my book. And there are subtitles coming up on the screen automatically. Burned into the image so, even with the sound off, it's clear what's being said.

My aunt can be so mean. Sometimes she throws bottles at my head. Glass ones. They never hit me, of course. She's too drunk to be able to aim properly.

They appear on the screen in big, bold font as Andrea reads from my book. From the slightly dark, but still clear, picture, you can see me looking uncomfortable in the armchair facing her. It takes me a while to realise what's going on. How this has happened. Then the penny drops.

She videoed it. The entire meeting. And she's put it online. I watch the horror show unfurl, the words burning into my retinas.

The truth remains that, if there is a murderer amidst this whole sordid mess, that person would have to be you.

I think I'm going to be sick. I try to calm myself down by breathing deeply. Danielle looks over and asks, 'You all right?'

'Yes,' I whisper, nodding. 'Just . . . got a headache. A migraine I think.'

She nods, but still looks unsure, so I stand up, stooping to grab the mouse and exit the YouTube tab.

'What were you watching?' she asks, glancing at my screen.

'Nothing,' I say, scooping up my phone from its charging pad, 'just something stupid. Spam I think, from an email. Not important.' I walk away from my desk towards the loos, trying not to break out into a run.

I'm not sick when I get there: the nausea seems to have subsided; but I still shut myself into a cubicle and sit down. Grabbing my headphones out of my pocket, I plug them in and navigate to my emails, opening up the hyperlink once again. I'm praying the reason for the subtitles is because Andrea hasn't managed to capture any sound. That means it's all her word against mine. But as soon as I press play, the audio arrives in my ears crisp and clear.

– Were you present when Adah drowned?

– Yes.

– Did you watch her drown?

(pause)

– Yes.

I drop the phone. The sound of the screen cracking barely registers with me. I pick it up off the ladies' bathroom floor and walk back to my desk.

Danielle's ready with a question as soon as I return. 'Katherine, dear, are you sure you're all OK? You look as white as a sheet.'

I just shake my head at her. 'Not well. I'm going home.' I grab my bag from under the desk, knocking over my chair, causing a loud clatter. Moira comes marching out of her office, her eyes wide. 'What on earth is going on here?'

I don't reply. I just leave. I walk down the road to my flat, climb the stairs, close the doors and sink down onto the floor. If the neighbours hear my screams, they don't come knocking.

Chapter 40

The next couple of weeks are hellish. I even think I go a bit mad, in my own way. I don't keep a regular sleep pattern. I only bother to shower because I find the warm flow of the water a comfort. Other than that, I barely exist. I don't leave. I eat my cupboards bare down to the last can of long-life soup. I ignore all the calls and emails from my publisher; my agent; Moira. I can see from the subject headers how serious things are getting: people are asking questions; journalists are reaching out to me for comment; Moira is alerting me to the fact she's terminating my employment contract. It all just washes over me. It's white noise.

My lowest moments come in the middle of the night,

when I dream of terrible things. Real things. Imagined things. Things that conflate dreams and reality. One night, after waking from a dream involving a stone maze filled with small semi-human-like creatures, each dragging a corpse of a little girl along the floor by the hair, I grapple around on my bedside table for my phone and dial my dad's number. The call is answered after six rings, and I immediately begin sobbing. 'I'm going to go to prison,' I cry, fighting to catch my breath and keep it steady enough to talk. 'I'm going to lose my flat. I'm going to lose everything.'

Silence follows for a bit. Then I hear a sigh. And that's when I realise it's not Dad on the other end. It's her. Amanda.

'You're a vile, nasty murderer,' she says in a cruel whisper. 'And you deserve to go to jail.'

I fling my phone across the room away from me like it's a grenade. I can't work out in my dream-addled state whether the screeching cackle I hear as the phone flies away from me is real or an after-effect of my nightmare.

My phone brings me another horror the next morning; a robustly real one that signals a change to my current day-to-day existence.

I'm not sure why I answer. It may be because it is a withheld number, and curiosity gets the better of me. I press the cool, cracked glass screen to my ear and listen.

'Am I speaking to Katherine Marchland?' a female voice asks in a businesslike tone. 'Formerly known as Katherine Carlson?' I tell her she is, and she continues. 'Ms Marchland, my name is Detective Inspector Cousins of Northumbria

Police. I need to ask you to present yourself at Wickton Close Police Station, Newcastle tomorrow afternoon at 3 p.m. to be interviewed under police caution. You are not under arrest at this time, but I have to inform you that you may be liable for arrest if you fail to turn up at the appointed time. You are of course free to bring legal representation with you, or you can access legal advice through a duty solicitor if you request one to be appointed for you. Please can you confirm you have understood this information?'

By some miracle, I manage to say, faintly, 'Yes. I do.' She ends the call after that.

Chapter 41

January 2020

'Can you talk us through exactly what happened on the 31 October 1987?'

DI Cousins looks at me as she says it, then looks down and swaps the two folders over in front of her. The older-looking folder is now on top. I find its faded, dark-beige cover unsettling and foreboding.

'Amanda really did suggest I ask one of my new friends round for tea. But it was just that. Tea. I don't think they had any sinister designs on her. So I did as I was told. I went out to find Adah and we played for a bit in the woods. Things turned sour a little later. Adah seemed to guess that I liked Levi. The boy my mother attacked with the knife. And I did like him – but not sexually; we were only about ten, him a bit older. She teased me about it. And then her teasing took a nasty turn.'

I feel the atmosphere in the room intensify. DI Cousins has ended her huffs of frustration. DC Malik is completely still. I take a moment to consider my next words, then carry on.

'Adah began to speculate on how Levi's sudden absence – the fact he had left the area – was my fault. That I had driven him away. Frightened him away, somehow. How the rumours were true. How the cottage in the woods was cursed, and I was the witch who had died there, and I had returned to take lives and terrorise the surrounding villagers.' I take a sip from my now barely-warm tea, trying to stop my hand shaking as I lower the mug back onto the desk. 'Adah's words, her stories, all the rumours and legend she kept talking about – all of it was too closely related to what was happening in my home. It frightened me in a way I cannot describe. I felt I had no escape from a constant, prevailing sense of threat. It had become so sustained and acute that I couldn't think clearly. The resulting fight was stupid and childish, but in that moment, I thought if I could just stop her existing, all the things she'd said would stop existing too.'

The tears return as I say these last words. And to my surprise, after some seconds have passed, DI Cousins speaks in a gentler tone than before. 'I'm sorry, Katherine. I realise this is difficult to talk about. But can you give me a clear answer to this: how did Adah come to enter the water?'

I shake my head slowly. 'I honestly don't know. There are times I think it may be my fault. That maybe I . . .

pushed her. We were shoving each other and arguing. And there are times when I think she took a misstep and fell in. We were already close to the river bank when we started arguing.'

DI Cousins nods. Then she opens the file. 'On the first of November, after Adah's disappearance had been reported to the police the night before, a child's body was found floating in the stream by the bridge you describe. It says in the details we have from the investigation that a family staying in a cottage nearby was questioned by police at their home to discover if they had seen anything or come into contact with the young girl. Each member of the family – a father, a mother and their daughter – said no, they had never seen or heard of a girl named Adah or recognised a girl matching her photo. They said they were just staying out in the cottage during the half-term holidays, during which time their daughter had caught the flu. They explained that they'd stayed longer to allow her to recover before travelling home. They were certain their daughter never went off into the woods alone.'

DI Cousins looks up at me when she finishes talking and waits for a response. And I have one to give.

'They lied.'

'Both your parents?' DI Cousins asks.

'The police only spoke to one of them. That was Dad. The woman they presumed was my mother was actually Amanda. Mum was upstairs asleep. She never saw the police, and they never saw her. That was how Dad wanted it.'

DI Cousins's eyes narrow. 'Did they tell you to lie too?'

I rub my eyes and give a little shrug. 'Sort of. Not

exactly. I don't think they really needed to. They didn't truly know what had happened in the woods. But they knew there was more to the whole thing than I was letting on. I had come back soaking wet, without the friend I was supposed to be bringing over for tea. I never told them everything. Over the years, we sort of had an unspoken understanding not to talk about it.'

DI Cousins nods, then takes out another page from the file. 'The postmortem report from the time says that there were bruises and cuts to Adah's right ankle, which fitted with what the police discovered when they removed her from the water. Her shoe had caught on a submerged piece of fallen tree. She had been unable to pull herself free. They never really thought the death was a homicide, but due to a previous murder in the area that went unde- tected due to police incompetence, they wanted to be sure. Everything tallied up, in their eyes. She was out playing, she fell in, she couldn't free herself.'

As a mixture of regret, guilt, and deep sadness rises up within me, I cling to the one small hope that I'd offered to Andrea a week previously. 'So . . . I couldn't have saved her. Even if I'd tried?'

DI Cousins closes the file and leans back in her chair. Like Andrea, she doesn't seem in the mood to offer reas- surance or absolution.

She folds her arms and says quietly, 'I can't be sure of that, Katherine. Nobody can.'

Chapter 42

I'm released without charge, but it's made clear to me that things aren't completely over. Before I'm let out of the interview room, DI Cousins says she'll be consulting with the CPS on whether they believe it to be within the public's interest to take further action against me based on the interview she's been given.

DC Malik volunteers to see me out, and once we're by the doors of the police station he turns to me and says in a low voice, 'Try not to worry. I know it's hard, but, based on my experience, I seriously doubt this is going to get very far.'

I turn to look at him, aware my eyes are full of hope. His nod releases a wave of relief across me, so powerful I think I grow a little unsteady. I use the door to stabilise myself and ask, 'I won't be arrested?'

'I probably shouldn't be telling you this, but our Super, he was one of the PCs involved in looking into Adah's death and he always thought there was something more to it.'

I nodded, remembering Andrea's threat about going to a certain police contact, but I don't say anything.

'He rather jumped at the idea of taking another look at the case,' DC Malik continued. 'And I suppose, in a way, he was right. I can't say for certain; it depends how the conversation with him and the team goes, and even if they think it's worth putting this to the CPS. But the way I see it, you were too young for any serious legal culpability to be laid at your door, and if there were any ramifications, it would be more along the lines of obstruction of justice. You and your family all getting together and lying to the police – that bit isn't good, if I'm honest; though as a minor, it's unlikely this will have any consequences for you. It's likely we'll be questioning your dad and Amanda. But again, I'd be very surprised if it ever reaches court.'

Words cannot express how grateful I am for him telling me all this. I shake his hand and thank him, and he tells me to take care. Then I walk away from the building in the direction of the train station, hoping I'll never have to walk down its dark corridors again.

★   ★   ★

My sense of relief doesn't last. I'm on the station platform when the aftershocks of the day start to hit me, like waves of electricity pulsing through my body. The things I've said; the experiences I've had to live through all over again; the constant nagging doubt about that day by the edge of the stream. Hands clutching, grabbing, pulling, hitting, shoving – then nothing. Just the sound of a young girl trying to cling to a life that is drifting away from her, carried off by the surrounding water.

My next moves come so naturally to me, it's as if my brain's on autopilot. I leave the train station, go back out onto the street and cross over to the car rental company I had passed on the way to the police station. I'm greeted by a young man at the desk inside and I tell him I need a car. It takes me mere minutes to show him my licence, get my details booked in and be handed the keys to a brand-new-looking Nissan Leaf. The man giving me the vehicle asks if I want some instructions on the 'best practice usage' of the car, but I say I'm fine. Then I drive off in the opposite direction of home.

I regret not getting advice on how to drive the car during the first half hour of my journey, as it takes me a while to get used to the automatic braking and intuitive driving settings. After a while, however, I grow to like the fact it's taking a lot of the thinking out of driving so I can cruise along the motorway, allowing my consciousness to sink down within me, steadily growing numb to the world.

I have a bit of a wobble at the service station an hour into the drive. I haven't got much further to go, but I haven't eaten all day, so I get myself a slice of pizza and some chips from the canteen staffed by two bored-looking women. It's seeing my book on the way out that does it, in the WH Smith near the exit, amidst a row of other new titles. I run to the car and unplug it in a hurry, leaving the charging lead swinging from the machine as I grab open the door, start the engine up and drive off into the dusk.

It's at the point when I think I'm lost that a road sign tells me I'm on course. The trees grow dense around me, the motorway ends and the road becomes long and winding, snaking through woods on either side. Memories from over a decade ago come back. Memories from when I was a child, and from when I did this journey in my twenties in an attempt to seek closure. It took me a long time to track down the right area of the forest then: a lot of wrong turns; a lot of trial and error. I thought coming back would help me make sense of things. Now, I've given up trying to properly make sense of things. I just need everything to be over. Finality. Closure.

I turn the car down the country track. It ends in a gate, now, with a car park. The whole area is managed by a company under licence from the county council, although it appears it's been shut up for the night. There's no security though, and it doesn't take much effort to uncoil the loosely wrapped chain and pull the gate open. I drive in and park my car in the deserted area, passing by the little bins and signs displaying maps of the woods and different paths visitors can take. The night is still around me, though the temperature has dropped again and the air tastes of snow.

I vaguely remember where to go from here, and I set off walking until I reach a dip in the ground that takes me down to a pathway. And there it is, the surface of it glittering in the moonlight, until a cloud moves over and turns the rippling silver into shimmering black. The Poison Stream. I've never looked up its proper name. If I was ever told it, I've forgotten it now. It's only ever been called that for me.

I move slowly, step by step, towards the edge where it meets the ground, its natural shallow entry blurring the boundary between earth and water. Where a merging happens between safety and danger; life and death; reality and dreams.

'Kitty . . . help me . . .'

I can hear her now. Slightly muffled, like her voice is going in and out of signal; like a radio that's not tuned properly.

'Help . . . please . . . please . . .'

I close my eyes, allowing the tears to roll down my face and drop into the water around me, becoming part of the body of the stream.

And then I keep on walking, past the water's edge.

I allow myself to fall under the water, its icy hands gripping my body like an old friend welcoming me back, until my face is the only part of me above the surface. I lean back and allow myself to be taken into its arms, and as I look up, I see large white flakes drifting down from the gaps in the trees. It's started to snow, and it's beautiful.

All of it is strangely beautiful. I'm grateful that the last thing I see of this place, before I let myself go, isn't the horror I've held tight within me all this time. It's something wondrous.

Then my vision blurs, and everything finishes.

Chapter 43

'It's OK. Hold on to me.'

The words come out of the blackness. I think I've imagined them at first, but then the feeling of disturbance, of something in motion, judders across me and I realise something's taking hold of me in the water. Something hard, strong and very real. I'm coughing and choking and water is pouring from my mouth, and suddenly I'm back, the night air stinging my face. I'm lying on the river bank, gulping in oxygen greedily and desperately; like I can't get enough of it, like I've been denied it for years.

'Can you walk?'

The voice again. A man's voice. Gentle, quiet, but with a reassuring strength.

I nod.

'OK then. I'm going to help you across the bridge here. We're going to get you some help.'

I nod again. I don't try to speak, but even if I wanted to I'm not sure it would be possible.

He helps me walk until I'm steadier, although once we've gone a little way up the path I'm shivering so much my balance is compromised. 'Nearly there,' he says, and then finally we stop to go through a little gate and up a winding gravel path. To a cottage.

'No,' I say, loudly, making myself jump with the sound. Then I realise this isn't the place I think it is. The brickwork on this is much newer, and nicer; and it's bigger, too. 'Do you want to stop?' he asks. I can't properly see his face, but I see his mouth open a bit as if something's just occurred to him and he says, 'Do you want to stay out here? You don't have to come inside. I can phone someone or an ambulance or something. I can bring out blankets. I'm sorry, I should've thought.'

I shake my head. 'It's fine, I can come in, I'm freezing.' I say it through chattering teeth.

Once over the threshold I trip over some tiny yellow wellington boots, and the man says, 'Sorry, watch your step.'

The normal me would be telling myself to get out, get out right now; but this isn't the normal me. She's lost somewhere, like a friend I've lost touch with. A friend I'm not even sure I knew in the first place.

'Go into the lounge – I'll start the fire up. The central

heating's already on, but this will get you warmed up quickest.'

He clicks about with some buttons near the mantelpiece and flames begin to glow in the hearth. I walk close and hold my shaking hands out towards the flickering warmth, feeling them steadily get their feeling back.

'Do you want me to call someone?'

I shake my head, not looking at him, focusing on watching the water drips grow and then fall from the ends of my fingers.

'Are you sure you don't . . . need to talk to someone? A friend, or family maybe?'

I shake my head again.

'I'll get you a towel and some clothes,' he says, and disappears upstairs.

I kneel down on the floor, bathing myself in the heat from the flames, and look up to the mantelpiece. Smiling faces of children beam down. School photos, some of them, but there are some family shots: a man, a woman with their arms around the little ones.

Something in the little boy's face stirs a memory deep inside my head.

The man's back, bringing with him a pink hoodie and tracksuit set. 'I thought these would be most comfortable,' he says. 'They're my ex-wife's.'

I take them from him and he stands there, awkwardly. I notice he's quite good-looking, with a severe jawline and short stubble with a slight hint of grey. He's probably a little older than I am – on his way to fifty. Again, that stirring of familiarity rises up within me. He jerks backward a bit and says, 'Sorry – I'll, er, I'll be upstairs. Just need to change out of these wet clothes.'

I turn away as he climbs the stairs and pull off my wet clothes, leaving them in a little pile by the fire, and tug on the wonderfully soft tracksuit bottoms and hoodie. I'm not sure if it's fabric softener or just the material, but they feel close to heavenly after the uncomfortable, cold wetness I've been clothed in.

While I sit by the fire, my shivering abates. A few minutes pass, and I hear creaking up above. I get up, walk over to the stairs and peer up. I need the loo. The landing is dark, but there's a light on in one of the rooms. I take the carpeted stairs carefully, listening to the movement. I wonder if the man's kids are up here, fast asleep, or if suddenly one will burst out and ask what a strange woman is doing climbing the stairs, like an evil witch from a fairy tale.

The landing gives full view to the room with the light on, and inside I can see the man, standing in his boxer shorts, drying himself off with a towel. The landing floor creaks and he turns to look at me. 'Oh sorry, I'm just getting dried off. I haven't abandoned you.'

I nod, and I'm about to go back downstairs, embarrassed for finding him undressed, before I remember why I've ventured up here. 'Erm . . . I was looking for the bathroom.'

He smiles and gestures to the left. I see the door and give a small smile in thanks.

Then I notice something that makes me stop and turn. There are two, distinct lines along the side of his torso – quite visible in the bright yellow light in his bedroom – and as I take a step closer, I see what they are. They are scars.

They disappear as a t-shirt is dropped over them. 'You all good?' he asks.

'Yes . . . yes, sorry.' I quickly walk into the little bathroom, trying to comprehend what I've just seen.

I end up staying the night on the sofa downstairs, the fire still on but turned down a little lower. Sleep comes surprisingly easily, my mind closing down, allowing so still and deep a rest to come it feels medicinal, like a healing blanket falling around me.

When I come to, the room is full of daylight, and the smell of toast and coffee is strong. I'm amazed at how good these familiar scents feel, even if my surroundings are strange and new.

'Good morning,' the man says, coming into the lounge. He's holding some toast in one hand and a mug of something in the other.

'Morning,' I say, straightening up against the cushions.

'Coffee,' he says, more as a statement than a question, and hands me the mug. 'I'll get you some toast, too.'

I shake my head. 'I'm fine. I mean, coffee is enough, thanks.'

'Nah, you should eat something.' He comes back with a plate topped with a freshly buttered slice. It looks and smells delicious, so I accept it without protest.

'Do you want to talk about last night?' he asks, his voice a little gentler, perching on the arm of the chair facing me.

I take a bite of the toast and chew it slowly, trying to work out how I feel. 'I don't think so. Not properly. I'd . . . just got myself into a bad place. I'm very grateful to you for . . . what you did.'

He smiles. A kind, genuine, warm smile. The kind I haven't seen in a long time. 'Happy to help. I go for night-time walks around here. I'm part of the team that manages the forest, and I own a few cottages dotted around its borders. Rent some of them out as AirBnBs, and the others have long-term tenants.'

Silence passes for a few beats while we both sip from our mugs, then he says, 'Do you live nearby?'

I shake my head. 'No, I live in London.'

He raises his eyebrows. 'Christ, that's a long way to come.'

'I know. I needed to get away.'

'Well,' he says, setting his empty coffee mug down on the floor, 'if you needed to . . . get away for a bit longer . . . you're welcome to stay in one of my places. I've got a small cottage free; just been done up, as well. It's nice, even if I do say so myself.'

I feel a sense of panic within me rise, like a distant alarm bell going off. 'Where . . . where is it? Is it in the forest itself?'

He shakes his head. 'No, just on the edge, this side of the stream. I can show you, if you like.'

I breathe out, worry giving way to relief. 'Is there still a cottage in the forest, right in the centre?'

He's on his way back to the kitchen, but stops. He looks back at me and gives me a slightly odd look. 'Yes.

Well, there used to be. How did you know? Have you been here before?'

All I can manage is a nod.

'Well, it's gone now. It sort of went to ruin, and it was unsafe, especially with families and Scouts and people doing things in the woods these days. It was demolished about five or six years ago. I think there's a children's play area on the site now. Slides and swings, that sort of thing, and a place to eat sandwiches. A picnic ground. It's probably for the best. It was a horrible place.' He shakes his head a little, almost like a shudder.

I don't respond at first. Just stare at the pattern on the blanket he gave me last night.

'Are you sure you're all right?' he says, peering at me.

I snap back into focus, and nod quickly. 'Yes, sorry. Just . . . a lot on my mind. I think I will take you up on your offer. To stay in one of your cottages. I think I'd like that. I'll pay, of course.'

His lovely smile returns. 'Splendid. Well, it's all kitted out with a shower and washing machine and tumble dryer. Let's get you over there – I'll get a bag for your wet things – and you can settle in.'

He goes into the kitchen but comes out again almost straight away. 'Sorry, that probably sounded a bit rude. I don't want to chuck you out . . . you're welcome to stay a bit longer . . .'

I hold up a hand in a little wave. 'No, no, I'd like to see the place. It sounds like a bit of a lifeline, actually.'

He gives me a thumbs up. 'I'll be with you in two

348

ticks.' He laughs a little and says, 'Sorry, I don't think you said what your name was. I'm Levi, by the way.'

Goosebumps flare along my skin like sparks. I hold on to the side of the sofa, steadying myself, then say, 'Lovely to meet you. I'm Katherine.'

Chapter 44

We walk to the cottage so I can have a shower and get my clothes washed and dried, then he says he'll come back later in the afternoon so we can go and pick up my car and drive it round. 'You must have forced the gate to get in,' he says, though he doesn't sound cross. He's grinning again, and I notice how it lights up his eyes. I confess to taking the chain off and protest that it wasn't even properly locked.

'That's on the to-do list. There didn't even used to be a gate, but we got it when we realised the car park was becoming a zone for, er, shall we say "adult activities". Quite a few cars would be parked there late at night at times. The gate was really just for show to nip that in the bud.'

We reach the cottage after about fifteen minutes. It's beautiful, framed by the trees from the forest and facing a country lane, with a road leading down towards some larger, older-looking properties. 'It's nice and quiet around here. And there's a Tesco Express just a twenty-minute walk away, or only about a five-minute drive. Do you have, er, money and things?'

I shake my head. 'No . . . I mean, I do, but my purse and phone are in my bag in the car. I can set up payment to you as soon as I get my phone.'

He looks embarrassed. 'No, that wasn't what I meant – I was thinking like teabags and milk and things. For supplies.'

'Oh, I know,' I laugh, and he does too, both of us trying to navigate the awkwardness. 'I'll be fine for now.'

He unlocks the door and shows me inside. The place still has that slightly solvent-based scent of new paint and wood. It's been very well kitted out, with a very comfy-looking sofa and a separate armchair. In the open-plan kitchen I can see a coffee machine and a dishwasher. 'This is wonderful,' I say, turning around, taking it all in. I'm suddenly aware I must look like Belle discovering the library in *Beauty and the Beast*, so I make myself stand still.

He looks thrilled. 'Brilliant. I'm pleased you like it.'

'Did you do all this yourself?' I ask.

He shakes his head. 'No, I had a company do it. I'm more into the sorting-things-out side of things rather than the artistic stuff. That's why I like managing properties, and the forest of course.'

'How did you get into it?'

He laughs. 'God, it's a long story. I used to live here in the village when I was young, in an estate just on the edge. It's been knocked down now. Awful place. I was a foster kid. I ran away to London when I was in my early teens and more or less lived on the streets for a bit. Got into some stuff I shouldn't have done, just to survive. But then this rich old bloke who I met allowed me to wash his car for money, so long as I went back to school. He sorted all that out – I don't know how he did it. These days the care system is more stringent, I think. But back then it was the best thing that ever happened to me. I got my GCSEs, and got an apprenticeship when I left and went on to do qualifications in bits and bobs. Then, when I met my wife, she had a bit of money saved and we moved up here and bought some property and started a family. That bit didn't go so well. The marriage bit. But the kids mean the world to me, of course. And I still run the houses and my ex gets a cut. It's all worked out in the end.'

His eyes glaze over a little, then he lets out another short laugh. 'Sorry, that was literally my life story. More than you bargained for.'

I smile at him. 'It's a lovely story. It's made . . . well, it's made me feel a bit better.'

He smiles back, then returns to showing me round, telling me a few things about the washing machine and tumble dryer. He's even brought with him some washing tablets from his house, along with a loaf of bread and a new pack of butter. I feel a rush of affection towards him when I see this, though I stop myself showing it.

'Right. I need to hop off and get my kids now from their mum's. You sure you'll be OK? There's a working landline if you need it. You can find my mobile on the laminated card thing in the visitor's folder in the kitchen drawer. Honestly, just call if you need anything.'

I tell him I will, and again offer assurances that I'll be fine. 'I'll see you about two-ish,' he says, and opens the door. But instead of walking through it, he turns and looks back at me. 'Do you know . . . it's a very weird thing but . . . I feel like I already know you.'

I laugh, and our eyes meet. I look quickly away at the floor.

'Hmm. Odd. Sorry, this is probably me growing senile already. See you in a bit!'

He closes the door behind him. I move to the window and watch his slim, tall form walk down the gravel path, back onto the country road and through the trees into the forest.

I turn back to the living room in front of me. Its neatness and serenity soothes me in ways I never knew were possible. It's like the world has been made new again. I know my positivity won't last. I know it's only temporary, and there'll be many nights ahead where I'll wake up thinking about the many monsters lurking in my past. But today, I feel glad I was pulled from the river. Glad I'm here now in this house, with the thought of him returning in a few hours' time.

I'm about to go and look round upstairs and have a shower when I hear a sound outside. It's the sound of someone walking quickly, followed by the crunch of gravel and a knock at the door. I rush towards it and open it. He stands there, a little breathless, looking at me with astonishment and realisation filling his face.

He says just one word. But it's enough.

'Kitty?'

I look into his deep, hazel eyes and nod. 'Hello Levi.'

A smile fills his face. A smile of warmth, amazement, and a thousand other emotions all rolled into one. Then he comes inside, and closes the door to the outside world behind him.

Acknowledgements

It would be possible to write a whole book-length of thankyous, but I'll try to keep this as disciplined as possible. First, thanks must go to my brilliant agent Joanna Swainson and the team at Hardman & Swainson, my editors Helen Huthwaite and Phoebe Morgan and publicist Sabah Khan and everyone at Avon HarperCollins.

Endless thanks to my parents and my sisters for their encouragement and support through the publication of my first book and for joining in with the excitements of each stage of the journey.

Becoming a published author has been a wonderful thing, but also a very challenging and at times disorientating experience, bringing with it difficult periods I didn't anticipate. I'd like to give special thanks to my wise and wonderful friend Rebecca Bedding for being so brilliant through both the good times and the less good times, and for our many joyous adventures to delicious restaurants, theatre trips, bookclub discussions and visits to cookie-dough bars (yes, they do exist).

On a similar theme, a big help to me during this past year has been the writing community, especially those who are so kind and generous with their advice, both within the Psychological Suspense Authors' Association (shout out to Emma Curtis for starting it!) and within interviews and Podcasts. There are many shows, publications and people I could mention, but two standouts are *The Honest Authors*, hosted by Gillian McAllister and Holly Seddon, and Sarah Painter's *The Worried Writer*. In my many moments of confusion, imposter syndrome, writing-based concerns and general unease, these podcasts are an absolute dream and have been a huge help.

Also, in the book world – from authors to booksellers and many others – I'd like to thank: Cally Taylor, A. J. Finn, Kate McHale, Bea Carvalho, Kate Skipper, Diane Jeffery, Rowan Coleman, Karin Slaughter, Helen Fields, Jane Corry, John Mars and Elisabeth Carpenter. A massive thankyou to all my colleagues at Waterstones and everyone in the Ecommerce team who have helped make it possible to be both an author a full-time social media coordinator. Thanks also to all the booksellers and retail workers who have helped my first book, *A Version of the Truth*, find its way into the hands of readers.

A big thankyou to police officers Steve Bowyer, Paul Scott and Tom Mitchell for their advice on the police procedure elements in *Hold Your Breath*.

This book was inspired by my love of mystery stories, horror movies, fairytales and weird fiction, so I'd like to thank my friends Meg Wallace, Martha Greengrass, Tom Bedding, Corinne Gurr and George Doel for being integral parts of my enjoyment in this particular area of storytelling – from cinema trips to reading recommendations to many movie nights and bookshop visits in between.

Lastly, thanks to our family golden retriever Rupert for allowing me to use his nickname (Kitty, because he curls up on chairs like a cat) for my main protagonist in this novel.

We all see what we want to see . . .

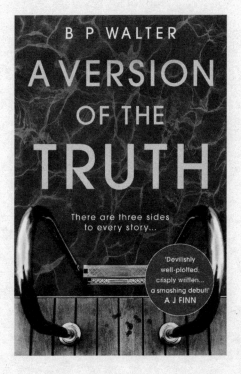

A dark and twisty domestic suspense novel that will have you hooked from the first page.